Critical praise for

AS WE FORGIVE

"SO POWERFUL THAT IT PULLS THE READER INTO IT."
—Baltimore Sun

"NEIL DAZZLES!…[the] plot is so riveting that her book can not be put down." —Best Sellers

"A HAUNTING, INTRICATE TALE….AN EXTRAORDINARY ACCOMPLISHMENT." —Publishers Weekly

"FASCINATING….The theme she handles with exquisite control, establishing an almost psychic relationship with her readers, an ability to show us only what we are willing to accept." —The New Republic

"BEAUTIFULLY WRITTEN, almost lyric in quality and intensely effective." —Nashville Banner

"THE POWER TO HAUNT…a lyrical work of wistful imagery." —Austin American-Statesman

"A GRIPPING NOVEL….A HAUNTING STORY."
—Wichita Falls Times

AS WE FORGIVE

A NOVEL BY

BARBARA NEIL

ST. MARTIN'S PRESS/NEW YORK

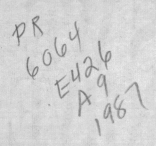

PR
6064
E426
A9
1987

AS WE FORGIVE

Copyright © 1985 by Barbara Neil

All rights reserved. No part of this book may be used or reproduced in any manner whatsoever without written permission except in the case of brief quotations embodied in critical articles or reviews. For information address St. Martin's Press, 175 Fifth Avenue, New York, N.Y. 10010.

Library of Congress Catalog Card Number: 85-25045

ISBN: 0-312-90138-0   Can. ISBN: 0-312-90139-9

Printed in the United States of America

First St. Martin's Press mass market edition/May 1987

10 9 8 7 6 5 4 3 2 1

For Andrew
and my mother, Jean Neil

1

In the past days the feeling had come to Lydia Evans again and she was trying hard to remember the precise moment it had returned. It was a feeling of not being alone, of being watched and of her actions being influenced by another will, stronger than her own. The sensation started as a nervousness, a twitch almost: she would be doing something mundane about the house then stop and look behind, as if disturbed by a subliminal tap on the shoulder.

Earlier this week she had been at a party given by one of the other masters' wives, had been enjoying herself, laughing, when suddenly she became grave and turned her head slowly to see ... what? Through the din there was a silence only she could hear, then she knew what voice, coming from nowhere, would break that silence if she dared to wait.

'Take me home, Eric, please,' she said quietly when noise of the present had closed about her again, and dear Eric, so concerned, took his pale and shaking wife away. Yesterday evening she had stopped reading to cross the room in which the only sound was Eric turning the pages of the books he was marking; she opened the door, looked through to the dim hallway of their rented Victorian house, closed the door softly once more. 'It's all right, dear,' Eric had said, drawing the curtains on the still, daybright, summer evening as if to shut out something that threatened. 'There,' he turned on a lamp, 'all right now.' So this time he too had felt it. Eric put away his books and settled his bulky figure on the floor in front of Lydia, forearms on knees.

At twenty-eight, Eric's fine, wiry hair had receded slightly, yet he retained a boyish appearance; he had a benign face with big, firm lips and as he began to speak now his eyebrows

gathered together in a little bridge of apology, his smiling eyes
glinting, nervous. Lydia knew the particular pawn he was
going to push out on the slippery surface of their conversation.
For the four years they had been married she had avoided
checkmate on this subject, although the specialist had been
adamant that conception was most unlikely.

'You know what I'm going to say, don't you? Goodness I
sound boring about it, but if only we could have one proper
conversation so I can, sort of, know exactly how you feel then I
wouldn't nag. Did you know that to get a white one, I mean an
ordinary, healthy white one, you can't be too old? I don't just
mean you, actually, I mean us, they're awfully tricky about it,
the authorities.' He paused to watch his fingertips tapping
rapidly, a faintly critical gallery to what he was saying, 'But
actually I wouldn't mind brown, yellow or anything. Really I
wouldn't.' She had not already interrupted so Eric rose
hopefully and went back to the table saying, 'Actually, Lydia
dear, I've got something here ...' He rummaged amongst his
books letting two fall, 'I thought you'd be annoyed or
something,' he chuckled, 'so I didn't show them to you before.
All sorts of papers telling about different kinds of adoption. I
know you don't want to think about it, but if you knew what
was involved it would be a start. I don't mean soon or
anything, of course you must take your time.'

He found the papers and was leafing through them himself
when suddenly the heavy curtain he had drawn across the
window billowed inwards knocking some of the leaflets to the
floor.

'What a funny thing ...' he began, but Lydia sat rigid, her
two hands clutching the arm of the sofa, her eyes searching the
room. She was waiting; the feeling had not left her and she
knew something else was going to happen. Eric had launched
again into his subject thinking she was listening.

Then the telephone rang.

Eric stood near it, papers in hand. '... I do understand it
would be upsetting for you with all the questions ... just a
moment ...' He reached for the telephone.

'Eric, I want to,' Lydia said, then almost shouted, 'We'll go
tomorrow. I don't mind what they ask me, but please don't
answer the telephone.'

Eric turned to her, his face beaming, receiver in hand. Missing the hysteria at first, hearing only the point, he said, 'Lydia, do you really mean it? That's absolutely ...' but looking at the receiver he remembered convention and put it to his ear.

'Please don't answer it,' Lydia said, hopeless, with her head sunk.

'Hello, Eric Evans speaking. Who's that? Hello?' He waited for a while; gradually his expression changed, became puzzled. 'Hello ...?' He paused, holding the receiver away from him he looked at Lydia, 'There's no one there,' his voice low, lifeless.

'It's all right, Love, it'll only be a wrong number.' She was now composed, prepared. 'I really do want to, you know.' She leant forward as if trying to push across her words, but Eric turned his back to her and replaced the receiver; she leant sideways easing the train of words around him, trying to recapture his interest from what now absorbed it. 'I'd like to adopt now. I'm ready to, if we can.'

'You asked me not to answer it, didn't you? Why?' he said, his arms hanging at his sides, the papers, now forgotten, still in his hand.

'No reason, Love.'

'Why, after all this time, should I be thinking of him?' She did not answer. 'Lydia?' Eric was still turned away from her.

'What is it?' she asked gently, trying to caress with her words because she was still not ready to cross the room.

'Was it him, do you think?'

She waited until she could answer calmly and said, 'No, of course not. He probably died ages ago.'

2

Lydia was alone in the house the next morning, and would be until late in the evening, because Eric had been obliged to sit on a Sports Day Committee, although neither thing was a strong point with him: sports nor committees, but refusing had never come easily either. They had agreed that she would make an appointment with the adoption society, however that was last night, then it had been necessary, appropriate to agree; now, alone, the thought of adoption societies, strange babies, was becoming again abhorrent. Having nearly had her own child she sensed that exclusive, prejudicial, irreplaceable feeling of mother-love and it was hard to believe she could make do with no deeper connection than that of protector and protected.

Lydia took her coffee through to where they had been sitting last night and sat again upon the peeling leather sofa. She liked this room, booklined, shadowed by a wisteria trembling on the other side of narrow French doors leading to a patch of green. Only today it was not the same, it did not offer the solace it had before in odd, lonely moments.

She thought about the wrong number, how she had communicated her fear to Eric. This morning, at last, she could admit that she knew very well what was causing all of this. Only last Monday had she not seen the figure on the corner for herself? Her neighbour, Mrs P, who suffered from a grotesque swelling disease, had swayed to Lydia's back door, blocking the sun with her massive form,

'Phew, the heat,' she had moaned to announce herself. 'Seen him, then, have you dear, The Watcher?'

'Watcher, Mrs P.? No. Come in and have some lemonade.'

'I won't do that, thank you, dear.' Mrs P. liked Lydia,

because she was gentle, fey and her frail form reminded her of
how she had once been. Lydia was kind to her and understood
how her condition immobilised her, making her vulnerable.
'He's been there some days now. Just watching.' The minutiae
of the street were her fear and fascination; for her, burglars,
murderers, rapists of elephantine women were everywhere.

'Waiting for his girl I expect, Mrs P. Don't worry.'

However, Mr. P. had been insistent, had taken Lydia by the
arm through the house to a front window where she pointed
out, away to the right, the legs, the hem of a coat, the
shadowed figure of a man standing beneath the dipping boughs of
the great oak, just there, on the corner of the street.

'You take care of yourself, won't you dear?' Mrs P. warned
as she moved, cumbrous, towards her own house, her tone
implying that no matter how much care was taken a dreadful
fate would befall them all.

At the time Lydia had only been concerned to allay Mrs P.'s
fears; even to herself she dismissed him as the clandestine lover
of some unpunctual lady living nearby. Nevertheless, she had
deliberately not looked for him after that, did not want to see
again that overclad form, obscure, yet with something
disturbing, anguished about the stoop of his great shoulders.
But since then she had felt the presence unceasingly. Yes, she
knew all right.

She decided to leave the house; get busy; see the adoption
people right away, never mind appointments. She would go by
the way of the other corner, never so much as glancing to the
right, in case … in case. If she moved fast enough in the cage of
her life nothing would touch her.

Then the telephone rang.

For some time Lydia watched it on the table the other side of
the room waiting for it to stop; yet she knew it would not. She
also knew it was not the Matron asking for help in the
sickroom or the Headmaster's wife enlisting cakemakers for
the Sports Day tea.

Slowly she rose and crossed the room, touching the
armchair where Eric dozed in the evenings, the table where he
worked. She sat down before the telephone screwing her hands
together until, supporting her forearm with her other hand she
reached out, lifted the receiver and listened. She heard

breathing, hands moving on the receiver at the other end, a chair scraping on a stone floor. At last a man's voice said, 'Lyd? Is it you?'

'Yes …' she said quietly, 'yes, it's me.'

'Of course it is. Thank God you're there. I tried last night, someone else answered.'

Lydia's body curled as if defeated. She covered her face with her hand and put the receiver away from her; and still she heard his voice, 'Please … please wait. Listen to me. I want you to know what happened. I only ask you to listen.

'I've been watching the house for some days now. I stand under the trees at the top of the road hoping to see you. I've seen a man coming from the house; I know what time he leaves and what time he returns. Is he really to do with you? It's hard to believe that I could be so near and yet you don't guess at my presence, don't come out to look for me, find me.'

'Yes, I knew you were there. Please don't, though, ring me or watch me. Go away, please.'

'This is the first time I've returned to England since we parted and the only reason is to find you. Do you remember the day we parted at Coalbarn, how I shouted after you? How long ago was it? A lifetime or a day? I don't know time any more.'

'It's been four years.'

'Why didn't you stop the car; turn your head? If you'd only made some sign, just a smile, that I was forgiven. As it is I am sick, you haunt me. When I walk, others in the street clear a path about me. I lumber into things and all because I'm blinded by your face, accusing and uncomprehending; but in truth the face I see isn't only yours, it's hers as well. Her face accuses and yours forgives; she'll let you do that for her, she'll let you forgive me. Will you do it? Please? You do hear me?'

She listened because this voice carried the scents and dimensions of rooms locked away in memory that only it could release; it moved the scenery, changed the set and took Lydia back four years to when she and Eric were living together in a shoebox of a flat off Baker Street in London.

Both Lydia and Eric were unusual types for modern times; they shared a shyness about life and a code of reticence which made others dub Eric mildly boring and Lydia a trifle dull, but

Eric knew what people thought of him, did not mind, even agreed, which made him seem to have a placid confidence.

Another common factor between them was that they had been only, lonely children, but that was where the similarity of background ended. Eric was seven when his mother had run off with a man nine years her junior and he never saw her again; his father, who owned a second-hand bookshop, took over his upbringing, devoting all his love, attention and money ('We'll do son, just you and me from now on'). They were very close and Eric, who felt a great debt of love and responsibility to his father, worked hard, went to a minor public school and on to a teachers' training course. One winter his father developed premature senility and had to be moved to an old people's home because they could not afford the expense of the twenty-four-hourly attention he required. The sale of their small house and the shop ensured a nice enough place for his father, but pushed Eric into the backwaters of London's bedsitter land.

Where Eric's isolation was the effect of one doting, over-protective parent. Lydia's was the effect of two uninterested ones. Her conception had come as an embarrassing surprise to her parents after nearly twenty years of marriage with not so much as a 'missed week' to hint at procreation. When her mother, a large, coarse-skinned, fox-hunting woman, who conversed freely about her bodily functions, discovered that she was pregnant she was mortified and disgusted by the strange, almost mystical state that came upon her. Although her life had been mostly spent coercing or restraining copulating dogs (she bred red-setters), mucking out her hunters and, for various reasons, pushing her mannish forearm inside her mare's backside, to find that now she had to be the subject of examination and interest was awful, vile. Blast George. Blast nature. She became a different woman and far less objective about her body. No more 'Scuse I, off to the lav. for me moment.' No more shouted bulletins on a frosty morning at the Meet: 'What me? Fine thanks. A nasty boil on me you-know-what started last week but better now.' She became sullen and introverted for the duration of the pregnancy, and after the birth, which was long, painful and dangerous, she went back to her horses and dogs as soon as she was able; but never again did they hold the same appeal. The breeding became distasteful to her and she could not longer hold a dog on to a nervous bitch when necessary, whereas before she had been able to grasp the locked animals with one arm, drink a mug of tea at the same time and say, 'Oh yes, she's receiving. I can feel it.' All these functions of nature started to touch something deeper in her. Despite herself she began to feel a feminine affinity with the mare, the bitch, and she did not like it at all, nor did she like Lydia.

It might have helped the relationship if Lydia had grown into a dog or horse-loving child, but these animals frightened her.

Lydia's father had been an Actuary Manager in a large firm of accountants. He was a small man, smaller than his wife, and it was from him and her mother's middle-life conception that Lydia inherited her slight form, delicately-boned, childlike even in her twenties.

He was a quiet man who liked a quiet life which, to an extent, Lydia stopped. So when she was eight she was sent to boarding school and to stay with whoever would take her during the holidays.

Although Lydia would have liked to be something gayer and more noticeable, she had been too busy surviving since the age of fourteen, when her parents were killed in an aeroplane crash, to worry much.

Her father's death exposed his gambling debts; Lydia's sheltered county life and private education were ended, together with most of what little confidence she had had. She was sixteen when she left the unwelcoming suburban relations who had housed her and went into the heart of London to share a scruffy flat with five other girls whom she did not know and hardly ever saw. She found a job as waitress in a cafe.

Lydia had been working at the cafe two years when she met Eric there. He was teaching mathematics at a North London Comprehensive. The other teachers were pleasant enough to this curiously aged young man, but the boys were hellish: ragging him, defacing his books and urinating in his briefcase. He would watch Lydia while pretending to mark books (... 'Please, Sir, is this tomato sauce or blood on me logrivums, Sir? Killed someone 'ave yer, Sir?' 'Oh, sorry, Barlow, sorry.'

'Don't keep apologising to the boys,' the Head was always saying, 'It weakens your standing.').

Eric liked the earnest simplicity with which Lydia went about her tasks in the tawdry cafe and he felt he understood her apparent shyness about life.

When at last he spoke to her his opening gambit was,

'If you don't mind me saying so, you've really stayed the course. The other girls seem to come and go like anything, but you're always here whenever I come.'

'Oh, thank you, and you've been coming here longer than most of the customers do, but I didn't think you'd noticed ...' Embarrassed by her accidental admission she became abrupt. 'What do you want?'

'Oh, sorry, baked beans on toast and a cup of tea, please. Actually, I'm Eric Evans,' he added quickly, displaying two diffident palms, as if he would be anyone else if the offer came.

'I'd better put your order in,' Lydia said.

'Oh, sorry, yes, of course.'

When Lydia returned with the order Eric rose to his feet and gestured to the empty seat opposite him. 'Would you care to ...'

'But I can't, I work here,' she said, amazed at the suggestion. Then she looked round at the empty, tatty cafe and back at Eric smiling daftly: 'Well, why not?'

Right away, Lydia liked this apologetic, well-spoken young man with his tweed coat, creased tie and amiable face. He shifted often in his seat and was seldom altogether still, especially his hands, which tapped, pinched and squeezed each other in an unending dialogue of carps and quibbles.

After some tentative conversation, he said, 'I suppose you wouldn't consider coming to the cinema with me?'

And with cinemas, the Tate on wet Sundays, suppers in his bed-sit, they grew close. Drawn together in part by their loneliness and their shared intangible immaturity, they became lovers. She was his first girl friend and he her first man.

One day in his bed-sit a few months later Eric approached Lydia in his usual way with tricky subjects, settling on the floor in front of where she sat, and said, 'You've heard me mention Greg, the Art Master at school, haven't you?' And she had, many times: she felt that Eric rather hero-worshipped Greg, which, although she had not met him, made her feel hostile. 'Well, he told me about a flat and I even went to see it today. It's small, dirt cheap, that's because of the dirt in it I expect,' he spluttered a giggle (just his kind of little joke), 'but it could be lovely. Will you come and see it and if you like it, sort of …!' he foundered.

'Marry you?' Lydia leant forward fascinated, 'Or live with you?'

'Well actually I did mean, don't be offended or anything, "live with" just for starters. Oh, God, I say …' He stood up nervously rubbing clenched fists together, 'Don't leave me 'cause I say "live". It's only just for the moment. I'll "marry" if you don't want to "live". It's only that I want to ask you when I've got a better job. More to offer.

'The flat would be a start but not enough to ask you. Will you, Lydia?'

'No, it's all right, really.' Lydia put her arms about his neck and kissed him. 'I would like to live with you, like you say, just for starters.'

And they moved in feeling suddenly part of a real world and happier than either had ever known.

The flat was at the top of flights of narrow stairs on which the carpet had been worn to no more than a stain between the battered treads. The rooms below were the offices and workrooms of unsuccessful solicitors and tailors; except for Mrs Leek, who occupied a first-floor room, but was rarely seen, only heard, when, from behind her door (on which a plastic number one had lost a screw and swung by its foot), there came the sound of springs straining to a tentative rhythm and the low tones of a male voice mingling with hers during some cursory transaction. By six o'clock in the evening it was possible to believe that London was empty and that the G.P.O. Tower seen blinking through the back kitchen window was for their own private amusement. With the eager intensity of children Lydia and Eric dressed the flat, two small rooms, kitchen and bathroom, from markets and junk yards and with some heavy Victorian furniture Eric had saved from his home. They hung moth-eaten red plush curtains, too large for the windows. Within a few weeks the effect was that of the props room of any theatre with all the bric-a-brac they had collected, as if to confirm by acquisition their life together.

* * *

Some of these objects were about Lydia now as she sat in this different room, in this different life, pressing the telephone receiver to her ear, her head sunk upon her arm listening …

'I'm at Coalbarn now. The sky and sea are as unending as ever. I love it. Be here with me? I could drive to you so quickly. I'd wait again under the tree like I did yesterday and all the days before. Didn't I always wait for you? Didn't you always come? What I have to say is hard without seeing your face. I wonder if you'll forgive me for what I've done to her. Yes. Yes, I think you will because you have kindness. You always had that.' Among the reboant sounds she could hear when he paused (again the scraping of a chair on a stone floor, the muffled slam of a door or shutter), there was another which made Lydia strain to identify it, as though a child had cried nearby. She assumed it to be the febrile call of a gull. 'Say something to me. Let me hear your voice.'

'I'm here. Still here.' Lydia said. 'Tell me what you have to, then please leave me be.'

'Yes. Yes, that's your voice. I always loved your voice. Think of the past. Of how it all was. Wasn't it all good though? Wasn't it? Meet? Please meet?'

3

She did not want to be living that past again, two pasts really, but she was no longer able to stop herself and was remembering first a dark, wet afternoon in winter London four years ago, shortly before her first Christmas in the flat with Eric. She had come laden from the warmth of a brightly lit department store into the swooping cold and stood for a moment taking her bearings in the pushing crowd. She had decided to take a tube train home when a hand grabbed her shoulder.

'Lyd, hello. I thought it was you. Goodness me, you haven't changed one jot.'

Lydia looked about her to see how the mistake was made, but that "Lyd", that awful "Lyd", struck its chord, and before she looked up at the man whose bulk now blocked the view all around her, she knew who it was. It was Ben Wavell, with felt hat pulled down and the collar of a great black coat turned up. She could see the lower half of his face, grinning, delighted, and smell damp wool cloth and limes: surely that other trace was limes? What a curious smell for wet, winter London. He clasped her elbow. 'C'mon, let's do some shopping,' he said, and guided her straight back into the shop she had just left. In that one powerful moment Ben Wavell made her, once more, into a ten-year-old girl.

It was to the Wavells' house, called 'Eden', set upon pristine lawns running down to the sea, that Lydia had been sent as a child during several summers. The first time was with her father who was engaged upon some accounting work for this man. He had asked if he could bring his daughter as her mother was not very well (not quite true), but that she would be very quiet and behave herself (true).

Lydia had been so liked by Ben Wavell's daughter, Nathalie, she was asked back for following summers. She had loved that house and the people in it, who laughed, teased and fought one another with wit and warmth; and she had longed for just a smear of the kind of confidence it bred. Although she had always been in awe of Ben and he used to tease her without mercy, calling her 'beautiful' and a 'siren', just for the joyous sight of her red face and confusion, he had captivated her.

Now, being steered by him through the food halls and wine department of the store, Lydia mentally re-adjusted her plans for the afternoon. This was her only free afternoon from the cafe and she still had to buy the special coffee she and Eric liked.

Finally, Ben stopped at a counter displaying gloves and scarves, behind which an irritable, grey lady stood muttering, folding silk squares and glancing at her wrist-watch.

'I want something pink with brown in it,' said Ben, apparently oblivious to the assistant's mood.

'Well, that's not good enough, is it? I mean, Silk? Large? Small? Formal print? Abstract? I take it you do want a "foulard", Sir?'

Satisfied with her amble into the foreign tongue, she rearranged her chins and bosoms and clasped her hands on the rotundity popping beneath the waistband of her skirt.

'Show me all of them,' Ben said.

This rounded off her ill-humour and she started to pull out drawers until twelve of them were piled on top of one another on the counter. Undeterred by this deluge of wares Ben started riffling through them, casting aside in a soft, rumpled heap on the counter all that did not appeal.

'This is all right isn't it, Lyd? You're not in a hurry or anything? As soon as I've got this we can talk. My God, it's been years … I say, this is quite nice.' He dropped a scarf over Lydia's head so that her face was completely covered.

'No I'm not,' Lydia replied. 'Well not yet anyway, but I can't be too …'

'Good, good. I knew you'd say that,' and he dropped another scarf over her.

She stood patiently, feeling ridiculous, and wondering who the scarf was for. After all, she knew it would not be for Viola,

Nathalie's mother. Lydia had heard about the divorce quite a few years before from her parents. Maybe the scarf was for Nathalie. That was sure to be it ... smooth-skinned Nathalie, glistening and dark, as vibrant and unpredictable as her father. No ankle socks for her in summer; bare feet in open sandals or just bare feet, and wherever she ran in all the secret, dusty, muddy places of childhood, the skin on her legs and feet was always soft and tender, seeming to belong to some much more dark and private area, her tactile body covered with something cotton and delicate; a cherished body moving with the loose confidence that, to adoring parents and a secure family structure, anything is acceptable.

'The woman I am buying this for has dark brown hair, so let's pretend yours is, Lyd. Let's see now.'

And Ben stood back stroking his chin, looking at the little figure, the breath from her hidden face slightly ruffling the swathes of silk.

So it might be for Nathalie. Her hair had been gold brown, but by now it was probably dark; Lydia's hair was no longer as fair as before.

'What do you think?' he said, turning to the assistant, who was busy snatching and folding. She was so amazed that her rancour had been ignored (funny, they usually packed off quicker with a few sharp words) and impressed that her opinion had been sought, that she launched into her new part as enthusiast and co-operator with zeal.

'Oh, Sir, it's lovely; but if it's brown hair you say, well what about this?' and she drew from a drawer out of sight something perfectly pink and brown.

'I'll take it,' he said.

Lydia was unveiled, but while under that silky pugaree a distant, remembered feeling had come back to her, one of not really being there for Ben; that she was just a convenient, familiar face whose name he might not even be certain of.

Now, bored with the scarf and the transaction, he quickly paid and took the scarf, while the assistant began to realize, crustily, the clearing she had to do for only one sale.

'Come and see my house,' Ben said to Lydia. 'It's new, I've done it myself. My car's just around the corner. You do want to, don't you?'

Yes, this was Ben all right, ploughing up the path of her day,
but she thought, too, that there was something sad about him;
something desperate in his enthusiasm. 'Oh yes, of course I do.
I'm very interested really.' Half an hour would not hurt, she
thought.

Lydia sank into the front seat of the claustrophobic and
pulsing car Ben had parked in a side street, trying to become
accustomed to being an adult in his company; but he was so
much a part of her childhood that, even now, it was hard to
call him Ben. She did make little forays into the world of adult
conversation, tentatively and shyly saying, 'I was very sorry to
hear about your divorce. You always seemed to me the ideal
couple, the ideal family really. I used to think that when I grew
up I would want my own family to be like yours.'

'You mustn't be fooled by people's little charades, Lyd,' he
snapped.

There it was again, that nasty nickname. Would she dare to
ask him to call her Lydia? No. It was not worth it. Could that
be true? The Eden, the Wavells she had loved so much as a
child, a charade? The happiness and humour pretended? She
wanted to ask more, but he had not liked her mentioning it.

As he concentrated on the mounting chaos of the traffic
Lydia searched Ben's profile for signs of age but the neon night
of town rinsed out the details leaving him spectral beside her.

She remembered clearly the first time she had ever seen him.
It was years before, when she was ten, during one of those
summers at Eden; until then he had always been away on his
many trips abroad. Lydia had been in the sunlit dining-room,
glittering with crystal, silver, and heavily scented with the fruit
arrayed on the sideboard. She had rushed into the room
thinking that lunch had begun and found it empty, and now it
was hard to leave because on the other side of the door they
were calling for her to come to lunch. Already at the table, she
had felt guilty and ridiculous. Suddenly, Ben Wavell's big curly
head looked round the door.

'Oh, there you are.' He shouted to others still outside the
room, 'She was in here all the time ... You are Lydia, I take it?'
he added quickly. She nodded. 'Well, of course you are,' he
said, banging the door wide open.

A rush of three spaniels halted their pace at a Persian rug, then sloped to their usual places under the sideboard. Another door opened discreetly on the other side of the large dining-room and the butler entered, immaculate, anonymous, positioning himself beside the chair at the head of the table, and waiting for the group to settle itself. There was Ben, who was huge, not fat, but with great limbs that constantly moved, describing, ordering, teasing, then always returning to one gesture, when his elbows would fly up like wings beside his head and his hands travel through his hair, down over his shoulders to his large chest, where they stopped; then his left hand would slowly massage his heart area, mental inventory: hair, head, heart, haven't lost them yet. Parts of the room that were not filled with his body were filled with his all-pervading existence. Nathalie came in behind him flushed with excitement at the arrival of her father; then her French governess, a greying unmemorable woman with neurotic habits. Preceding Viola Wavell came her guest, called Millie. She was a little older than Viola, in her early forties but plain by comparison, slim and faded-pretty. And then Viola: very dark, beautiful, she came from an old White Russian family and was brought up in France.

Viola had never lost the courtly manners of her European upbringing and tried constantly to instil them into Ben and Nathalie, who resisted firmly. But with her formality went all the passion and vehemence of her race. At any unexpected moment it would spring out as laughter, fury; she might suddenly dance or sing, or cry; she was mercurial and Ben seemed to adore her, almost as much as he adored his daughter.

Viola ushered her guest, Lydia and the governess to their places with graceful gestures and with brief finger movements, a semaphore on a different plane, indicated to the butler to start serving the food. Ben sat at the head of the table.

'By the way, Millie, this is one of Nathalie's friends,' Viola said to her guest.

Somehow the introduction required nothing from Lydia; it made her inanimate. Viola might as easily have been saying, "That picture we bought at auction, the chairs were in the family and that, that little girl, is something Nathalie picked up," which in a way she was.

Ben studied arrangements for a moment and said, 'No, no, this is all wrong, Viola. Hopeless seating. Not who I want next to me at all, and after all I am the one who has been away for three weeks. You must spoil me at least until tomorrow.'

Viola shrugged to her guest and held up her hand to the butler to stop him serving the first course. 'All right Ben, have it your own way,' and let her deep voice trail into a weary sigh.

'Everyone stand up again. Now, Mamzel ...' Ben addressed the governess in studiedly bad French, though he could be fluent, to show that he was not frightened of her which, like all Englishmen with governesses and their ilk, he was. '... boojay voo lah, silver play.' He pointed to the other end of the table. 'I want you two girls next to me, Lydia one side and Natta the other.'

"Natta" he pronounced with a heavy "a", making it sound rich and Italian. Millie was compelled to go to the other end of the table too and she looked put out to be moved away from his right side.

'I'm not coming all the way down there,' Nathalie said. 'Don't be so spoilt, Daddy, and stop moving everyone around.'

'Come on, Nathalie,' Ben pleaded, 'you only have to move all of three feet and I haven't seen you for ages. Every time that hole of a place called school lets you out I seem to be away.'

'Oh, all right, Daddy. God, you are a bore,' she said, smiling that particular smile that defied offence.

That was all typical of Ben. He loved to rearrange scenes just as they had been set and everyone thought they knew what they were doing. He could reduce anything to chaos if he wanted to. The only person who was never confused, and only pretended irritation, was Nathalie.

'Hawes,' Ben abruptly addressed the butler, 'No one to help you serve? Where's Maggie? Isn't she in today?'

'No, Sir, her boy is not well again and she was obliged to ...' The butler inclined his face towards Viola to indicate that all of this had already been gone through.

'Ben, Ben, please not now. I know all about it and it's all right. We can manage,' Viola said.

'Of course we can. I just wondered, my imperious darling, that's all. I shall serve you myself as you have never been served before. Watch out, Hawes, you'll soon be out of a job. Give me that dish, give me those things. Right.'

Ben grabbed the napkin thrown over the butler's arm and started a foolish performance delighting Nathalie. The butler was unperturbed, he was entirely used to this kind of behaviour and whatever the joke, however chaotic things became, he remained still-faced and efficient. The only time he showed himself to be aware of the reactions of those he served was when he served Lydia, if she became hopelessly muddled with the spoons or with helping herself from something he offered he would gently guide her through the correct procedure and give a trace of a wink when her frightened face looked up at his.

As Ben served he banged, dropped and rattled the accoutrements around, and just as Millie, plainly irritated, was poised, hands mid-air, to serve herself from the proffered dish, he swung away from her.

'I saw you, dog! BLOODY DOG! GET BACK! GET BACK!'

Millie, still further ruffled, re-settled her hands in her lap. It was always the same here. The overwhelming energy of the family; so involved with themselves, so sure, so inexorably Wavell. 'Come to lunch and see us. Enjoy us.' No time to enquire into anyone else's life. And Viola pretends to be annoyed, but she loves it; his buffoonery makes her look more regal than ever and that poor wretched child of theirs becoming more spoilt by the day.

'I'm sorry, Ben, I was miles away. Did you say something?' Millie looked up at him and asked as he offered the dish to her once more.

'Yes, Minnie. Sorry ... MILLIE. How are you? I mean, how are you really?'

'Well, I was going to tell you about the trip to Calif ...'

'GET BACK!' Ben roared at a venturing dog. He handed the dish to the butler, 'Hawes, you do this. I'm fed up with it ... GET BACK!'

'Dad, do shut up. Don't shout, you're frightening the dogs. Look how they're cowering. Animals and babies don't like you, you're too noisy and bossy.'

'They're not cowering, are you doggies? They love me. It's nasty, whiney little girls they don't like. My voice is firm and commanding. They know where they are with me, don't you,

doggies?' He bent sideways in his chair addressing the dogs
and putting on his "doggy" voice; the youngest crept forward,
head close to the ground and slightly turned, making sucking
noises with its tongue. One leg, now another. Steady. What's
this? Is it a game? Is it food? Not too fast. A little further ...
'GET BACK! BLOODY DOG!' It dashed back and sprawled,
head on paws, watching. Get the next signal right.

'There! There you are, Mummy, Lydia. Did you see that?
He's mean. You're a bully. Lydia's frightened of you, aren't
you, Lydia?'

'Well, Lydia,' asked Ben, 'are you?'

Lydia swallowed and blushed. She could not say 'no', that
would be disloyal to Nathalie, and she could not say 'yes', that
would be rude to Ben.

'She is, she is,' cried Nathalie, bouncing on her chair,
thrilled with the silence, the implied affirmation.

'Why don't you shut up, Natta?' Ben said. 'No one can think
anything with you around, you won't let them. You'll have to
be a Trade Union leader when you've grown up, which of
course you think you already have, and, my darling, you might
have noticed that your friend has not yet had a chance to
speak. I should like to get to know her a little ... Let's see now,
"Lydia",' he considered, 'it's a nice name but I shall call you
Lyd, because it's friendlier. Is that all right?'

'Yes, quite all right, thank you,' Lydia said, flinching. She
had always thought that was the trouble with her name: you
couldn't do anything with it.

'I should like you, Lyd, to give me an opinion. I like
squeezing opinions out of little girls. It's very easy with Natta
because she's full of them, the wrong ones of course. Tell me,
do you believe in "pre" or "post" marital sex?'

'Really, Ben, you're intolerable,' Viola said.

There was a cough from the governess and an exasperated
sigh from Millie, but Lydia was going to try to rise to the
occasion; however, in her eagerness to respond she became
muddled with the 'pre' and the 'post' and she said, 'I believe in
pre-marital sex ... I think.'

Ben slammed his hand on the table and shouted 'I SAY,
WELL DONE.' Then he gave a mock frown and said, 'But you
shouldn't.'

Although all the adults were amused by the child she felt that somehow she had blundered.

'I believe in sex too,' Nathalie chipped in, ' "Pre" or "Post", or anything.'

'Stop showing off, Natta,' Ben said, then half rose from his chair and pushed his head into the slope of her fragile shoulder, drinking in the scent, the throbbing proximity of his darling, his wonderful, brave, precocious darling.

'You're an awful, awful, repulsive little girl and I adore you.'

Nathalie turned her head away and swept her hand through the air to cover, from a distance, a mannered yawn.

'You see, don't you Millie, they never change?' said Viola, and turning to Ben and Nathalie, 'Darlings, do stop now, Millie wants to tell us about California. Was it nice? Did you have a chance to look up Aunt Hilda?'

'Do what to WHO? Oh, Mummy!' Nathalie pressed her hand over her mouth, spluttered and turned red in an effort to control the delicious giggling hysteria, but laughter spilled out and over.

'It's "whom", sweetheart, and what is so funny, anyway?' said Viola.

'I thought you said … I thought …' Convulsed again.

Ben watched Nathalie with his chin cupped in his hand, and shaking his head he said, 'Dirty little girl,' but his eyes were smiling, smiling.

'This is really very silly, isn't it, Lydia?' said Millie, turning to Lydia, searching for an ally, but Lydia, lost in the jokes, longed to be drowning in that laughter too and to be freed from merely observing.

'Enough.' Ben raised his hand and smiled placatingly at his frowning wife. 'Enough filth, Natta. GEMME?' he said emphatically.

'Gotcha, Dad, Gotcha,' Nathalie replied, making a supreme effort to control herself.

'No, don't. Both of you. I can't bear that awful slang.' Viola put her hands over her ears. 'They say it such a lot, Millie, don't they? I'm sure you've heard them before, and I know they only do it to annoy me, but these things stick and become a habit. You don't let your boys say that sort of thing, do you?'

'Well, no, not if I can help it, but I must say …'

'Okay, point taken,' said Ben. 'Gotcha, one might say,' and instantly slapped his hand over his mouth, rolled his eyes and raised his eyebrows at the giggling girls. 'Sorry, it just slipped out. Now what I want to know is, what are you going to wear at the ball? Something lovely; hundred's spent? Mmm?'

'What ball, Daddy? Where?'

'Here, of course. We are going to have a Viennese evening. Didn't you know? You should, because, after your Mother, you will be the most beautiful young lady there.'

'Mummy, why didn't you say? Oh, Lydia, think of it.'

'Ben.' Viola's voice cut through Nathalie's excitement, 'The girls will not attend.'

'Oh, Viola, why? It would be such fun and Natta would look so lovely. I'll help her to get the dress if she hasn't got one.'

'Yes, Mummy, why? It's not fair.'

Viola lengthened her neck, pursed her lips, prepared for the onslaught.

'I could go. I'm twelve and everyone says I look older. Daddy wants me to go, don't you, Daddy? And Lydia would absolutely love it, it's just her sort of thing, isn't it, Lydia?'

'You are not twelve, you are eleven and too young. I am not discussing it now.' There was a sudden flare in Viola's eyes and she said between clenched teeth, 'I told you not to mention it, Ben. Why can't you listen?' Adding, in order to soften her anger in front of Millie, 'Hopeless man.'

Millie's eyes flickered between Viola and Ben, picking up the nuances in every phrase and look that passed between them. Ben sank in his chair in sulky defeat and when Nathalie saw this she ran from the room sobbing.

'Now look what you've done, Ben. How could you? Poor little Natta. Never mind, Paris will make up for it,' Viola said.

'Paris? What Paris? Oh, never mind, tell me later, I've just thought of something to dry the tears. I'll give her my present.' He jumped up and left the room.

With Ben and Nathalie gone, lunch proceeded tediously and Millie at last told them about her Californian trip. When they had nearly finished Ben re-entered and stood behind Viola's chair with his arms clasped behind his back. Millie's talk trailed off as she looked at Ben standing, grinning. Viola looked behind her.

'What is it, Ben, why don't you sit down? We'll never finish lunch at this rate and there are fourteen to dinner tonight.'

Ben kissed the top of her head where her hair was swept into a knot. He came to her side and facetiously knelt on one knee, removed a fork from her long fingers and pressed her hand to his lips. Viola leant back in her chair allowing him to kiss her languid hand while she prettily tapped her mouth with her other hand pretending her smile was a yawn. It was easy to see who Nathalie copied.

'A little Nothing from the servant of a Queen.' He placed a river of diamonds on her wrist. Viola snatched her hand from him and held her wrist close to her breast while she studied the bracelet. She looked down at Ben, who was still kneeling; there were tears in her eyes.

'Ben, I asked you not to ...' her voice quavered. For a moment she pressed his huge, curly head to her shoulder, then she, too rushed from the room sobbing.

'Good. That's all right then,' Ben said when the door closed and delightedly helped himself generously to food and wine. 'Now then, if she had said "Thank you, darling, it's lovely", it would have been no good; would have had to change it right away for something better, but tears are a mark of approval. You do see my women are potty, don't you Lyd? He leant across to Lydia and said in a stage whisper, 'It's the foreign blood that does it. Wogs, you know.' Then added, 'Oh, Christ, I still haven't heard about the dreaded Aunt Hilda. How is the old bag?'

'It's all right, Ben,' Millie said with controlled impatience, 'don't worry, I have to go. I suppose I'll see you at the ball.' When she reached the door she turned and looked at him in silence until he glanced up at her enquiringly. 'You're blind, Ben. You think you know why she's crying, but really you've no idea what's going on at all.'

'What's she mean by that, Lyd? Anyway, they're both crying. Interfering baggage.'

The governess rose and Lydia made her escape with her.

How exciting Ben had been when she was a child. He had a way of rattling the key on the locked door to the adult world, hinting that he might let a little girl enter and Lydia had thought she would never tire of watching him, hearing him;

but on that day nine years later, sitting next to him in the car while he was eager for her attention, she was worried that she would be late home.

Ben stopped the car in a quiet, tree-lined street. 'Look, that's it.' He pointed to a house opposite with some steps leading to the front door. It was impossible to see more in the heavily falling rain.

'Please don't think I'm rude or anything, but I can't stay long, it'll take me ages to get back,' Lydia said.

'No, it won't, I'll call a cab. Where do you live anyway?' He gave a penetrating look at 'off Baker Street' but said nothing and she found herself excusing it. 'Oh it's not very … of course, but well … well we've made it … home.'

'We, eh?' he said.

She followed him up the steps, intrigued, despite her desire to be getting home. The street lamp did not help Ben much as he fumbled for the right key. 'Bloody little thing,' he was muttering and 'Ah, got it,' as the door opened.

It flashed into Lydia's mind that he had aged; dealing so fussily with a key, acting the way old people do, as though the incidentals of life are ganging up on them: plugs, handles, especially keys and locks not responding the way they used to: setting out to trick and make life difficult. He switched on the lights and ushered her quickly from the narrow hall into the sitting-room, saying, 'Now, let me give you a drink. Let's see. I know, a Moscow Mule. Do you know what that is? Ginger beer, lime juice and vodka.'

'Whisky and water, please.'

'You can't mean it?' he said.

That was the first time he really looked at her, as if the request for such a downright drink had thrown her into focus (young girls liked to play around with alcohol, didn't they?) and then to see her, little Lyd of years ago standing there in his own room with no other reason for being there than that he had invited her. He deserted the drinks tray and held her shoulders between his hands; narrow, vulnerable shoulders.

'Lyd. Lyd. It's wonderful to see you. Standing there you look like … well, you just remind me of things I thought quite dead in my mind. You are a little bigger, I believe. Not much. You must be twenty, but you still look twelve, well not quite, but still at an age when you're not eyeball to eyeball with maturity.' He tilted her chin up to him. 'Lyd, little Lyd,' he said again. Embarrassed, Lydia lifted her head and turned it away.

'Right,' he said, and forgetting the drinks, snapping his concentration on her face, he began to describe excitedly how drab the room had been before he transformed it into this richly coloured, chaotic cave: scarlet walls and a huge sofa massed with cushions. Books littered everywhere, some open displaying prints of birds, some spread and lying face down, piles of new ones with pristine dust-covers. The room was designed for comfort; it was easy to imagine Ben here, alone, reading and smoking, with his feet on the wide stool in front of the sofa. He's probably lonely, Lydia thought, must be. The only orderly thing in the room was a large desk standing like a temple to virtue amidst abandon, with silver letter-knives, pencils and pens, immaculately lined up beside half-full filing trays. An austere desk, very proud of its purpose, the schizophrenic spot in this otherwise sensual room.

Ben noticed Lydia's interest in the desk. He stood beside it and tapped the leather top. 'Oh, yes, work,' he said. 'Trying to give it up, you know, semi-retired and semi-retarded, that's me.' They laughed.

'What do you do? I mean, I could never make that out as a child, or are you really retired?'

'Damn it all, thanks, Lyd, I'm not that old. Not quite. I'm in electronics. My father backed the firm in the twenties when electronics was the smart new thing and after university, he pushed me onto the shop floor, letting me work my way up. My strongest point is I can sell anything to anyone, that, and man management. What else can I tell you? You've a right to ask. I shall ask you all about your life in a minute.' But before she could have asked any question, he said, 'Hey, come this way, I want to show you my cellar.' He led her back into the narrow passage and opened a door to reveal rows of red-necked bottles craning from racks. 'It's only a cupboard really, but it does.'

Lydia was enjoying how easy it was, after all, not to feel childish, beginning to regain some of that hard-won confidence that had deserted her when she first heard his voice. His enthusiasm and eagerness to show her everything in the house made her feel he was the child and she the condescending adult.

'Come on, I'll show you upstairs. It's not grand but all right for a bachelor.' He mounted the stairs in twos, threw open a door to a single-bedded room clearly unused, 'Guest room, but no one ever stays there.' He opened another, letting Lydia peer through while he leant against the passage wall lighting a cigarette.

The curtains were already closed here. In the gloom she could make out a wide bed with a red cover. On the dark walls gold-frame drawings hung in pleasing disorder. A door on the far side of the room led into a large bathroom where the light was on; a towel hung limp from the wash-basin, clothing was dropped about the floor, the wardrobe door gaped. He had been dressing here in a hurry, but it was a cold chaos, yesterday's disarray; obviously, whatever he was doing last night, he had not woken up here. Lydia felt strangely cheated. Maybe he was not quite what she had assumed him to be: a redundant dad. And what about Nathalie, anyway? He had not mentioned her yet. She dared herself a little joke.

'And so this is where it all happens?' She said it to draw attention to the fact that she had grown up and to lead into telling about Eric, but his matter-of-fact reply, 'Of course,' left her face and neck burning. She wished she had never said it; it was not her sort of remark anyway. She felt a rill of resentment. He obviously was not lonely, he had people to buy scarves for and more; so there was no good reason for making her late when she had so much to do before Christmas. She changed the subject.

'I see your bathroom's as untidy as Nathalie's was. I remember you coming to say goodnight and going on about how she left things around.'

Ben looked at her with such urgency she was startled. 'Do you though? Because I do. I remember all of those things, Lyd, and I think about them all the time.'

Although she did not share his desperation, she shared the pleasure in the memory.

Ben had visited the girls in the bathroom the evening after that tearful lunch. He came wearing a dinner jacket and sat sideways on the empty bath, still warm and steaming from the girls' riotous splash. Nathalie's bedroom and bathroom had been Lydia's favourite rooms and bathtime was the nicest ritual of the day. With his legs hanging over the edge of the bath Ben ticked them off for not putting the top on the toothpaste, aimed damp sponges at them and pretended to trip Nathalie as she walked up and down the bathroom brushing her hair idly and reciting 'The Lady of Shalott'. She, of course, stepped quietly round the outstretched foot without even looking.

> 'She left the web, she left the loom,
> She made three paces thro' the room,
> She saw the water-lily bloom,
> She saw the helmet and the plume …

'… and she … erm … she …'
And Ben continued:

> 'She looked down to Camelot.
> Out flew the web and floated wide;
> The mirror cracked from side to side;
> "The curse is come upon me," cried
> The Lady of Shalott.'

'I thought shallot was an onion. Do you think the onion was named after her breath? I'll bet that's why she was shut up in a tower. Bad breath.' Nathalie said.

'God, your humour's tedious. Are you all like that at school? It's a tragic poem, Natta. You don't appreciate the symbolism.'

'Show-off,' she said.

Followed by Ben, Nathalie whisked into her bedroom and while the girls climbed into their beds, Ben toyed with the silver hairbrushes and little glass bottles on the lace-clad dressing-table. He picked up clothes and books, looking at each one carefully, then over to Nathalie as if already mystified by the trappings and private world of this miniature woman. He turned off the light and went to sit, huge and hunched, on Nathalie's bed, spreading her hair in a tawny halo on the pillow, silhouetted in the darkness by a roundabout nightlight casting minacious shadows in the room. From her dark corner Lydia saw Ben's black shape grow another smaller head as Nathalie wrapped herself around him.

'Don't go, Daddy! Don't go! Lydia doesn't want you to go either, do you, Lydia? Tell us about that man you used to know, that tramp, the one who put his warty hand in a bag and asked someone else to open it so that they would catch the warts. You know the one.'

'I can't think which one you mean, but I must go now, we have hordes in the house tonight, but listen ...' the black shape moved its big head, the little one nodded and the blackness separated, became two again.

Ben crossed the room to where Lydia lay listening to the pillow's heartbeat and ruffled her hair. 'G'night, little Lyd.' The door slammed. A tear had traced its way round her temple and broken in strands of hair.

When she was a child night-time and sleep had brought horrors into Lydia's mind that divided it. Its search for light and warmth drove her somnambulant body into rooms and passages that, if she suddenly woke, were far colder and more threatening than any dream landscape. Later that night Lydia was seeing from some curlicue on an elaborately plastered ceiling her flimsy white form standing in the moonlight spattering through a huge latticed window. She felt herself abruptly swirl down in relieved reunion, but the shock awoke her body. She stood terribly cold in the dark room amidst furniture that breathed out the warmth and scents of recent occupation; she was in the oldest part of Eden, an Elizabethan room sometimes used as a drawing-room.

She was used to waking and finding herself beached on the shores of reality, so she waited for familiarity to seep back. It did when she heard a voice somewhere over in the darkness.

'Do wait. Come here, just a moment. Please. Come on.' A quiet voice, so easy and strong that the darkness lost its paralysing power. Oh yes, she would come over, but where? She moved through the room, found a door partly open. The half-light in the hall revealed two figures, and it was not so easy to run to the source of that voice.

Ben stood at the bottom of the stairs and Viola two shallow steps above him. He was holding her wrists, looking up at this woman, whose tall, languid, black and white beauty made this bear of a man seem angular and earthbound. Somewhere in a past of hers she had been a ballet dancer and the training still enabled her to conquer empty space with a fluency that made those around her look like counter-stream fish. The light from a lamp swinging outside the front door threw their shadows high up the wall and down, glowing the folds of Viola's blood-coloured crepe-de-chine gown.

Ben spoke again, 'Come on, darling, talk about it now, please. You can go to Paris anytime. Why tomorrow? I'm only here four days, until the ball, and Natta goes back after that and then I'm away again. Is it really only shopping? Please don't go.'

He pressed his head onto her stomach and wrapped her narrowness into him. Lydia saw an elongated shadow with head cast back on an undulating neck and heard the bitchy whispers of silk.

'No, Ben. Stop it. I don't want to. Do stop.' Then she heard footsteps and silk moving away upstairs. There was silence.

How different was this man, this night-time Ben, with his attention not distracted by silly little girls. He spoke in another voice, serious, sadder, moved less recklessly, as if chastened by an evening of adult company. He came towards the door behind which Lydia stood so still, giddy from holding her breath, terrified and hating being the bird strung in the wires of other people's relationships. Ben stopped to light a cigarette and drew the door shut; but some sense, some instinct about the tone of silence in that empty room must have made him re-open the door to look in at the blackness.

There was a little, luminous tremble of life standing, just there, and it was gone as clouds swept across the moon. He stood trying hard to see what was really there, then stepped forward a little.

'Lyd? Is that you?' Not sure, not at all sure. 'Good God, it is. How the devil did you get in here?'

He crossed to her and knelt down looking into her face; she stared back and through him, and felt herself being seen as something incomprehensible. Ben slowly put out his hand and traced away a fall of stringy hair from her forehead, then lightly let his fingers rest on that quivering frame. His other

hand came forward and the largest part of this little girl's body
was surrounded and covered by this man's two hands; not
held, for his touch was so tentative she only felt the pulse from
them spreading through her. Almost imperceptibly his hold
tightened on the thinness of her flesh, the division at the top of
her rib cage under his two thumbs; hip bones at the bottom of
his palms; and her spine (no longer than his forearm from
small head down to the very last, tiny, diamond vertebra)
curved out, in and away under his fingers.

And they were caught these two; she by a terror of this
familiar man in the unfamiliar night, his touch, his scent, so
overwhelmingly close; and it seemed he by a fear that to grasp
this form might extinguish its fragile life; leaving him holding
a crumpled mound, like a puppet dashed to the ground by a
distracted child. It was as though something else too kept him
from leading the child away from this dark room; that some
horrible thought had come to him and despite shaking his
head to clear it, it still hung sinister within him. He quickly
grasped and raised her, bearing her body in front of him like a
disgraced dog that he did not wish to touch his clothing.

He set her down in a passage upstairs and disappeared into a
brightly lit room.

'Darling. What's-her-name's been sleepwalking again. I
think you'd better put her back. Be careful, she's still asleep.'

Almost instantly Lydia was being borne to her bed in Viola's
smooth arms, her loosened hair brushing against her face.
Kindly, firmly, she was settled in the camp-bed set up for her in
the corner of Nathalie's room, and Viola crossed to where
Nathalie herself slept coiled in her blankets, bent and kissed
her daughter.

'Goodnight, my angel. My darling angel.'

Lydia did not know whether Ben had remembered precisely
what she had, and she was too disturbed by the feelings it left
to ask, but when she turned her face to his he whispered, 'Little
Lyd. You were so frightened of the dark.' To relieve his
embarrassment he changed the mood swiftly, 'Natta's very
well, you know. At least she is by all reports. I haven't seen her
for a couple of years. Two years, eleven months and nine days,
to be precise.'

'I'd love to see her again.'

'So would I.' The thirty-five years separating their ages revealed themselves with alarming clarity, the broad shoulders collapsed, the lines about his mouth etched deeper. Lydia felt she should not ask, let him tell what he chose, and he altered yet again, 'And still no drink. Forgive me, I'm an appalling host.'

They returned downstairs. Having placed the glass in her hands with a 'Can't get over it: you and whisky', he telephoned for a taxi to take her home.

So that's it, Lydia thought, it's nearly over; this might be the last time she would ever see him. After all, it had been years and then only chance.

He poured himself a drink, seated himself on the edge of the sofa holding the glass with his fingertips, like an actor with a prop he had not been warned of. He became ill at ease. It was possible now to see there was a man other than the extrovert; the teaser, the dashing dad with the savoir faire.

'Lyd?'

'Mr. Wavell …?' She was berating herself in silence for not taking the opportunity to call him Ben, but he did not seem to hear, and said simply.

'I'm desolate.'

There was silence. She waited for the joke, the wink, the reprieve from seriousness, but it did not come. The tone of his voice was a chink in a wall through which a wilderness was visible. Still looking down, he said, 'When you knew me before I had everything. My beautiful family, and they were beautiful, weren't they, Lyd? Viola and Natta. My home, my work. Everything with me, before me. And where now? Viola married to some Swiss banker; of all things a bloody gnome. Natta far away. Won't see me. Won't speak to me … best really I suppose, but I thought she was perfect. I'm not saying it just because she's mine … was mine. You knew her. There'll never be anyone like her, will there?

'Do you know that that summer when I met you was our last summer? Viola left me to marry that bloody man and took Natta with her. And when she was gone Eden no longer had a point. I mean I only bought the house for her. It was a perfect setting for her. Viola was the sort of woman who required a setting. For myself, I'd have lived in London. My work was very demanding then. Sometimes I'd be away for days. So, anyway, after waiting for months, knowing she'd never return, hoping she would, with the rooms laughing at me playing families alone, I started to lead a bachelor life at Eden. Parties and things, people, you know.' He looked at Lydia to see if she did. She knew. 'But it didn't feel right there. I might be with some woman or another and would suddenly get an image of Viola and even me there too ... I'd actually see these things going on as real before me. People thought I was mad. The rooms were ashamed of my treachery too, except by then they were just squash courts with all the stuff that Viola had managed to remove. But the laughter was still there in the walls, love all cupped-up in the cornices. I mean, Lyd, we did love, didn't we? And laugh? So I sold it and here I am with walls that don't even know or care who I am, they have been stripped, papered and painted so often, poor little raped rectangles; even my work doesn't hold the same excitement.' He looked up at her. 'And then I saw your little face in all that hubbub this afternoon and a string of yesterdays met together and, God knows, I can see myself more clearly through your face than through any glass, and I'm desolate.'

So, late in life, at nineteen, the last nursery rug was pulled from beneath Lydia's feet. There was no such thing as the iron adult; if anyone was, it was going to be Ben, and here he was before her with his head on his arms, dejected, finished.

The transition from child, in his company, to woman was an easy one: one moment politely enquiring, admiring, and the next standing with her fingers in his warm hair, pressing his head against her womb hard to take away all his pain. To lose him in herself. Nothing will touch you. I'll take your desolation. I'll live out your loneliness. Wear it out on me; use it up; go back to where you belong: in happiness, I'll take you to the door. She was strong, his misery made her invincible.

After some moments Ben reached for Lydia's wrists, freed his head from her hands and rose. He towered above her again. Still with her hands and wrists lost in his grasp he looked down at her. He had switched again to his other self.

'You're a sweet child, Lyd. Haven't I always said you're a sweet child? You must give me your number ... perhaps if

Natta gets in touch or something ...' He shrugged. Lydia wanted to say, 'You don't have to be polite and take my number,' she knew it was only that, but she did not like to say it. He scribbled it on the corner of the blotter in the centre of his desk. 'Now, have you enough for a taxi? Here.' He pushed a note into her pocket.

Pulling her collar up he gazed into her face as though it was a screen through which he stared past any consciousness of her. He cupped the back of her head drawing her to him, walled her face with his other hand. She was lost in a cave of warmth, drugged by a scent that had haunted her since childhood: a mixture of limes, nicotine and male, that came to her once when she was lost in a room.

'If I did ring, if I did ask you to come back, you say "No" to me. Gettit?'

'Gotcha,' she whispered. They tried to laugh and he shut the door.

* * *

'Lyd, are you still there? I want to see you. Please meet?'

'No. Don't ask. I can't.'

'Well, listen then and see if you won't change your mind. When you left me here four years ago (I can see the road from where I sit now and almost the ghost of the car with you in it disappearing round the corner into the village), I packed up then and flew to Rabat. The deal I did there was disastrous, because by then I was only thinking of her, and by then, too, I had decided that I wouldn't go to England and wait for her, because your own words kept coming back to me. You said, "She won't come back, you must see that ..." I went to Paris to find her, hoped, even, she would come to the airport to meet me, but only Millie turned up. Poor old girl, she seemed to have aged terribly. Her manner with me was very different, rather reserved. I spent a few days cajoling her; bought her things; took her to dinner, she'd always been easy to please; but whatever I did she wouldn't give me the address I wanted, until one evening we were walking back to the hotel from a restaurant, there was a sudden downpour and we went into a bar for shelter, there she suddenly softened and I found the reason for her cold manner. She told me the child had never been adopted and was living with his mother after all, that he was two years old and that the resemblance to me was uncanny. She looked at me for a long time, tears in her tired, hurt eyes. I know she was waiting for me to say something to help her disbelieve the obvious, but I could think of nothing as she sat there looking remote, betrayed. Without a word she scribbled something on a scrap of paper and passed it to me; it was the address. I took her to the airport the next morning, put her on a plane for London. She seemed very anxious to go. Funny: after all those years of friendship we suddenly had nothing to say to each other. But it didn't matter much to me, then, because I had the address; all I wanted to do was go there.

'I suppose Millie had been almost my only friend, real old friend, that is. And you, of course. You were only a child when I first saw you at Eden and I think I loved you then. I know it. I don't think "friend" is the right word for someone who is part of your being, as you are of mine. You knew I was coming back to you, didn't you ... please meet? ...'

4

In the taxi returning home from Ben's house after that chance meeting Lydia had examined an old addiction to Ben's presence, insisting to herself that it was only the memory of a feeling. She had, as a child, secretly coveted his attention, although it was not in her nature to set about gaining it, and when she had been left at Eden for two days without Nathalie or Viola she had at first believed that attention might be focussed on her. They had gone to Paris, as Viola said they would, despite Ben's pleas. Lydia pretended for all she was worth that she was Nathalie, that Eden was her real, her only home.

However, the two days did not go as she had pictured. The weather suddenly became extremely hot and the sun brought a quiet drowsiness about the house which emphasised the absence of Nathalie and her mother. The governess had been busy inside her own room, not transferring to Lydia the hennish fussing she lavished upon, and maddened Nathalie with. Ben only appeared at one meal and seemed then withdrawn, hardly speaking a word.

By the second afternoon Lydia had been to all the 'camps' and 'bowers' and other exciting places she and Nathalie had made or discovered. None seemed the same without Nathalie to bring them to life. She went into the long attics where the dust shimmered and spun in the sunlight slanting through the round windows. There again, without Nathalie it was not filled with the possibilities, the endless games of imagination; it was just dirty, rather frightening among the trunks, the dressmaker's dummies, the superfluous furniture swathed and swollen in sheets. Having rooted there a while Lydia found a violin with the bow tied to its neck by a piece of string. She had been learning the violin at school for several terms and loved it, but played only at school because her parents could not stand the sound of her practising at home. Now in the attic she scraped away happily on the out-of-tune instrument until she ran out of remembered music. Then she had looked about in the old trunks for some music books, but found none. She was going to put the instrument down when she had an idea. Lydia took the violin and bow out of the attic to a long upstairs passage where, under a tall, narrow window, stood a piece of furniture that had always fascinated her. It was a marble-topped commode, the front of which was marquetry depicting musical instruments and scrolls of music, the detail such as to depict actual notes on a staff. She listened hard for signs of anyone who might hear, but Hawes would have been in his cottage at that time of day, the governess shut in her room at the other end of the house and Ben she had not seen since lunch-time on the day before, so she doubted that he was in the house at all.

After studying the piece of furniture, twisting her head this way and that to read the scrolls with their tiny dots of shiny, black wood to show notes, and smiling at her own silly game, she had started to play, improvising where she could make no sense at all. It absorbed her attention completely. She forgot about Nathalie being in Paris, about going home soon, and she did not notice a shadow fall across her as she knelt on the soft, thick carpet in the blue afternoon light. Only when he was crouched beside her, peering at the scrolls on the commode himself did Lydia realise Ben was there.

He looked from the commode back to Lydia with amazement, said quietly, 'I can see exactly what you're trying to do. What a good idea. I'd never have thought of such a thing, but it sounds awful. I don't think the cabinet-maker was any musician, do you?' He laughed gently and then frowned, as if observing her face for the first time. He moved the fall of hair from her eyes and touched her cheek, 'You're a strange little girl, Lyd. So strange.'

There was something different about him. Ben had always used two voices, his public and his private voice. The public voice was for when he was telling jokes or talking to people he either did not really like or who bored him; he also used his public voice on Lydia. His private voice he used when he spoke to Nathalie or Viola, and once when Lydia had passed a partly open door she had heard him using it on the telephone. It was a gentler voice, without pretence; and for the first time he had used his private voice with her.

He rose briskly, picking up a file he had placed on the floor beside him and disappeared down the passage.

'Won't be long now, eh?' he shouted back over his shoulder, 'They'll be back tomorrow. Isn't it horrid without them?' Public voice.

She asked the taxi to drop her on the corner of her street and, feeling flush, because of the tenner Ben had given her, overtipped.

The moment the ground floor door shut behind her she heard, from the top of the house, their own front door open. Eric shouted down through the stairs, 'Lydia? Is it you, Lovey?' He thumped down and Lydia rushed up to meet him, bringing with her the scent of evening and rain. She clung to him tightly on the landing. 'Goodness, I've been so worried,' he said, removing her hands from around his neck and holding her at arm's length. 'You are all right, aren't you?'

For a moment, while he was moving her hands, it was as if a slide had slipped in Lydia's mind and through a transparency of reality there was another of Ben holding her the way Eric did now, except that her small hands had been lost in Ben's large ones.

'I'm sorry,' she said at last, 'I met someone I haven't seen for ages and went back to his house in Holland Park for a drink, and Eric, it was awful, it really was …'

'Holland Park? Miles away. I must say you look pretty shattered, you poor thing, and then crushed to death on the tube.'

'No, not really, because …'

'Tell me all when we're upstairs and you can rest,' he said, and feeling strangely guilty she thought that the stairway was no place to tell him she had been given the money for a taxi.

When they reached their door Eric said, looking pleased, 'By the way, Greg's here.' And Lydia's heart sank; all she wanted was to be alone with Eric and to push over some of the pain communicated to her from Ben so they could analyse it together and diminish it, but when she followed Eric into the sitting-room, right away the knot of coldness, emptiness within her softened. It was a low-ceilinged room with an oval black iron fireplace at the far end, where Eric now bent puffing fussily upon the smokeless fuel to produce more flame; red plush curtains drawn, it was glowing, cluttered home and Ben's misery began to seem a far thing.

Greg was leaning against the mantelpiece. He was very tall and smattered with ginger hair on every patch of flesh that showed. For a moment he looked like a genie as he stood suffused in an alley of smoke from the long clay pipe he held aloft in greeting, hand haloed in red fuzz.

'And here she is,' he cried in mock music-hall tones, 'the Little Thing herself,' and added genuinely, 'Oh … it's lovely to see you.' He picked Lydia up, crushing her to him and his beard, and spun her round the room; the little gold ring in his left ear pressing into her cheek.

Since they had invited Greg for a meal, to thank him for telling them about the flat, he had lurked a lot in their life; appearing at unexpected moments and filling them with animated chatter about his own unstable existence with a Danish wife, not his own, and the dramas they liked to create for themselves. But while he pranced and gesticulated (a toothbrush in his top pocket as a badge of his footlooseness), a shadow within him watched Eric and Lydia for signs of tarnish on the silver harmony in which the couple lived; not from any malevolent wish, on the contrary, so long as their happiness existed he had an example to hold up to himself. But there was part of him that, not accounting for his own easily bored nature, considered Lydia as the perfect woman for him: so quiet, happy to please, gently loving, the ideal panacea for his turbulent spirit. If she should show any shortcomings it would not only offend his dream of perfection but would spoil this refuge from his own life.

Lydia had overcome most of her reservations about Greg and she told herself that any doubt she had about him must be based upon jealousy of Eric's affection for him, and anyway he was their only real friend, the only person who, other than Eric's father, came to their home.

'Tell us all about it, Love. Who was this chap you met?' Eric said over his shoulder, still tinkering with the fire.

'He's just a lonely old man, really, but I felt terribly sorry for him.' And as she said it Lydia felt there was an inaccuracy there, yet both were facts: he was lonely and he was old. She explained how she knew him, how the Wavells' life had been, and about the meeting. 'I never knew there was anything like that in your childhood, Lydia, rich people, butlers and things,' Eric said. 'How nice. I would love a butler to serve my food, it's quite different from a waiter, isn't it, Greg? A waiter sort of slops it out for you and you sit there like a bit of a ninny, but a butler proffers, doesn't he, and you wave him away when you've got enough.'

'I've never thought about it,' Greg said, 'but if Lydia would proffer-off now and make a nice spaghetti I'll proffer for you all you want. I'll be butler for the night.'

Lydia went into the kitchen annoyed because they wouldn't seem to listen or take it seriously. But why should they have time for another man's misery? They were too young, too busy. She wouldn't try to tell them any more. It was not fair to show them that a life so full, so perfect, so hopeful as Ben's had seemed, can really be ... what was the word Ben had used? A charade.

Eric followed Lydia into the kitchen which led straight off the sitting-room and offered to help her. 'I'd rather do it alone,' she said sharply, then gently, 'Really, Love, it'll be quicker. You talk to Greg.'

He put his arms about her from behind and kissed her cheek. He smelt faintly of T.C.P. A minute later she heard him say confidentially to Greg, 'She is a bit upset, I think. Mustn't tease.' And Lydia smiled to herself

A while later when she went into the sitting-room carrying a tray Eric jumped to his feet and took it from her.

'Listen, Lovey,' he said excitedly, 'Greg had the most marvellous idea. Obviously that old chap has fallen on rather hard times ...'

'What "old chap"?' Lydia said, quite lost.

'You know, your old chap, Ben, isn't it? Well things have obviously gone very wrong for him, no more big houses and servants and divorced and all. Well, Greg thought, we thought, why not ask him here for Christmas? And it would be very good company for Dad.'

Lydia stood dumbstruck. She knew she had not given every detail about Ben, but that they should get him so wrong was ridiculous. The very thought of Ben in her own untidy, crowded little flat, and him with Eric's father, who could scarcely speak a full sentence any more and had to be spoon-fed, was awful.

'I've never heard anything so stupid,' she said angrily. 'If you hadn't been so busy making jokes about butlers you might have understood more about him. He's not like that at all ...'

'Not like what?' Eric said through her words, but she did not hear him.

'... and he's not poor, not in that way, and he's not lonely. He bought a scarf for someone today so he can't be that lonely and anyway he couldn't possibly come here.' She gestured at the room and grimaced.

The two men looked at Lydia and in the silence Lydia heard her angry words again and saw herself standing waving deprecating arms at the walls of her home.

'There's nothing wrong with our flat,' Eric said, hurt, with his head hung and rubbing a finger into the grain of the table where he sat. 'Sounds as though you're ashamed of it. I thought you liked it.'

'Oh, I do. I do.' Lydia was near to tears as she sat down beside Eric and put her head on his shoulder. 'Please, please don't let's talk about it any more. I love the flat and you and everything and I never want any of it to change. I'm sorry I shouted, I'm just terribly tired, that's all, and Ben and all of that is not important, let's just forget him.'

'Oh, sorry, Lydia, really. There, there, of course we'll forget it. I'm sorry.' And the two of them laughed shyly at their silliness in front of Greg, who had stood, still leaning against the mantelpiece with his arms crossed watching the whole scene. The smile on his face was cynical.

But over the following days Lydia had begun to feel a restlessness. At first she thought it was because she had completed her Christmas preparations rather too early for what was, after all, a very small celebration. One afternoon at the cafe while she was slapping rectangles of cheese between sparsely buttered, grey bread ('crusts orf? CRUSTS ORF?' the owner exploded the first day she ever prepared sandwiches, 'you've only been and gone and cut orf me profit, incha?') she examined her feelings and decided that the restlessness was not for change but perversely for continuation and she smiled as she thought how easily that was achieved. It was Wednesday, the day Lydia always met Eric from the school and went with him to visit Victor, Eric's father, in the rambling, dead-hearted 'Home'. They walked together along a comfortlessly saffron-lit residential street where the detached houses of Neo-nothing architecture stood primly behind over-attended front gardens.

'I've seen something so nice, Eric,' she began, 'and I've looked at it every day and it just gets nicer. I want to buy it, but with you, I only want it if you do. It's that sort of thing.'

'Oh, good, good, what is it?' Eric was pleased. They both loved buying.

Lydia paused, then said, 'It's a cradle. Made of oak and carved ...' she went on quickly to give him time for a convincing excuse should he need one, for even now their relationship had a tender reserve, '... and it has rockers, it's very low and awfully old and it's ...'

'Do you mean the one in the shop on the corner where the two old ladies are always making tea?'

'You've seen it then?'

Eric pulled Lydia's hand into his pocket with his own and walked on, as always looking at his feet, but she could see from a quick glance, which was all she dared, that he was smiling.

'Actually, I've bought it. Your present.'

They stopped briefly to hold each other and, in silence, seal their faith.

When they arrived at the Home, which always cast a pall of depression over them both, they were met by the Matron, a wide, big-boned lady hewn from rock, but with a gentle voice. 'Your father's in the lounge, Mr Evans. He's been a little confused today, but we think it's the excitement of going out for Christmas.'

The lounge was full, but the only sounds were coughs, groans and the occasional laugh, infectious, genuine, caused by nothing and stopping abruptly. The visitors talked in whispers. It was a home for the extraordinarily senile, not simply for the elderly who had nowhere to go; and Victor was by far the youngest inmate, he was only sixty-six, but his condition qualified him. When Eric had visited the place prior to his father's admission he was upset by the interminable grey and green of the walls, 'But Mr Evans,' the Matron had said, 'the paint was free and these people's lives are coloured by memories, the walls don't exist for them. No matter the colour, they will dissolve the walls and see what we can't. They want to be on their way out, Mr Evans, and a pretty wall won't keep them in.'

'Mr Evans. MR EVANS, your son is here. Come along now, wake up.' The Matron bent over the thin, erect, seemingly somnolent body.

'Shove off you dirty bitch.' He leant forward pushing his lean face towards the Matron's, '... see if I care.' Blank-eyed he pointed a finger towards Eric. 'If you think that young pup'll keep you, you're mistaken ... He'll be off ... Eric? Eric?' He addressed an empty space in a womanish tone. 'Marks haven't got the winter ones so you wear two summer ones 'till I say.'

'All right if I leave you then?' the Matron said, turning brightly to Eric before she whisked away. Eric knelt and stroked his father's hand.

'Hello, my son,' Victor said quietly. 'Your mother's just left. She won't be back this time, but we'll do, won't we? You and me.'

'We'll do, Dad, we'll do. It's all in the past now.'

Intelligence and a little shame worked into Victor's face, 'Yes, that's all over, isn't it? Now then ...' He studied Eric, 'How are the boys behaving, bet they don't dare play you up, eh? Be firm with them, that's the way.'

'No, Dad, they don't dare.'

Lydia then stepped forward; her habit was to stay removed until father and son greeted each other, and Victor had emerged from the confused past in which he lived between their visits.

'We're taking you out on Monday, Dad. Home for Christmas with us. And Dad, we've got some news ... we're getting married as soon as we can in the New Year. What do you say to that?'

Victor grinned broadly and nodded, 'Well blow me, blow me,' pretending for their sake it was a surprise. 'She's a good one, that one is, you'll be all right.'

On the day that Victor was due to begin his short Christmas stay with them, Eric left early to collect him and Lydia rushed to do her shopping in order to be home on their return. She was supporting a bag of shopping between herself and her front door while fishing for the key with her free hand; inside the flat the telephone was ringing. She let herself in and quickly put down the shopping, sure that it would be Eric to say that Victor was not well enough to come out, something that frequently happened. Although Lydia was very fond of him she was never as disappointed as Eric when this happened, because more often than not it was she who dealt with the bedpans and the spoon-feeding and, although she did not mind, it tired her, and at a deeper level than the physical. But she knew how to make Victor happy, enjoyed amusing him, and had planned many little ways to make this Christmas a particularly pleasant one for him. She lifted the receiver and answered, while absent-mindedly gazing at her image in the mirror above the telephone-table.

'Lyd, is it you?'

It was Ben's voice and she knew it but said, 'Yes, it is. Who's that?'

'It's me. Listen. Meet? Please meet. Today at four. You don't have to answer me, just come if you possibly can. Goodbye.'

There was no face in the mirror now, only mist, as she stood staring and listening to the burring of the vacant line. The voice had been unmistakable, severe. She was lost; her own home seemed an unknown place, her hand, still upon the receiver, someone else's, and that girl, now beginning to materialise in the mirror before her, she did not know and did not trust. The sound of heavy footsteps on the stairs shunted reality into place.

'Love? Love, we're back. Can you come and lend a hand?' Lydia retrieved herself; she knew her own image again with the sound of Eric's voice. Before she opened the door she paused to use her last moment alone. The manner of Ben's invitation seemed to make acceptance an admission, a capitulation, because he had not waited for an answer; but that was a good thing because he could not be offended if she did not go, which, of course, she couldn't; wouldn't.

'All right love, I'm coming,' she called down the stairs to Eric louder than was necessary.

Victor was ashen-faced and shaken from his journey; he did not know where he was and shielded himself with the proud and introspective expression he used whenever his wayward limbs were being arranged by others, as now these two young people placed his arms around their necks guiding him up sordid stairs where he did not want to go. They will carry me, yes, but I will leave my mind downstairs, I'll stay at the bottom, see if they can lift that. And he nodded fiercely at the excellence of his plan. 'That's right, Dad. Nearly there now,' Eric said.

For some time Victor sat where they put him with a rug over his knees in front of the fire muttering to the passers-by in his mind. Lydia watched him and thought, as she often did, that he was more handsome than his son, taller, leaner, a nobler specimen to look at physically. Eric must have taken after his mother.

Several times Lydia sought the moment to tell Eric about the telephone call, but it never came; Eric was too busy attending to his father, unpacking his few belongings and talking gently all the time to ease him into the present. When they were preparing lunch Lydia said, 'Love, you know Ben?'

'No, I can't remember a Ben, do you mean the new chap in the cafe?' Eric was preparing a tray for his father, but when Lydia did not answer he looked up and saw on her face the same pent-angered look that he remembered from that evening with Greg. A strange expression that he did not know as one of Lydia's and he was anxious to dispel it.

'Oh, yes. Yes, I do. Sorry, I wasn't thinking. Have you changed your mind, would you like him to come on Christmas Day? Or sometime?'

She remembered the evening too and felt the same irrational anger at Eric's suggestion. All she had to do was explain to Eric, give him some details, and yet she resented his need of explanation and her own confusion.

'No, no, no. Just forget it. It doesn't matter.'

'Sorry. Listen, I'll just help Dad with this.' He held up the tray with a bowl of soup on it, 'or do you want to?' Lydia shook her head. 'All right then. Will you do supper? He does like it so when you help him.'

'Yes, I'll do supper,' she sighed.

She stood and watched Eric feeding Victor, then went to the

window and looked out. There had been many little things she
had intended to do, all concerned with Eric and Victor, but all
she was doing was looking at her watch, working out how long
it would take to get there, and how long to return. At last she
said, 'Eric? Would you mind if I went out for a while. I don't
know why, it's just that ...'

'Do go out. Really,' Eric said, relieved that she had found a
way of dispelling her own mood. 'I do understand and I will
concentrate on Dad. He'll be all right by the time you get back,
after a little sleep and a talk. Honestly, Love, you have a nice
walk.'

Suddenly Lydia was happy. She was happy that Victor was
there, that Eric was so understanding, that he was the man she
was going to marry. She was happy and she was strong again;
she had the strength to share. She kissed Eric and held herself
tightly against him.

'Dear, dear Eric, I won't be long. I only want to think for a
bit. I'll read to Victor when I get back. He loves that.' She went
over to him and put her arm around his shoulders, 'I'll read to
you when I come back, your favourite "A.J. Wentworth, B.A."
Remember?' She tossed her head back to Eric, 'That always
makes him laugh,' she said, laughing herself.

Lydia walked for a long time still feeling elated and free. Eric
had wanted her to go, the relief showed on his face and when
she returned it was going to be easy to please him and his
father. It was good to feel the power and pleasure of making
people happy; it was a talent not to be abused. Or wasted. Her
only loyalty was to Eric but his, of course, was divided between
herself and Victor. Would Eric understand if she found other
loyalties? The answer had to be 'yes' because of his
preposterous invitation for Ben to spend Christmas with them.
She even shuddered again at the idea, then looked about the
street briefly aware of how deep in thought she had been; but
there were a lot of people and all too busy to notice her. She
had come a long way from home and could no longer pretend
she was walking aimlessly. She stopped and looked back along
the crowded street and it seemed that on the corner she could
see, amidst the shoulders of the throng, herself, a shy self that
wanted to turn towards Eric and home, peering curiously at
the one who was walking away.

Lydia walked up dilapidated stone steps to Ben's front door and was about to ring when she noticed it was not quite shut; she pushed it and walked in. Inside it was hot; soft lights were on everywhere and the curtains were drawn across the window at the top of the stairs. Here day had already been dispensed with, the house had settled for evening. The sound of lute music drifted with the scent of jasmine. Each tread of the stairs at the end of the short passage had a plant upon it; little stunted cactuses popping contorted growths, jasmine and ferns casting their foliage casually back over the stairs and the other plants.

The thick pile carpet muffled the sound of Lydia's entry and she stood taking in the atmosphere, detailing this place created by Ben before his massive presence eclipsed the setting; a harmonious, gentle setting at odds with this earthy man. She checked herself with a looking-glass that returned an antique flattery and walked to the door of the sitting-room.

Ben was on the far side of the room with his back to her; he was leaning with one arm stretched up against an alcove twiddling the knobs and dials of a stereo system. His movements were of a man who was entirely comfortable in the world: walls were there for leaning against, floors to sit on and space to be filled with great gestures. His thick, curly hair had been rich brown, but now, although not grey, was paled; his wide shoulders bore the ghostly weight of past years, almost, but not quite, imperceptibly. He turned his head and looked down, divining Lydia's presence like a blind man.

Quietly, to the floor he said, 'So, you came.' Then, as if awaking, he turned to her, arms outstretched, in a manner Lydia knew much better than the solitary, 'Lyd. You came. How sweet of you. I really wasn't sure if you would.' It was obvious from his voice that he was trying to quash the private urgency of the telephone call – let that be something she imagined.

Now her other self had caught up: Lydia Shy tugged at the sleeve of Lydia Free.

'I can't stay long, I'm afraid. It took ages getting here.' Ben stepped forward and put his hand on her shoulder. 'I quite understand,' he said with his head on one side prying into her averted eyes. He seemed amused. 'Come and sit down.' He crossed the room, pausing to light a cigarette, then sat on the edge of the wide stool in front of the fire. Lydia did not move from the doorway. 'Well come on, Lyd …' So she sat uneasily on the sofa before him.

'The reason I called,' Ben said investigating the palm of his cigarette hand, 'was that after you left I thought about our meeting. It was such an incredible coincidence, even to recognise you after all this time, that somehow it seemed a waste not to talk to you more. There were so many questions I meant to ask … and it brought back so many memories, my God. How is your father? He was a very meticulous little man, I remember. Good accountant.'

'Dead,' Lydia said abruptly. She never liked this subject because she could never conjure the pain people assumed it must have for her; she said again quietly, 'Dead … actually.' She knew the 'actually' softened the blow for the listener. Ben expressed all the usual sentiments without conviction as though he suspected her true feeling but said genuinely, 'If only I had known I could have helped in some way. You should have got in touch …' ('Scuse me, Aunt May, I'm going to ring my friends the Wavells, rich clients of Father's. They'll take me in.' 'Lydia speaking. No, your accountant's daughter. My parents are dead. Can I come and live with you or would you rather send money?') '… so then what happened?' Ben asked.

Lydia related carefully the details of her life up to the time she arrived in London, but when Ben asked her about work she hesitated; he would not understand. 'In a cafe,' she mumbled.

'In a what?' He was already leaning forward incredulously.

Lydia raised her eyes from her lap and stared at him for a moment. With a nod and a frown Ben encouraged her to go on.

'I said "a cafe", Mr Wavell, I'm a waitress in a cafe …'

'Ben, for Chrissake … Ben.' She did not hear his irritation.

'… and it's not even a smart one and I've worked there for two years because I couldn't get another job. No one would take me. I tried to be a receptionist, but you need bosoms for that …'

'Yours are O.K.,' he said with a smile.

'… and I couldn't go for shorthand typing because I couldn't do it.'

'Do what?' His hand hiding the broad smile this time.

'... And don't ask me why I didn't go to a finishing school in Switzerland, or somewhere, and learn something useful, as I am sure Nathalie did, because there wasn't any money. When my parents died it was discovered that the "meticulous little accountant" was a gambler. Everything went to pay his debts. Everything.' Lydia was shaking and she thought she was going to cry, which was strange because she had never wanted to cry about the injustice of it before.

'All right Lyd, all right,' Ben said kindly. 'I must say I think you have shown great ...' with a little difficulty he selected the word, '... determination.' He rose. 'Come, let's make some tea and while I totally mess up the kitchen we'll talk some more.'

The 'messing-up' turned out to be a studied operation, and because he appeared to be engrossed with cups, slices of lemon and a silver sugar bowl, Lydia talked more easily and began to tell him a little about the flat. As Ben raised the tray to take it through to the sitting-room he said, 'And do you live alone or share?'

Lydia was shocked that through all her talk she had not mentioned Eric and said quickly, 'No, no, I share. I've got a ... well ...'

'Lover?' Ben helped, mocking eyebrows raised.

'Yes,' Lydia said vaguely, musing over the word where Eric was concerned, 'I suppose he is really.' But when Ben went past her with the tray his expression was not mocking or amused, it was sour, lips tightly drawn.

When they sat down again he did not want to talk about the present any more, only the past they had shared and maybe, she thought, that was natural. Perhaps the present did have a tinny resonance when she referred to it; it was more fun to share his adult's eye upon her childhood.

Every time the conversation lulled, Lydia felt a mild surge of alarm: now then, this was it; time to go; to say goodbye; he was becoming bored. So when he rose and crossed the room to a pile of leatherbound photograph albums and said, 'I must just show you these before you go,' she knew it was near the end.

Lydia joined him by the table where the first album lay open. There was a picture of Viola, younger than Lydia had ever known her, playing with a baby that could only have been Nathalie. There was another, with Ben there, too, all of them laughing in a pile of straw; Eden when they first bought it, looking very derelict (before he made it the setting for the woman who required a setting); and gradually, as the pages were turned, some pictures began to appear with Lydia, looking tiny, grubby, dishevelled, just as she had always felt. Ben's voice softly drew her attention to details. 'See that puppy? I gave her that on her seventh birthday. That's Viola when her hair was short before she swept it into that sort of thing at the back. I loved it long, how it was at the end. There's you and Natta by the tree house; Natta teasing the dogs ...' His tone was as if they were spying on a past that might hear. Softly, softly; they must not know I still watch.

Lydia saw his hand covering a page of fixed yesterdays, very large and square, with clean but unmanicured nails. On his brown skin near the knuckles were two browner spots and a thin white scar traced across from the V of thumb to wrist. They stood in silence. He closed the book while she was still looking and turned her towards him. His brown eyes gazed into hers, reading them now, no longer looking past, but searching, piercing and vague like the eyes of a sailor, a traveller, someone who has spent years fixing their sight for a finer but distant sanity.

'Lyd, I can't see you as the child in these pictures. You come here now, not as a friend of Natta's, but as a woman. When you came last time I revealed my feelings in a way which is rare for me ... all the more rare these days ... and if it was embarrassing for you, I'm sorry. The sight of a pathetic, disillusioned old man must be disgusting to someone of your age.' He waited for a reaction, but Lydia stood silent before him. He lowered his voice and there was an echo of the same urgency she had heard on the telephone. 'But you did something that made me think I might not be entirely repellent to you. You held my head against your body; your little body and ...' he touched her cheek with the tips of his fingers, moments passed, then he said brightly, changing course entirely, 'I kept some things too. I'll show you.'

His habit of looking hard at her, immobilizing her with his eyes while he scrutinized hers to see what was in, through them,

and then releasing her and charging down some new trail of
interest, was beginning to fascinate Lydia. At first she had riled
against these searches and could not return his gaze, but now
she looked forward to the moments when he stopped
mid-sentence casting aside conversation as mere insulation
against the winds of feeling, searching about them for gaps
through which to blow; he would slam the shutters, by
movement and talk, or draw her attention to some book or
object. While she obediently studied the offered diversion he
watched where her hair broke about her shoulders, how it
hugged her skull, a few strands parting where his breath
touched, the top of her head level with his heart. Lydia now
used those searching moments of his to carry out explorations
of her own. Because he studied her as a painter does his
subject, or a collector some prized and coveted addition to his
collection (ah, the form, the detail, the strange familiarity of
the long awaited Netsuke piece; now quiet, let me see, let me
see), it was possible to look at him without being seen to look.
He had always been lined, that was his make of face. In
smooth-skinned youth, before Lydia had ever met him and as
he had been in some of those photographs, he must have
seemed bland while his face was running through those
expressions which eventually wore their own permanent paths
as a celebration to his enthusiasm for life: the fan of lines at the
corners of his eyes, more on his forehead which winged down
to two short ones between his brows, this network had not
been eased into his skin by a dreary trudge, but from running
alongside, beating life at its own game.

'Well, don't you want to see? Or is it time you should go?'
Ben was standing at the top of the stairs and Lydia at the
bottom, not realizing she had been meant to follow.

She went up and into the bedroom, where he was now
reaching on top of the wardrobe. 'Look at that one over there,'
he said, nodding towards one of the gold framed drawings on
the wall, while he bore a battered, brown leather suitcase on
his head and let it drop onto the bed. 'She's just like you. I'd
never thought of it before. When I bought it I thought she
looked like Natta standing there, all little and bare-footed,
busy being a child, but come to think of it she's more like you;
Natta was never absorbed in childhood. She pretended to be,

but kept a weather eye on the adult world. Now this little lot will make you laugh.' Ben opened the suitcase, letting the lid drop its film of dust onto the red blanketed bed, then triumphantly pulled out a music case, the metal bar still faithfully pressing down the floppy leather flap. 'There now. Recognize that?' Yes, she did. It was Nathalie's, and Lydia was shocked at the vividness of her presence through this tatty object; it was as if Nathalie had walked into the room and found her here with Ben. What would she have said? Probably she would have laughed ambiguously and left, then Ben would have rushed after her. 'Angel, don't go. What's the matter? It's only Lyd.'

Ben stood entranced before the open suitcase and Lydia went forward and looked down into the profusion of nursery relics. Peeping from behind 'Prayers for Children' was a green velvet jester, his three-pointed bell-topped hat was sewn on and stuffed so it became one with his head. One arm was detached and tucked into his belt, but this old doll from the past was still smiling his odious smile. And why not? He never expected his luck to turn from being gnawed by the dogs, forgotten under the bed and, when remembered, produced for experiments conjured out of the imaginations of little girls, to a life of cosy seclusion with one of the be-coiffed, be-slippered, be-jewelled foreign beauties who had stood so haughtily on a shelf in the nursery and who was now grubbing in the bottom of the suitcase with him. There were chipped china dogs and a squashed tennis shoe, an exercise book, which fell open at 'MY HOLIDAY IN BIARRITZ'; the remains of coloured crystal flowers in a crystal vase which had been a wonder to Lydia when Nathalie had produced it, because the flowers changed to tell the weather, purple for rain, pink for fine. A tarnished, silver-backed brush jostled with a toothbrush in the folds of a white nightdress embroidered with pink rose buds. Lydia touched the pieces reverently, things she had not been allowed to touch when Nathalie had cared for them, when she had said, 'No, you look. Just look, that's quite enough. You might spoil it. You can be a bit clumsy, you know.' Gently she lifted the dress. How she had longed for this when Nathalie had worn it, 'Dozens of nuns sewed on the rosebuds, you know, dozens of them just sitting sewing on *my* rosebuds, on *my* nightdress. See?

Each one has a stem and its own little leaf. See?' As Lydia now
raised the dress a small box fell from it. A tiger was inlaid with
ivory on the lid and around the sides elephants marched trunk
to tail. This was not Nathalie's. This had been a cherished gift
from Lydia's grandmother, who had died when Lydia was
seven. She had taken it to Eden to put it proudly beside her
camp-bed and was delighted when the sight of it produced
from Nathalie, 'Gosh, you *are* lucky, I wish I had one.' Then it
had disappeared from the chair on which it rested and here it
was nestling in Nathalie's cast-off prides.

'You like that, don't you?' Ben said. 'You can have it. I like
the idea of you owning something that Natta once cherished. I
found all this stuff littered in her bedroom and bathroom after
they had left Eden. On the floor, at the back of drawers, and
dusty on the darker patch where her bed had once been. She
took that too, you know, the bed, or at least her mother did.'

The telephone started to ring. Ben and Lydia were startled
from the past. He dashed to answer it beside the bed but
before he reached it, stopped, looked at Lydia and changed his
mind.

'Join me downstairs in a moment, Lyd,' he shouted as the
stairs shook beneath him. A door slammed somewhere below.
The little white light on the telephone stopped flashing and
shone steadily, indicating a conversation in progress. His
subservient rush for the telephone the moment it sounded
seemed undignified. What was there in the outside world,
Lydia wondered, that claimed his attention so thoroughly? A
lady with dark brown hair? Work? No, not work. He had said
that that no longer interested him and his reaction when the
telephone rang was not uninterested. She went to the stairs,
from there his voice came muffled, 'I know, I'm sorry. I got a
bit tied up. Can I ring you back? ... Yes, of course I do ... Tell
you what ...'

Lydia went back into the bedroom suddenly depressed. She
dropped the ivory box back into the case and lifted once more
the beautiful nightdress. She could remember the day Nathalie
had first shown it to her, the day she returned from Paris after
Lydia's short time alone at Eden: The return of Mother and
Daughter had been heralded by the crunching of gravel as the
car drew up. Lydia had stood leaning against the balusters of

the first floor landing which ran the length of the hall, with the staircase at one side curving down to the marble-floored hall; from there she had a bird's-eye view of the front door. The butler had heard or seen the car too and was already outside when Ben came rushing from a downstairs room to stand with his arms raised in greeting, even before they were out of the car. His great frame now blocked Lydia's view, and when Nathalie ran into the house preceded by her voice – 'Daddy, Daddy, I've got so many beautiful things, I can't wait to show Lydia.' … and into her father's arms, Lydia could only see her friend's hands clasped at the back of his neck still clutching several seductively wrapped boxes and bags on long coloured strings.

Ben set Nathalie carefully back on the ground when Viola came into the hall. Lydia had wanted to watch them greet each other; she was always intrigued to see these two particular adults display their love for each other physically, because in her own home love was shown by a dry kiss from her father to her mother when he opened his packet of birthday socks. 'Thank you, dear, just what I wanted. Kiss, kiss?' And he would plant it on the safe place she offered. Or it would be shown when her mother opened a present from him, 'Oh George, you did get the right one. Very nice, dear,' and she would pat his hand while still looking at the scarf or cardigan. It was always something like that; and present-giving was the only thing that brought on these parched displays of affection. Beyond these tight-lipped kisses and pats the degree and intensity of love had to be assumed. So to see the way Ben let his hands rest upon Viola, the light pressure, the release, and again the anxious touch, feeling her, knowing her, her shoulders, her back, her neck; seeing those hands speaking had mildly thrilled and outraged Lydia; they hinted, somehow, at the kind of love she had heard the girls at school whispering about, the kind of love she and Nathalie had wondered about. ('But they couldn't do THAT. It would HURT,' or simply, 'Ergg, how disgusting.'). But this time Nathalie had prevented Lydia from watching with wet-lipped fascination the implied intimacy between these two by bounding up the stairs and shouting for her at the same time; she prolonged the ascent by dropping parcels and retrieving them and bounding up again.

When she reached Lydia she said, 'Oh, Lydia, you must see, you simply must, but first could you get those other parcels? There, on the long stool by the door near Mummy and Daddy.'

Nathalie had gone into her room and Lydia had descended nearer and nearer to where Ben was standing with Viola, but now she could not watch them, she was too near and not an observer but an intruder on the field of electricity the couple exuded. They were not even touching at the last moment Lydia dared to look at them but there was an exclusive privacy in the way they confronted each other and if they were speaking the embarrassment suffocating Lydia was such that she did not hear. With an almost crippled sideways shuffle she approached the long stool, and praying for invisibility, reached out for the parcels.

'OH, for Christ's sake, Lyd, take the bloody things and go. Stop shuffling about ...' Ben shouted at her. In her terror Lydia pulled a large parcel from underneath and brought the whole lot tumbling to the floor. She knelt amongst them, tears beginning to blind.

'Not the dark blue ones, Lydia,' Viola said calmly, 'the striped parcels are Natta's, if that's what you are after.'

'Dad, stop shouting at my friend. She's my friend and you're not to. I don't shout at your friends. I can hear you all the way in my room.' Nathalie was shouting herself as she stood gripping the banister and looking furiously down at him.

'Sorry, sorry, sorry. Here you are, Lyd.' He piled the parcels high on her outstretched arms and pointed her towards the stairs. Lydia tottered away with her view obscured by her burden.

'God, he's beastly sometimes,' Nathalie said when the door to her room was shut. 'Here, this is what I want you to see.'

Nathalie was holding up the long white dress scattered with embroidered rosebuds. Lydia was entranced by the ethereal garment and put out a hand to touch it.

'No, don't do that. You might dirty it or tear it or something, but listen, I worked and worked on Mummy but she still says "no, no, no" to us going to the ball, and I said it wasn't fair on you and all that, but still she said "no".' Lydia had felt a deep relief. 'But, you see, this is what she said I could wear. It's a nightdress really and she said we can stand and watch everyone arrive and when they look up and see me I'll be wearing this. Won't that be nice? Don't worry, Lydia, I'll give you a nice one too, I've got lots of old ones ... Actually, it wasn't Mummy who gave it to me, it was a frightfully nice man called Erik, some old friend of the family or something. He said he had brought it all the way from Switzerland for me. And do you know what? ... God, it was funny ...' Nathalie had then related wondrous revelations, mostly gathered from unchaperoned wandering in the wide and hushed corridors of the George V.

When the day came and the guests began to arrive for the ball their first sight was of two girls standing peering through the first floor balusters. Most of them did not know who the little girls were gazing down at the chattering, glamorous adults billowing in from the warm summer night; some of them ignored the pair, others pointed and said, 'How sweet,' and 'the one in white is Ben's girl, you can tell at a glance.' But they did not know who the other one was, the one in rather shrunken blue pyjamas with Donald Ducks all over them: 'Sorry, Lydia, Mademoiselle says I can't share anything as personal as a nightie.'

An hour later the girls were kneeling and leaning against each other in an effort to stay awake when the butler appeared with two glasses on a silver tray. 'Your father asked me to bring champagne, Miss Nathalie, for yourself and Miss Lydia.' They drank it delightedly and on their way to bed, giggling and hiccoughing, they made faces behind the governess snoozing before a blank and flickering television.

As she drifted into sleep, even through her sleep, Lydia had heard the sound of the music climbing in the still air and wished that someone ... Ben, would come to say goodnight.

The next morning Lydia had watched Nathalie standing on the steps of that serene house waving and shouting, 'See you next summer, see you next summer. Don't forget to write.' And Lydia was waving frantically back through the window of the big black car that was taking her to the station.

That was the last time she ever visited Eden.

Slowly Lydia closed the lid of the old suitcase and buckled the cracked leather straps. Go to sleep Past, please lie down;

I'll shut you in now and strap you so you leave me alone. She glanced at the telephone. The light still shone. She lifted off the case and brushed the bed with her hand, the telephone gave a faint click and the light went off. Ben was already thundering back upstairs.

'That was kind of you, Lyd. I didn't mean you to put the case away. I can do it later. Come on down.'

He switched off the lights and stood aside in the doorway. Lydia stayed across the room looking at his silhouette blocking the amber light that filled the rest of the house. Far away a train gave a two-note howl into the evening, rain started to beat onto some leaves of a plane tree outside the window: dead vestiges of summer clinging to an impatiently beating branch. A small spring whined in the door-handle that Ben was twisting backwards and forwards trying to wring from it a decision he could not make. He shut the door softly and sat on the edge of the bed; pushing broad hands through his hair he said, 'You say nothing, child. You must know what I am thinking and what could happen, and your silence is invitation.' He spoke into the palms of his hands. The only light in the room came from a street lamp shadowing his hunched figure. Lydia stepped towards him and immediately he grasped her looking up but he would not be able to see her face between the falls of her hair, only feel her hands, cold and slightly rough upon his forehead.

'Go, please,' he said. 'Go away and hide yourself. I am more than twice your age and, God knows, three times your size. I could hurt you.'

She did not hear him. All Lydia knew was that now he was accessible; this Ideal, this God, who had given so much love to those others when she was a child, was now beside her: it was her hand on his face, that dear face, and her own head bent towards his shoulder; that the arm now gripped about her waist and the hand moving inside her thigh were his. All the time as his hold became stronger, as so easily he laid her down he was pleading in a whisper, 'Please go. Please go. This mustn't happen.' But she was not leaving. For once the moment was for her, not Viola, not Nathalie, not a lady with dark brown hair. Now she was going to take what she had craved as a girl: the love that Nathalie had owned and paraded; those childhood years of longing for a demonstration of love from her own father; all of this she would condense into one act. The man she had seen rejected on a darkened staircase in some haunted corridor of childhood was, at this moment, her own; it was his caressing mouth on her body. But when she saw his face in the light of the street lamp, still shining as it had in a history ten minutes before, his expression was incredulous, maybe of his own abandon or hers, or else he was making a mistake, a mistake of identity. He could not have been able to see her face lost, as it was, in the hills of the pillows and her own hair; and still he allowed her hands no freedom to return his touch or clear that hair, to show her face, to say 'It's me, it's Lydia. It's no one else.' He said, 'Don't be frightened, I won't hurt you. You'll see … you'll see.' But he did hurt her and the pain was the joy. She was still under the ecstasy of his weight when, before he came, Ben suddenly released her hands, held her fiercely by the hair, pulling her head away from him and into the stream of light. He stared hard at her face, shaking in some moments of doubt. Lydia knew then that it was not her he was seeing at all but still she laid her hands upon his back and pulled him down.

* * *

'… The address Millie gave me, Lyd, was a little street in the Montparnasse area. There was a great double front door with a postern set into it. Directly inside was a deep arch with a wide stairway leading up, and beyond was a sunny cobbled courtyard. It was very quiet until I stepped through the postern, then there was a sudden burst of laughter and my courage gave in. The laughter was far away, deep inside the building, nothing to do with me; but you see it was her laugh, I knew it; then I heard her voice calling something, couldn't make out what. She sounded so happy. A man's voice answered her, there was more laughter. That was when I left. For a while I stood in the street, already sick with jealousy. I couldn't think what to do but I had to get away from the building because some of the windows of her apartment could have looked down into the street, I couldn't risk her seeing me; not before I was ready. I went into a cafe on the other side of

the street and settled myself in the glassed-in section in front of
the cafe. It was warm there with the sun shining through the
glass and there was no risk of being seen; for my back was
towards the road. I suppose then I should have decided to go
away, leave her alone, or even before that: when I heard her
laughter. I should have gone but I didn't even contemplate it
as I sat viciously stirring my coffee burning with hatred for that
other laugh I heard. All I did was plan how I could get her
alone and get her away. Then I had a little bonus, I took it to
be a hint from fate that my desire was not to be totally
thwarted, it was a good omen: reflected in the glass window on
my right, the window to the cafe itself, were the great double
doors that led to the courtyard; to the apartment; to her. I
turned to look through the glass on my left, on the street side,
to be certain that I was not mistaken; and I wasn't. I could sit
for as long as I wanted watching that second-hand reflection
rendered richer by the dark cafe behind. No one could come
or go through the postern without my seeing and who would
look twice at the hunched back of a lone and elderly man
passing his hours in a cafe?

'I stayed there for the whole of that day and although a few
people came and went there was no sign of her. In the quiet of
the afternoon I went over to count how many apartments there
were in the building; there were nine bells, only some had
names. Her name was not there, or at least no name that I
knew to be hers.

'It was the patience I learnt from those days of watching for
her that has helped me to watch your house, although this time
I haven't had the comfort of a cafe and this time, too, my
anguish is greater ... Then, you see, I could have gone away
and lived without her, oh yes in utter misery, but lived anyway.
But now that's impossible.

'Lyd ... are you listening to me? ... please help me ...'

'How can I help you, Ben? I feel your sadness but I don't
understand. I tried once before to give you happiness. Do you
remember that? Because I do.'

5

Lydia walked home sorting her mind; it had been embarrassing afterwards, passion subsided. She had not been able to look at him for fear of seeing again the vague disconcerted expression; but anyway he had not tried to look at her. It had been a very final and shy goodbye but suitable punctuation, Lydia thought, to end that path of her short history. Whatever Ben's confused intention had been when he made love to her, Lydia's had been to acknowledge all her young years of loving him in the background while Nathalie had basked in the warm sunshine of his pride; it had been a retrospective gesture and did not occur to her as infidelity. After all, she would not be seeing him again.

As soon as her own street door shut behind her the sound of laughter and music oozed down the stairwell; it was an unusual one for this house and was certainly the last one she had been expecting. Her vision had been of herself breezing into the flat where Eric and Victor would be awaiting her arrival, certainly a little worried; she would still be exuding this unusual confidence and elation, she would still be the Happiness Dispenser, would read to Victor, please Eric. Now it seemed the flat was already alive and she climbed cautiously towards the door. No one heard her when she entered and she stood in the doorway watching, amazed. Victor was dancing with a voluptuous, round-faced, thirty-ish woman and Greg was standing with his arm flung around Eric's shoulder, the two of them convulsed with laughter. Eric never looked good when he was laughing, but he was redeemed by the infectious, shoulder-shaking, thigh-slapping, tear-streaming abandon of his laugh, and despite her initial resentment at this unexpected party Lydia began to smile and then to laugh herself.

Greg stopped laughing abruptly when he noticed Lydia and changed to the challenging smile he reserved for her. He poked Eric in the stomach and flung his arms up in greeting; 'Look, look, she's here, she's back.' And Lydia stood in a fleeting moment of fear and shame, disliking where Greg placed her: as intruder, but Eric instantly lifted her off that shelf by saying, 'Lydia, we've had such a time, I can't tell you.' He came forward, listing slightly. 'Greg has brought the last of his Retsina, the real thing, from his summer in Greece and, well, my goodness …' He waved an unsteady arm at Victor still dancing, 'Look at Dad,' to demonstrate the result of the Retsina. Then in an excited whisper he said, 'And look, there's Vebeke,' as though there might have been a dozen other women in the room to pick her from.

Vebeke, aware of the third person introduction, kicked a large leg and waved a hand in Lydia's direction using Victor's elegant arm bent about her waist as support. Victor bowed to Lydia and smiled in the same coyly irrepressible way that Eric had.

The first few occasions Lydia encountered these times of total lucidity in Victor she could not understand the change nor could she look to Eric for explanation because he would never explain, excuse or discuss his father's condition. The changes seemed to make the shuffling senility a voluntary abdication of his senses, a sham. The Matron had told her, with candour and compassion, that, yes, maybe the senility was a voluntary thing but it was a decision made at a level where reasoning, as we understand it, could not reach and that the state (called pre-senile dementia) while it was upon him, and however he arrived at it, was genuine and had to be treated so. The changes obviously engendered great affection for Victor at the 'Home', for the staff there seemed to care for him with a particular attention, each one hoping, maybe, to share in the softly distinguished man, who stepped occasionally from his cell of senility.

Greg snatched Lydia and whirled her about the room not very much in time with the Russian folk music that was playing, then Eric took her and whispered, 'Vebeke's not at all what I expected. What do you think?' 'Not at all,' Lydia said enthusiastically, pleased to have something to be adamant about. 'She looks more wholesome than Greg made out.'

Victor walked over. 'May I, Eric?' he said, arranging his arms towards Lydia. Victor danced well, so did Lydia, and for a while they enjoyed that while the others watched them, then Victor said, 'So at last it's marriage, Lydia?' He held her a little away from him to examine her face. 'I suppose it is, yes.' Lydia tried to lose herself in the formal intimacy of the dancing stance, but Victor held his arms firm so Lydia could come no closer and hide her face.

'It is what you want, isn't it? You seem a little doubtful.'

She turned her face to his. There had been times before this that she had found Victor easier to talk to than Eric. 'Yes, it's what I want but ...' Her lip trembled and tightened and again she tried to go deeper in his embrace to avoid real contact, and still he would not let her. 'Go on, they're not watching now and they can't hear with the music anyway.' The other three were all slumped on the sofa and talking loudly. Greg and Vebeke seemed to be having a mock row and Eric was laughing again.

'I'm frightened of hurting him.' Lydia looked towards Eric. 'Sometimes I feel I want to test what I'm really like, go to the limits of myself and look over the edge, just for my own interest, but I'm frightened of where that would leave Eric.' Lydia surprised herself. She had said something she did not even know she thought, and was it fair to talk to Victor like this? Should she not be painting a picture of perfect certainty so there would be no cause for worry when he was lucid and alone? But he was smiling down at her, 'Of course you will hurt each other, nothing wrong with that. Sadly, people never mature at the same time, however much they love each other. And those limits you talk about, well they seem as far away at my age as they do at yours. Maturity never really comes, it just gets easier to pretend you know the answer.' He made a few neat turns about the room and drew Lydia into the closeness she had sought before, and they danced a little faster turning and turning to impress. Lydia let her head fall back enough to see his face and said, 'Victor, I'm so glad there's you and Eric.'

'Hey, Little Thing, I never knew you could dance like that.'

'You're only as good as your partner,' she laughed back at Greg, but even as she said it she felt Victor's shoulders draw down towards her own. He missed a step or two; she tried to see his face but now he gripped her to him with the same rigid arms that a moment ago had held her away. 'Victor?' Lydia whispered, 'Victor, let's sit now.' But he did not stop the shuffling that his dancing had become. He was leaning so heavily upon Lydia that she could no longer move.

Eric and Greg came quickly to where she stood supporting the old man, her head lying against his now dropped upon her shoulder.

'Come on, Dad, sit down. You've overdone it, you old show-off.' Eric's voice came high and broken as he eased Victor into the chair by the fire and wrapped a rug about his knees, more to control them than to warm them. Eric saw the embarrassed faces of Greg and Vebeke and straightened. 'Sorry, it's always a bit upsetting however much you know it is going to happen. Like lots of goodbyes and I'm never quite sure which one will be the real one.' A tear was breaking in the corner of his eye as he wiped his nose, cracked his finger joints.

'We'd better go,' Greg said.

'No, no, please don't,' Eric sounded alarmed. 'Honestly he'd hate that and you see he can still hear, he understands, really. I'm sure he does. It's awfully early, please stay. They must, mustn't they, Lydia?'

Lydia was kneeling before Victor with his long-fingered hands in hers; she arranged them tidily in his lap and did not take her eyes from his face when she said, 'Of course you must stay.' She went through to the kitchen to be alone. 'I vill help you, dja?' Vebeke sang out from the sofa when she saw where Lydia was going. 'It's all right,' Lydia said, letting the door slam behind her; there had not been much danger of those great legs stirring, anyway. She did not turn on the light but went to the window and stretched her arm against the frame, resting her forehead on the frosted glass. If someone passing below had chanced to look up at the series of grimy back windows they might have been curious about the figure stretched against the window-frame in such listless dejection.

The kitchen door opened and closed. 'Oh Eric, if only he would stay right ... if only.' Lydia spoke without moving.

'Yes, if only ... but would it be rude to ask what made you so late? What keeps little off-duty waitresses so busy in the early evening?' Greg's voice had it's usual sarcastic edge.

'I thought you were Eric.' Lydia turned quickly. 'Switch on the light, will you?' She started to busy about the kitchen while Greg lolled against the door.

'Well?' he said, after watching her for some moments.

'Well what?'

Greg sat down at the table with his hands behind his head as he rocked on the back legs of the chair.

'Where were you?'

'Just walking.' She was tearing and rinsing a lettuce. Greg stroked his gingery chin with feigned wistfulness; 'I thought you looked a little ... let's see now, what's the word ... distraught? ... that's it: dis-traught, when you came in earlier. Everything all right, is it?'

'Move, will you please? I can't get to the cupboard.'

'Here,' Greg said languidly pouring olive oil into a bowl, 'let me do the dressing. Got any herbs?' Lydia passed him what he needed and used the opportunity to deflect his talk.

'You're right, I'm bad at dressing, I must watch you. I see you use lemons. Are they better than vinegar?'

'Sometimes it's easier to talk to an outsider and you know how fond I am of you. I wouldn't like to think there is something upsetting, something you couldn't talk to Eric about, perhaps?' His insidious voice persisted. 'It was your eyes most of all that impressed me when you came in. There was a wild look in them ...'

'Stop it, Greg,' Lydia flashed, crossing her arms and turning her back, 'I get sick to death of you painter types ...'

'There are more like me, are there?' He sliced an onion.

'Dozens, just like you.'

'In *your* life?'

'They come into the cafe and they are always holding forth about life and love and things like that and their would-be arty friends hang on their every word just as though looking at a few nude models or the ability to paint a bit of a picture gave them some extra understanding of life. And it doesn't. You can think and feel and understand just as much without a brush in your hand.'

Greg tapped his fingers in mincing applause, 'But did I mention love or anything of the sort?' The door opened and he dropped his hands quickly while guilt glowed and faded instantly on his face.

'You're not teasing Lydia again, are you?' Eric beamed round the door.

Christmas passed quietly and as Lydia had planned. Victor had long periods of lucidity which was an unexpected bonus and their card games became quite spirited in the quiet way the three of them had.

One morning a week after Christmas they were all in the hall preparing to take Victor back to the Home when the telephone rang. 'What's the betting it's Greg cheesed off after Christmas?' Eric lunged for the telephone with obvious pleasure. Victor was in his other diminished world and Lydia was trying to put his awkward arms into his overcoat.

'Hello, I know; you're bored or you've had a row with Vebeke, or both.' Eric grinned round at Lydia while waiting for the reply. The teasing faded from Eric's eyes and brow, but a formal smile stayed on his lips, 'Hello? ... Who's there? ...' All the pleasure went from his face. 'For goodness sake who is it?' He pulled his head sharply from the receiver as the suddenly vacant line rattled like invective. He slammed down the receiver, 'I hate that, I really do.'

Lydia turned from buttoning Victor's coat and reached for a scarf. 'Well, didn't you hear? You must have heard,' Eric said to her. She studied Eric at last aware of his state.

'I thought it was Greg,' she said.

'No, it wasn't. Don't you see? Didn't you hear? There was no one there, or at least there was, that's why it was horrible. I could hear breathing but no one spoke.'

'Eric, Love, really it happens all the time: wrong numbers. People are funny, they don't like saying "Sorry wrong number". I think they feel silly or something. I know, I've done it myself.'

Eric's face had become strained, he was pulling at the hairs on the back of his neck. 'Well you shouldn't, it's unkind. It's like an intruder. I feel as though someone has come into our home, Lydia, our life. Someone voiceless has slipped in.'

Lydia was going to protest but she stopped, affected by Eric's agitation. He was a man to whom tears came easily, whether from mirth or sadness, he shared his emotions openly like a child but the things that moved him were always logical, until now.

'I know I'm being silly. Sorry.' Eric put his head on one side and lifted his hands towards Lydia and she took them in hers.

At first Lydia had been nervous that Ben might pester her, that the situation might become difficult, but as the days had passed she realized she was safe from him. After some bitter amusement at her own vanity for thinking that anyone should ever pester her, let alone Ben, she had some days of confusion, regret, something like sadness. Now, with Eric's hands still resting in hers, she found herself hoping. 'Don't worry,' she said to him, 'it's no one, nothing.'

The next morning Eric was still lying diagonally across the bed (the position he adopted as soon as Lydia arose on those luxurious mornings when there was no school), when the telephone started to ring. He rolled to release himself from the coils of sheet about his legs, but the manoeuvre became complicated in his sleepy state so he lay listening for Lydia to answer. It continued to ring oddly persistent and too early for Greg. Of course it could have been the Home about his father, maybe, but that was not the thought that made Eric rise suddenly and trail the sheets with him to the hall. At the same moment Lydia arrived by the telephone. They stood looking at each other. 'Are you going to answer it?' she said. Eric was nervous. 'I know it sounds silly,' he said, 'but I think it's that "wrong number" again. Will you?' Lydia raised the receiver and put it to her ear, 'Hello?'

She heard lute music in a distant room which came into sharp focus and Ben said, 'Lyd, I know what I said, that we wouldn't meet, that I wouldn't ring, but please … Please. Mid-day today.'

Eric grabbed Lydia's wrist, 'It's him, isn't it? It's the "wrong number". Put it down quickly, don't listen to that silence, Lydia, it's horrible and poisonous.'

She replaced the receiver and stared at Eric. His face seemed changed and the tide of the everyday, of the familiar, was ebbing within her, soaking away with it all of the interests and routine which structured her day; a hundred little projects and promises slipped away in that retreating tide leaving nothing in the bay of her mind but a longing: unexpected, unfamiliar, irreducible.

'... I'm so sorry,' Eric was saying, 'I was a coward, and it's such a little thing too, I should have answered but I didn't think it would upset you so much. Next time I'll ... well I'll think of something. Have the number changed, maybe.'

Greg arrived during the morning. Eric was going to sit for a drawing before the three of them went to lunch and then while Lydia worked at the cafe, Eric and Greg planned to go to the cinema. They had tried to persuade Lydia to ditch the cafe during the school holidays but she was not made that way and, besides, she only had to work out the month before she left for good.

While Greg was drawing Eric, Lydia stayed in the bedroom. She did not want Greg to see her face. She could hear their voices: Eric talking about his application for a post in a boys' boarding school in the country, then he began to talk about the calls, the 'wrong numbers'. Greg was very interested. 'But do you have any idea who it could be? Think hard, Eric, come on, there must be someone who wants to upset you ...' He paused, 'or Lydia?'

'No, Greg, it's not like that at all. It's just some fool who's picked on our number and I suppose he heard I was a little perturbed, let's say, at no one speaking, and he's done it again for fun. It's my own fault for reacting. Next time I'll be prepared, but even so it leaves me uneasy. Unlike me, really.'

'Did he speak to Lydia?'

'Not a word. Actually she was more upset than me by the look on her face.'

'I expect she was.' And then no sound came but the soft rasp of charcoal on paper.

Lydia left the bedroom closing the door softly. She wanted to leave without notice, sort it out later, or not at all, but Eric appeared at the sitting-room door and over his shoulder ranged Greg's pale blue eyes.

'Hello. We were going to ask if you are ready to go for lunch now. You're not going somewhere, are you?' Lydia was wearing a lichen-green overcoat that made her look like a Tyrolean schoolgirl. 'Where are you going? Please don't.

Greg's finished the drawing and he was going to do one of you. Lydia …? Love …?' Eric's words had the effect of an invisible buffer pushing Lydia against the wall beside the telephone table. The folds of her coat brushed the receiver from its cradle and it swung in mid-air gurgling a muted, inane laugh.

The two men stood amazed at the stricken retreat as Lydia backed towards the door groping the air with a hand behind her and only when, still facing them, wide-eyed, mouthing silent syllables she slipped through the door to the stairs did Eric run forward and throw it open shouting down the stairs after her, 'Lydia, Lydia, where are you going? What's the matter? For goodness sake, please. Don't go.' But the only reply was the sound of her descent engulfed in echoes and the slamming of the street door.

Ben's front door was open just enough to show anyone who expected entry that it was to be gained by a mere finger of pressure. Lydia entered and leant against the door which closed behind her weight as far as the frame, where it resisted, then gave with a thump, which killed off reality stretched out in the daylight streets on the other side. She looked up the stairs, where the plants trailed lime-green tendrils, to a window through which day filtered in two even blocks down to where dimness soaked it away. At the end of a short, dark passage in front of her a string of onions hanging from the kitchen ceiling was silhouetted against a small window. The house seemed to be ailing; it was quiet, grey and smelt of stale cigarette smoke. This was the first time she had been there during the day and it was a night-time house, when the amber lights cajoled the plants into wasting scents on absent bees.

She went to the sitting-room door and Ben was before her, seated in a large chair with his hands spread on the arms, rigid, poised to raise himself.

'It's nearly one. I've been waiting.' He spat the words and then, 'I'm sorry, I didn't mean to sound impatient but I was so sure you would come and then twelve arrived and twelve-thirty and I began to think …' He shrugged and turned his face from her. 'I've been very weak, shouldn't have called you.'

Lydia went to him and took his hand. So easy this time. No need for pretence. No need to waste time.

The hours went past them while they discovered the inevitable, eternal coincidences of lovers' lives, 'You don't mean it, Lyd, but I was there then, too … No, no. Staying in that hotel at the top of the hill. The big white one with the one-legged commissionaire who was always pissed. To think of it! You must have been, what? Fourteen? I might have seen you sitting sipping citron pressé with your arms brown and marked by the pattern on the white metal table. Look how they are marked now, just by the folds in the sheet.'

She would have seen him, though, if he had passed with his shambolic stride, moving demonstrative arms through the hot Mediterranean air, as Latin in his exuberance as he was English in his reticence. Who would have been beside him then? Don't ask.

They lay close in a tumble of bedclothes, whispering, exploring, dreaming with exquisitely exhausted senses. Lydia's skin shone in the gloom, where it was not covered by his hand, his thigh or his cruising mouth on the planes of her neck.

Parts of that morning floated into her memory: Eric's hand clutching her wrist, his shadow falling through the half-open door as he sat by the window posing for Greg; and Greg's eyes, those assessing eyes, as though he guessed there was another dimension to her life. But these pictures did not intrude, they had no significance, no relation to reality. Reality was here in this room, in the navy-blue cloth-covered walls, in the people who gazed down at her and Ben from the pictures, especially the little barefooted waif who was supposed to look like her. Reality was Ben talking in a low and gentle moan, while his fingers threaded through her hair and his warm palms encased her head so that she could not quite hear what he was saying.

'We're going to go, Lyd …' He stopped to let his mouth brush the corner of her lip, 'to a place where the skies are so high …' His tongue traced the valley where her arm lay beside her breast, '… that you feel you're flying when you look up.' He raised himself and looked down at her. 'Little Lyd. You can't know about the loneliness, the emptiness. Thank God for you now.' Slowly he lowered his mouth to hers and held her head between his hands with such fierceness that Lydia felt the pain of possession. He then sat back on his knees and said with bright finality: '... and we go this week-end.'

She raised her head. Half of her face was obliterated by strands of hair, but Ben could see in one eye and part of her mouth panic and confusion. He was the murderer; he was the one who had mentioned time and killed their peace beyond time.

The words 'this week-end' had suddenly focused the situation for both of them. Now it was as if they too watched from the walls and in a spotlight saw a girl and a man with a sea of years between them, a ludicrous difference in their ages and sizes. Ben saw, too, in this sudden, unwelcome illumination, a young man unknown and faceless but threatening; threatening his happiness and his vanity. Lydia saw Eric broken and alone.

"But I can't do *that*,' she whispered.

'Do what, for God's sake?' That easy anger of his was rising again.

'Go away with you at the week-end. There's Eric.'

'I see. You can come here for secret afternoons; a quick P.M. screw, a little cinq-à-sept, but to come away with me, to see if there is anything real between us, you can't risk that. You're not married to this man, are you? Children or anything? What's his name? Eric? What a terrible name.' Lydia shuddered at the implied insult. 'Is he an "Eric"? Have you picked a right "Eric" to live with?'

'Don't, Ben. I told you I lived with someone and we are supposed to be getting married at the end of the month. I can't bear to hurt him. He's not at all like you though. It's not like when we are together. It's different, it's ...'

'I don't want to hear.'

Ben rose and went to a chest of drawers where an oval mirror reflected his face. He picked up two brushes and started pushing them furiously through his thick hair, as if trying to brush out thoughts and leave them gasping like fish on the floor. He replaced the brushes and started to speak, indistinctly at first and without turning, 'There we are, jealous you see, but Lyd, I can't not-see-you anymore. Can you understand that? I tried not to ring you for what seemed like days, but I had to ... Blast it.' There was fury and misery in his voice, but when he turned to face her it was with a new energy.

'Now, look.' He walked up and down the room cutting his words in the air with stiffened hands. 'Do you remember when you first came here I said, "you come here now as a woman"? Good. Well, I tell you honestly I want you and I can't do without you ... just now. I can't promise not to ring you because I shall. I need you, Lydia. But your situation at home ... I mean your "what's his name". I can't help you there and I desperately don't want to hurt you or spoil your life in any way, but you must sort that out on your own. Tell him what you like and if you think you shouldn't see me, then don't.'

He glanced round to assess the likelihood and saw a little figure kneeling on the bed with head bent under the current of his words. He dissolved and was lost again, just as he had been a while before by her touch, this time simply by the sight of her. He drew a sheet around her shoulders and held it tightly under her chin.

'Look at me,' he whispered. 'Forget what I've just said, it's going to be all right, little Lyd. Don't worry. I'll leave you alone now. Thank you for coming back ... and ... thank you for finding me.' He held her into his shoulder and gripped her with the same fierceness as before. 'Sorry. I'm hurting you,' he murmured. 'Always have been a bit clumsy.'

He drew the curtains against the evening and moved round the room turning on lamps. With the warmth of the light, soft and flattering, the nightmare of their realisation faded. Why couldn't she be with him? Who did it hurt? Who was to know? Lydia decided she would stay a little longer. After all, if this was to be the last time ... She would stay with him for the evening, then go home. She watched him dressing through her hair. When he had finished he went to the door and turned, then smiled. She heard him moving around the house, lighting it, preparing it for evening. The telephone rang and was answered instantly. He spoke briefly and she heard the receiver replaced.

When Lydia went downstairs Ben was different and she could not announce that she would spend the evening with him, do him that little favour. His manner was now 'there's nothing between us that the whole world could not know about', a 'don't come too near, don't ask too much' manner.

They stood just inside the front door. Ben buttoned her coat and turned up her collar.

'Here. Take this. You really should have one round a little neck like that.' Ben pulled a red woollen scarf from a brass hatstand and tied it round her neck. One of the hats on the stand was a black felt one she had seen him in before. When was that, though … how long ago? She remembered it had been raining. Tiny droplets of rain had glistened on the brim and disappeared; but that must have been years before, perhaps when she was a child; or was it only the other day?

Rain blew in as Ben opened the door, easing her outside. He pulled her collar up again.

'Hey,' he said, drawing her back quickly, 'just tell me one thing before you go. Why didn't you ring me when your parents were killed? I'm hurt you didn't even think of it. You would now, wouldn't you? If anything went wrong in your life, rely on me. I'm very good at that sort of thing, dependable, you know.'

The telephone started to ring inside the glowing house.

'I must go,' Ben said, and closed the door.

Lydia stood, the cold and wet closing about her and heard Ben's loud voice answering the telephone; she could not hear the words, just his unmistakable tone. For a moment she thought, hoped, that he would open the door once more.

How could she have asked him for help when her parents died? What was there to be done anyway? Losing both parents at a tremulous age had been like the backdrop accidentally falling behind a stage. Even if, with shouts and effort, it was raised agian, it would be too late: the reality behind had been glimpsed and the play of protected childhood was done for. Even when you are seventy, if you have a parent, you are someone's little girl. At that time she had ceased to be anyone's. Ben had no idea how unapproachable he had seemed to her as a child, yet to tell him now, now that she could say anything to him, would hurt his vision of what he had been to the children in his life: 'What will you do when I leave now?' 'How will you spend the evening?' 'Who rings you when you rush to answer the telphone?' If she ever mentioned Viola or Nathalie in any context but the past his face would change like a pack of cards displayed by a conjurer, that, with a flip, swish to their blank, secret side. 'Don't pry, Lyd,' Ben would say. 'Don't pry.'

She walked down the steps into the street, only looking back once, but when she did Ben was standing in a crack of yellow

light, watching. She turned to walk back and he closed the
door. Again they had said goodbye; again Ben had told her
they would not meet and again she believed him because what
Ben said was so; was the unalterable truth, not to be discussed.

It was the very least of her that walked through the dark,
glistening streets: her little body. Her mind was still in that
vivid house and her senses imbued with the sound of Ben, the
touch of Ben, the way he moved and the way he had
disappeared when that crack of light closed.

Not to meet again; not again. It began to hurt, but she
stowed the pain in folds of memory to die.

It was nearly nine when Lydia returned home and the flat
was in darkness; even the open fire in the sitting-room was
quite dead, the ashes and skeletal coals exuding a coldness
greater than if there had never been a fire. Familiar shapes of
things she and Eric had acquired with love gathered together
in the gloom with sad innocence; the phonograph they had
never played but bought for the fluted horn; a bent-wood
hatstand; a three-tiered table cluttered with shadowed
treasures; and a glass case within which small dead birds in
rigid flight went about their perpetual business. A stray and
roaming light grazed the brilliant wing of the uppermost bird
and Lydia followed the light when it sped, cross-barred across
the ceiling to the window and vanished. It was then she saw,
protruding from the folds of those humped, heavy and
undrawn curtains a shoulder: Eric's shoulder, and his head;
his frizzy hair hazed in the orange light of a phosphorous street
lamp.

Lydia stepped noisily on boards until she reached the island
of carpet. It seemed that between them nothing existed but a
deadness, while their relationship, that loving thing, lay
deposited about them, convulsive and smothering in the
furniture, the floor, the air. And for the sake of that struggling
thing they wanted to reach each other, and Eric more than
Lydia because for him there never was nor had been anything
but that; so he was the first to speak.

'I saw you coming down the street.' He knew, that was for
sure. 'Greg only left a little while ago.' And who had made it
clear was also sure. 'We looked for you at the cafe several
times ...' he waited while a police car spread its sound in the

streets, '… but you weren't there.' And that he said with such lack of guile that she shared his disappointment at not seeing the Lydia that he sought. She wanted to share his sadness at losing his love; yet she did not speak but stood with her head bent waiting for Eric to pass judgement and one that she knew he would not have formed on his own, without help. At last he asked the question they had both been waiting for him to ask. 'Where have you been … Love?' begging her to tell a lie. She wanted to answer but it was too soon; she only wanted to talk about Ben: how he wanted her, how she was happy to feel such misery; she wanted to boast about the way she could make him laugh; to describe his lined face; to say she was jealous too, jealous of someone with dark brown hair; jealous when the telephone rang and he, Ben, so eagerly answered it; but Lydia merely raised her arms and let them fall in a gesture of despair meant only to articulate the conversation she was having with herself. However, now that Eric had gathered his courage and asked that question he was ready to ask her more, to tell her more. 'Actually you don't have to tell me 'cause I know. You've been with that man, that old man you told us about, that Ben.' He spoke haltingly and the strain of remembering the points he had to make drained all emphasis, '… and it's not the first time. I mean, you have been with him before; that day Vebeke came, you had been with him then and I know that because … because,' he stopped, wiped his forehead and crossed the room to turn on the light; as he passed her Lydia smelt T.C.P. and the hollow scent of stale alcohol. He snapped on the overhead light they rarely used and stood with his hands pushed down in his pockets, looking at the floor, '… it's no good. I can't remember why I'm supposed to know that you've been with anyone at all. It's not something I'd ever guess … I don't think.' He raised his head and his full, rubbery lips used a smile, but only his lips. 'Where have you really been, Lovey? Lydia? I've been so worried.'

At last she said, 'With Ben.'

'*With*? Really *with*?' Quietly, thoroughly, he rinsed every connotation from the last word.

'Yes. Really with.'

'*With*,' Eric mumbled as he shuffled to the kitchen. 'Oh, my God. Really with,' as the door shut behind him.

Lydia stood in the middle of the room with those words hanging in the air about her and those possessions waiting to feel the custody of the relationship they knew. She went to the kitchen.

'I was going to make some tea. Would you like some?' Eric sought the safe lines, the well used ones that meant nothing.

'Please.' And she sat politely at the table.

As Eric took the kettle to the tap, he said, 'Lydia? The calls. You know, the silent calls? Well, they were him, weren't they?' Supporting her forehead in her fist she nodded with her eyes tight shut. 'I knew someone had come in, there was an intruder. Do you mind me asking you, are you going to go to him? I mean "live"; leave me?' He turned the tap on harder to drown the answer.

'Not unless you want me to.'

'Why aren't you? Doesn't he want, or don't you?'

'We agreed we wouldn't meet again. I said I couldn't. I said there was you.'

Eric looked at the peeling wall above the sink, placed the kettle fastidiously on the draining-board and went to the table.

'Is there me? Is there really me?' He pulled out a chair and sat. 'Only you see, Lydia, I don't think I could do it on my own, I mean: get along.'

'I believe, really, there's only you. Ben was another thing and it's done, finished now, anyway.' The pain, sickness, she felt when she said his name did not show and, if it had, Eric would not have seen then because he was looking, in the eternal fraction of one second, at Lydia with a man mysteriously old and potent, and two of them trying to decide what to do with Eric the Encumbrance and, as he watched, a delayed desire to hurt came to him.

'Of course, Greg says I shouldn't say that, he said,' and Eric's eyes swivelled to and from Lydia several times before he offered the second-hand insult, 'he said that I was the strong one and that you were ... spineless. That's his word, not mine.'

But it worked perfectly well. She was irrationally wounded and Eric moistened his lips several times before he moved away from her to finish making the tea.

After that there seemed little left to say, to explain; little left to do but what they might have been doing anyway at that time: perhaps eat something. Fill their stuttering mouths with food. But it did not work and after trying to bring the evening into some familiar shape Lydia went to bed, leaving Eric introspective and unapproachable at the table.

In the London-bright night of the bedroom she tried to feel what was in her that she could hurt Eric, why she had left the flat that morning; why she had ever gone to Ben after that first encounter and what it was that made him so compelling. Now in this silence smelling fustily of objects well used by others, with Eric somewhere through that door and the next it was impossible even to remember Ben's voice. It seemed unlikely that he existed at all; only Eric existed and that great hurt she had dealt him.

'Are you asleep, Lydia?' Eric came into the room and shut the door, an ungainly black shape whose edges melted somewhere in the wall. He spoke gently, 'Love, I'm sorry; I'm sorry about "spineless", I shouldn't have told you. Anyway, I don't think you are.' He climbed onto the bed beside her and bent his head to hers. 'And let's go on, Lydia, with everything, all our plans. And I love you, you see. I do.'

Lydia put her hands on his face and felt with the edges of her thumbs that familiar mouth and his little lashes brushing the tips of her fingers, and the hot, moist corner of his eye where tears had sprung while he was alone.

A small storm and nothing broken that would not mend in a while. But somewhere in sleepless hours that night when Eric was breathing gently, evenly beside her, a thought drifted in. Why spineless? Was it her size? Was it her reticence? She looked at Eric's face half submerged in the white pillow, lips parted, his eyes moving rapidly under closed lids, safe from pain in his sleep.

Why? Why, Eric? Of everything you might have used to hurt, why something that came as abuse only to reappear as plain fact? To harbour an insult, even once removed, so suspiciously accurate, was hard to bear, but a powerful weapon. And Ben? She would forget him. She could. She had more strength than anyone knew.

During the following weeks there was a constrained politeness between Eric and Lydia which eased with the passing of every hour. It was as if they were acting out their happy life as it had been before, trying to remember all the little words and deeds that made life together so pleasant; like insomniacs who feign sleep hoping to wake in the morning to find the feigning became fact.

They planned carefully, too. They planned their wedding for the end of February in a Register Office to be followed by a lunch at their usual Italian restaurant; Greg, Victor and the owner of the cafe (which Lydia had finally left) would be there. For some days Greg had stayed clear of the flat and Lydia, but soon he began to visit again; at first only returning with Eric from school and then arriving unannounced, as in the past. Eric encouraged Greg and Lydia towards the old relationship; he would laugh and say, 'Really, Greg, you must not tease Lydia like that,' when Greg had not been teasing her at all. He treated her altogether more seriously, listened when she spoke and watched her a good deal.

One day a letter arrived asking Eric to go for an interview for a post as Mathematics Master at a boys' prep. school in the Midlands. It was sometime since he had applied and they both thought he had not been considered, although they had never discussed it. Eric arranged to take a train after school the day before the interview and return late the following night. Lydia went with him to the station. 'Wish me luck, won't you; wish luck,' Eric kept saying, and she did, but they parted with a curious certainty that the job was his.

That evening Lydia was disconsolate. She wanted to feel more excitement but only felt apprehension. She spread the contents of drawers and shelves on the floor to see what from their vast collection of bric-à-brac could be thrown away: after all, if they were to leave ... Late in the evening Eric rang, his voice sounded small, remote, unreal, but she could hear the excitement still and even felt it a little herself when he spoke, but kneeling again amongst the clutter on the floor she was filled with a deep loneliness, despair. After the parting with Ben (to which she and Eric never referred) there had been a strange, dizzy sadness inside her, it was like a painful confusion, but this other thing, this unending emptiness, was new. Of course, she had been aware of something at the back of her mind, something that wanted to be noticed, but she had eluded it until now; and now, her life with Eric spread about her in their possessions on the floor, this something presented itself. She set the carved oak cradle, her gift, rocking, one touch and it had a momentum of its own, backwards, forwards on the floorboards, wood on wood resounding. Lydia put her hand into its low darkness then suddenly jumped up and rushed to the far side of the room, standing horror stricken rubbing that hand to clean off what she had felt: for it had not been the smooth hardness of the wood that her fingers had touched, but something warm, soft, pulpy; something that moved. Step by step she went across again to the cradle and standing with her head averted, ready turned from what she might see, she let her eyes move across and down into the little darkwood cuddy. Nothing lay within its rich, high-polished depths, the cradle was quite empty. Lydia knelt swiftly, seeing and touching its emptiness, she set it to rock again and leant back on her heels watching, this time, intently. The reflection from a side lamp was caught and thrown about in the shining, deep-brown cradle, rocking again on its own momentum; and from that light, spinning in the grain of the wood and the shadow, an image knitted itself. There was a child in the cradle: a little boy, naked and soundlessly crying. When Lydia put out her hand to touch him she touched only wood, but the image remained. The boy was quite grown, maybe two years, and if he had existed more than on the lower deck of reality he would have been too large for the cradle. The boy lifted his arms to Lydia, but from afar, removed by the patina rubbed from years of soft weights in soft shawls. In moments that patina shimmered and closed like waters over his head leaving the cradle once more empty, but even then it was too late for Lydia to forget that beautiful little face with fine black hair clinging about it and one eye slightly cast, a lazy eye following the direction of the other just a moment late; his face, too, had an odd familiarity.

Lydia washed and held her head under the tap for a while to clear away all this fantasy, and when she went to the window there was early light in the sky: she had been up all night.

During the next morning she was awakened by the telephone. It was Eric, who was almost inarticulate with elation; it seemed that the job was, after all, his, barring a few formalities, and that he was going to see the house that would be available to them. Not to worry to meet him because Greg said he would fetch him from the station and bring him home, it would be very late and he couldn't tell more because he had no more ten pence coins.

Lydia made coffee and took it through to the sitting-room, she was shocked at the untidiness: every movable object in the room lay strewn upon the floor. She tried to remember what she had been thinking during the last night but could only remember what she had been feeling, because that was still the same, undiminished, even strengthened by the light of day. She set about clearing things back to where they belonged, reshelving her life. As she did so that feeling ceased to be an introspective thing (and, in a sense, controllable because of that); it went out of her and began to fill the flat with an unease, a fear, as if there was a stranger standing waiting for her to move. And yet she was alone, was she not? Could there be a burglar; an intruder?

She went into the hall. There was no one there. She looked into the bedroom, the kitchen, the bathroom: no one; and yet the feeling was stronger. She stood in the doorway between the sitting-room and the hall listening, not moving, trying to divine where, why that feeling came. Slowly she turned her head to the source of her disquiet: the telephone. She watched it, mesmerised. Blunt sounds came from deep inside the instrument as somewhere a connection was made, then it rang; one terrible, piercing ring.

Lydia shook her head to settle her imagination, she went back to the sitting-room, closed the door and leant against it. The telephone started to ring again. She turned her head until her ear touched the door. She could hear in detail the sound she must have heard at least once every day of her life. It rang only twice, echoing round the walls and vibrating in the air long moments after the sound had stopped. Still rigid against the door she felt a dim pain, and yet not quite a pain; it was a sense of loss, that somewhere she had left something innately part of her; the feeling of a mother of a stillborn child when she leaves the hospital with empty arms. Now that Lydia was aware of it, it seemed to have been there always. She dressed, took her coat from its hook beside the door and left the flat.

* * *

'... Lyd, you know that I could have come to you. You're in that house alone now. But I want to tell you what happened, to explain why you'll find me so changed; to prepare you for the stooping, wasted and balding man that I have become. Do you remember her joke about the toupee? Well, I really do need it now. I've been in a sanatorium in Switzerland for this past eighteen months, maybe just a little longer, I don't know. I lose track so easily now.

'Where was I? Oh yes: waiting, waiting in the cafe outside her apartment just about two short weeks after you left me at Coalbarn. The very next morning, after the first day, I returned to the cafe and settled myself in the same position with my uniquely private view: the reflected entrance to her house. The first thing that interested me was a group of young people who stopped at the door and began a noisy and animated discussion about which bell to press and through all their words I heard her name. Curious really because nothing else they said was distinct. Yet not at all curious. Even if I hadn't heard her name I would have known they were to do with her, there was a likeness to her in some of them and a kind of sympathetic difference from her in others. Finally they tumbled through the postern, laughing and jostling. Always laughing; I can still hear, but, now only hers.

'An hour or two after that the same group reappeared and I scrutinized them in case she might have been hidden behind some of their bulkier forms; I even turned in my seat, discarding the reflection and looking with nothing but one pane of glass between me and reality. Nothing was real to me but what was to do with her; and I knew that only minutes before they had been with her, seen her, heard her. I waited for a while but couldn't stand the anguish, so I prepared myself to cross the chasm of that narrow street, to enter that house. But as I did so the little door within the gates opened and there she was. I was so shocked that I stood and stared without the protection of a single reflection; and if she had turned her head even for a second, she would have surely seen me. She was wearing the same clothes as when I had last seen her, the little leather jacket jingling with buckles and those beige leather boots with her jeans tucked in; her hair as cropped as ever. So dangerously, secretly feminine. Then a man came through the door and the shock of his appearance brought me to my senses. I returned to my seat and began to watch them again through the second reflection on the inner glass, turning occasionally, when I felt it safe, to confirm or clarify a detail. The man was wearing a black coat that went to his ankles and a red scarf wound about his neck, and still it trailed. He was as young as her and taller, as tall as me, and his jet black hair was far longer than hers, touching his shoulders. They each had thin, fine-boned bodies and they were made of the same fabric, the kind where you can almost see the life pulse coursing through them. He had gaunt features and her mouth: wide and not too full. They were perfectly matched physically, and at once I admired, envied and hated him.

'At first it was hard to see why they kept going back through the door, then holding it open and waiting; they had an air of tender impatience. Then a beautiful, dark, curly-headed child, about two years old, came struggling through the postern, resisting their help and amusing them by his efforts. He tripped, fell onto the pavement and cried. The man picked him up and swung him at arms' length above his head; then the child laughed and the man hugged him; their two heads became one mass of black hair. She came forward and put her arms about the two of them and the three walked away. I damned the man's proprietorial air with that child. It was, after all, hers and not his; it was the child who was to have been adopted.

'Do you begin to see, Lyd, how hard it was going to be for me to get her away from that place and that man? But I still believed, then, that I was the only one to give her real happiness, and I wanted the child too.

'I know you are listening to me. Yes I remember how it was with us. We were very happy for the time we were together and if we were happy again she would leave me alone, I know it … do you hear me? …'

'I hear you.'

'Then see me too.'

'I have a life.'

'I wonder if you really do. I know you, Lyd, your voice; there's emptiness somewhere, I hear it.'

6

On the way to Ben's house Lydia planned what she was not going to do: she was not going to ring the bell or try the ever-open front door; she was not even going to pass by the house; she was just going to see if by standing on the corner near the railings she could glimpse the house between the bare branches of the plane trees and whether there would be visible signs of the anguish she had sensed ringing around her in the flat.

It was cold again, with fog which moved in clouds, obliterating and revealing, so that when she could see Ben's house it seemed to stand alone, separate from its terraced sisters. The windows looked blank. But there is the reason: the shutters inside are closed; the house is empty. So there could have been no cry of anguish, no telephone call. There is no one there. He is gone.

She stood in the empty street holding on to the railing, crisp leaves blowing around her feet.

'Lyd!'

Yes, that was his voice. Easy to imagine it now and yet some time ago when she had just been with him it was quite impossible to recall.

'Lyd. Over here.'

She looked around her and saw no one. Was this the beginning of madness? Was madness the price for a few hours' living?

There was a car over there. She could see it through the railings that curved round the corner in front of her. Its engine must have been running, because a layer of steam clung over the long bonnet and the frost on the windows was dividing into rivery strips. Ben was leaning across the passenger seat and opening the door.

'Get in, Lyd,' he said.

They drove for hours not speaking, not touching. Ben looked severe and seemed to be driving with intense concentration further, further away from anywhere that Lydia knew. He drove very fast overtaking everything with no sign of impatience, but with a determination not to be delayed by slower travellers. Lydia thought that if they crashed and if they died that would be all right; she had had quite enough, there was nothing else she wanted.

Occasionally Ben looked over to Lydia; her hair was stringy and dull, her hands rested in her lap. He would have seen an oval, purple bruise on the bluish inside of her tiny wrist. Lydia felt him look and moved her hand to hide the bruise; the mark of her reconciliation. He looked quickly back to the road, then pulled onto the hard shoulder of the motorway, switched off the engine and turned round in his seat to face her. Quietly they faced each other, while trucks thundered past shaking the car, until they could bear the distance between them no longer and held each other with desperation.

'I didn't believe you would come. I was going to wait a little longer and then leave without you. You heard my ring? You knew it was me, of course you did. I won't let you go now, you know.'

After that some joy crept into the journey.

'I say, you don't know where I am taking you, do you? Well, it's to Coalbarn, my place, my peace. It was a rackety building left deserted for many years except for a few fishermen keeping their boats in there and I restored it. In return it restores my sanity. It used to be the building where they stored coal for the village as it was brought down the coast from the Yorkshire coal mines, but with trains, and God knows what, it fell into disuse. I want you to love it there, Lyd, because I do.'

Three hours later they sat in the car at a petrol station, stiff and weary, while the attendant outside in the pouring rain fiddled with the lock on the tank.

'You must be hungry,' said Ben. 'It's not far now, but I'd rather not stop, if you don't mind. I just want to get there. It's quite a job to warm the place up so we don't want to arrive too late ... except we must get you something more suitable. That's hopeless.' He nodded towards her skirt.

The attendant was tapping on the window. Ben opened it partly and pushed some notes through; the attendant took them and stuck his head horizontally through the gap, the rain bouncing off the plastic shoulders of his donkey-jacket.

'Would the little girl like a Smerf, then?' he asked, baring black, disarrayed teeth.

'What did you say?' said Ben, horrified.

'No, no, Sir, one of these,' and he pushed a little plastic man through the window letting it fall on Ben's lap. Ben drove off with a jerk, splashing the attendant who stood on the forecourt still grinning.

'Was that a joke, do you think?' Ben said as he threw the little man onto the dashboard, where it rolled with a bottle of pills.

In the late afternoon they arrived in a dingy town where they stopped at a brown, one-storey department store and a lady with grey hair sold them two pairs of jeans, two jerseys, some T-shirts, gum boots and plimsoles. Ben asked for it all, examined it all and paid for it all. Lydia had nothing to do with the transaction. While the lady wrapped the purchases in brown paper her eyes occasionally fluttered at Lydia, wondering.

Lydia was startled from a shallow sleep when the engine of the car stopped. It was night and there was no moon, no light of any kind to break the impenetrable black. Ben said, 'We've arrived.' He spoke timidly, almost apologetically. 'I shall go in and turn on some lights. It will take a while because the generator broke down just before I left last time and I'll have to use oil lamps until tomorrow.'

He opened the door and turned again to look at her. He was about to speak but was suddenly alert and very still; he was listening, and Lydia listened too. Above the moan of the wind, above the sad, ponderous gusts of rain thrown at the windscreen, and through the darkness came the sound of a telephone ringing, shrill and persistent. Ben moved quickly without looking again at Lydia. The night gave one gasp inside the warm car when he opened the door and was shut out with the velvet click of expensive machinery.

She listened for Ben's footsteps moving away but there was only the wind. It frightened her that she could not hear him. Why couldn't she? You can always hear people moving away;

sometimes they approach softly, unnoticed, but when they leave their footsteps echo and echo across a room, down a passage, a lifetime; even the most clamorous railway station reserves a resonance for the departing footsteps of the one most longed for. Here there was nothing, and Lydia had no idea where she was. It was then the panic began to skirt around her; panic as dark as her surroundings but studded with crystal clear questions posed in a voice that was not hers. 'Why, Lydia, did you ever leave?' Questions that came in waves to the front of her mind and roller-coastered down for another to rise. 'Where are you now?' 'What have you left in that life behind you?'

What had he said about a generator? She could not see the direction he had gone or any sign of light. She started to wrestle with the door, which gave unexpectedly, letting her fall onto sand. A light inside the car wavered for a moment and died when the wind slammed the door. Lydia's unconquered childhood fear of the dark possessed her again; the wider she opened her eyes to see any glimmer, anywhere, which would mean safety, the more the darkness pushed through her eyes into her head, eclipsing reason. She got up and started to walk against the wind. This was, maybe, a dream. If you wait, just wait, like in the old days, familiarity will seep back, you will find yourself somewhere you know and will trace your way to bed. 'Whose bed this time?' the same voice said.

Still her feet laboured in the sand, the wind carrying away cries she uttered; and she could hear nearby the sea. She went on, having forgotten where she was. She fell against a cold, hard mound and crouched, letting terror take her, unable to speak, unable to move, until at last there seemed to be a light, unstable, pale, faltering between shadows and very far away.

Ben came back, a lamp swinging in his hand, and found the empty car. He let the wind press him against its side while he held the lamp high. Nowhere in the landscape full of furious sea and sand-whipping gale could he see the figure he sought, and now there came to him through all this night and all this noise a memory with curious clarity: a room where a little girl in a white nightdress stood so still, and the memory brought with it the tuneless humming that a child sometimes makes for itself when absorbed in a world more real than the real. He put down the lamp and fought his way with slowed motion towards the sea, shouting for Lydia all the time, but his voice was forced back down his throat as soon as he opened his mouth because now he was turned towards the core of the gale. He climbed over a low stone wall and slithered down onto sand; from this slight shelter he scanned again and again the mudflats being quickly covered by the incoming tide.

He was about to rise and search near the sea when he sensed that she was nearer than that, that she was watching him from a place in the angle of the wall and the cold shifting sand. He groped towards her, unable to see, and cut his hand on a stone; the blood spilt fast down his sleeve. He reached out and gathered only sand and a mound of marram grass. He reached again, the gale now pushing him back to the wall. This time beneath his fingers was Lydia's thin and rounded shoulder.

'It's all right,' he said, pulling the limp body towards him. 'It's all right, Lyd, I've found you.'

He clutched her body to him and carried it back to the cottage, stumbling and bleeding. Inside, he meticulously bathed his hand, extinguished the lights and took her to bed.

A canescent light filtered into the room, falling across the white covers and onto Lydia's face. She lay awake in bed (not quite a double bed, but referred to in the trade, the furniture trade that is, as an 'occasional double') unsurprised at finding herself alone.

The room was very bare with fat, whitewashed walls that bellied inwards. There was a chair loaded with Ben's clothes, a chest of drawers supported on one corner by a nicely bound volume, and beside the bed a round, water-stained table on which stood an electric lamp and an oil lamp; nothing more, no pictures, no books, not even curtains at the window.

The thick walls prevented any view from the window except by looking directly through it. As Lydia put her feet to the floor she found the only embellishment in the room: a flat woven rug worn through in parts, Caucasian, with colours of singing vibrancy. She walked to the window and there between the battered casements, hanging wide like modest, presenting hands, lay an expanse of roaming grey sky and restless sea going away together for uninterrupted miles. There was a wall around the cottage, but that was simply a statement of possession, for nothing grew within it that did not grow beyond it; and it was too low and hunched to be serious protection if the sea grew wild and reached to claim more. There was no crisp Cote d'Azur division of land and sea, sea and sky; they blended into each other with a slow moving turbulence of soaring beauty and utter loneliness. A bird hung in the sky, rose higher and trembled in some isolated current, then plummeted to the sea, apparently for the sheer joy of falling, except nothing in nature is for sheer joy, always and only from necessity.

Her new clothes had been laid out with Nanny-like care and precision. She pulled on the jeans: too long, too large; a T-shirt, a jersey, and went in search of the bathroom. Before she pushed up the latch on the door the thought struck her that none of this was new. What she would find on the other side of the door she had seen before; this room, this scene, that view of unbroken desolation was all hers from somewhere.

She opened the door: a small, dark space. There was one door in front of her closed, and another to her left also closed; a flight of narrow, unbannistered stairs sunk away on the right casting back a smell of stale biscuits and creosote.

She walked forward listening; plimsole laces trailing. What she expected to hear was movement, and whistling perhaps, or frying. God, she was starving. But no sound came. Wait, yes there was a sound from behind that door; it was moaning. Ben was in pain and he was hiding it from her. Oh Christ, a heart attack. She touched the latch and listened again before opening; a rhythmic moan, deep and awful. She rushed in seeing an image of herself falling upon a writhing body, but stopped dead in the doorway. Ben was bent double in striped underpants and red socks, a dumb-bell in one hand, the other held carefully aside in a magnificent bandage, huge, white and so neat. He looked at her from between his ankle bones with red face and bulging veins. Lydia instinctively turned her head to the up-side-down preparing to communicate.

'Get out of here. Do you hear? Get out,' Ben screamed with surprising force considering his position.

Lydia slammed the door and dashed through the only other one which had to be, and was, the bathroom. She rolled against the wall, hand over mouth, hilariously happy at finding him human and, good Lord, figure-conscious too.

The bathroom was obviously an addition, with everything new and scrupulously hygienic; even nestling shyly on the other side of the lavatory, a bidet. The sight of it reflected in the mirror in front of her made Lydia stop brushing her teeth and examine the toothbrush she had picked up without thinking. It was new, it was yellow, and the one next to it was brown. That toothbrush and the bidet created a sum in her mind: 2nd toothbrush + bidet = Woman. But although there might have been 'woman', she was that for him now.

She opened a corner cupboard, the door jarred, then gave, spilling forth a rush of brown glass bottles which clattered noisily on the floor. Lydia sensed she had come upon something mildly secret and waited to see if the clatter would bring Ben. No sound, so she started to examine the contents; little shiny orange pills, opalescent yellow globules, big powdery white tablets, delicious-looking purple capsules, a beautiful array of shapes and colours. There was another shelf of more commonplace bottles and tubes, mouth-washes of several different varieties, insect-bite cream, pile ointment, athlete's foot powder; and these were not just-in-case supplies, every item was well used. She replaced the bottles and shut the door, closing off a certain pulpy intimacy she wished she had not found. Did people like Ben have athlete's foot and piles?

'What are you doing?' Ben put his head round the door. 'Listen, you won't touch that cupboard, will you? I'm going to get breakfast, don't be long.'

He retreated halfway down the stairs with his usual thunderous step, then stopped. He returned and crossed to where Lydia stood beside the basin and took the flannel from her hand, still holding his own bandaged one awkwardly like a half-completed salute. He folded the flannel on the side of the basin and with infinite care began to wipe her face. Not so as to cleanse, but with rapt attention as if to discover, to remove something as intangible as time. He placed some strands of hair back from her forehead and watched them fall again. He then retrieved his gaze upon a world quite past Lydia and kissed her. Again he said, but this time quietly, 'Don't be long,' and again he retreated, but this time slowly.

Downstairs was just one huge room with a large stove at one end and at the other an open fireplace in front of which sagged an exhausted, debauched old whore of a sofa strewn over with rugs. In the centre of the room was a scrubbed table with four chairs round it. Shrimping nets, saucepans and oil lamps hung from the ceiling. Two deep windows gave glimpses of the haunted landscape sighing outside.

Ben watched Lydia move into the room and seemed to be gauging her reaction to her surroundings, but she just smiled at him shyly, indicating that only through him would she acquaint herself with the place. Her long jeans made a swishing noise on the flagstone floor and the arms of her jersey hung long. Lydia pushed her hair from her face and rolled her sleeves a little. She did not like being watched and was not quite sure how to behave. Anything she did to be helpful, like unpacking boxes of food or making coffee might seem a little too proprietorial and that would not do at all.

When she considered how she had arrived here, how they had both arrived in this situation, with no pacts nor promises, with no words at all about what they were doing, either to each other or to anyone else, Lydia began to lose confidence. As long as she had been going somewhere, either from Eric to Ben and back to Eric; or while she had been travelling all that long yesterday, questions had not seemed relevant. Now in the light of day, facing each other with nowhere else to go, she felt there might be some explanation of the terms on which she was there. And she waited but it did not come.

'And now I'll show you how well I can cook. Put all those things from that box on the table and I'll tell you where each one goes,' Ben said, as he started to break eggs onto the hotplate of the stove.

So her instincts had been right, she thought, he was the boss around this place, he was no foundering male and any interference on her part would not be well received. She was quite relieved to feel that whatever she was there for it was not in the role of little housewife.

Ben ordered her about while he prepared fried eggs, bacon, tomatoes and sausages. The smell of all these drove away the smell of damp and the room started to come to life. With the appearance of food and ordinariness Lydia grew less frightened of where she was and what she had done and began to quite like the place, and herself in it.

They ate with relish and in silence until at the end of the meal Ben made a calculated sweep with his arm and pushed to one end of the table all the breakfast clutter between him and Lydia. He leant across and took her hands.

'Do you like my place? Do you really like it?'

'I love it,' she said, and kissed his hands holding hers, not only because she loved it, but also because he minded.

Ben looked at her head bent over his hands and in one fearful moment he realised she was in love with him; she felt his reaction like an electric shock and withdrew her hands. She must hide what she felt. She had to remember that, because with every uninvited show of love he would withdraw for a while only to venture forward later. It was all right for her to respond, that was essential; even if he chose the most impossible moment to caress her, she must not show it or laugh it off because even the most gentle or trivial rejection would throw him into a sulk. The pitch of their togetherness was always set by him; she must not give in to moments of wild joy and throw her arms around his neck and kiss him just where his hair curled onto his collar, not unless by a glance or gesture he had invited it. All this Lydia knew by instinct. They never discussed the tidal limitations of their relationship. She would just watch and judge which role he was playing and fall in with that. Now he wanted to be the lover and not the loved, but she had got it wrong, and he found that offensive, so nothing would pass between them for a while.

They started to clear and tidy. Ben stood wiping a dry plate with a cloth and uttered occasional thoughts thrown up by the ploughing in his mind.

'I'll never understand how Viola could have smashed our world so completely.' Lydia knew it was her presence that provoked the dwelling on his past but was too curious about it herself to distract him and she feared that if, when he turned to look at her, he did not see his past he might see nothing and dismiss her. 'I remember her little face looking back at me as they accelerated away from Eden in that Buick of Viola's. The end of our life together. Natta had a scarf on because the car was open, it was one that I had given her; she loved scarves.

But the wind pulled it from her head and it floated onto the gravel.' He paused to examine the scene in memory. 'They didn't stop.' Lydia sat still and quiet, looking over his shoulder, as it were, at these events, these wounds. He began to speak angrily, 'But she was jealous of Natta. She didn't like people admiring Natta more than they did her, which was beginning to happen and so she broke up our world to go in search of admiration.' His face flushed. 'Oh, and I know she found it time and time again, but she took Natta with her. Away from me.' He swung round and gripped the edge of the table, frowning at Lydia, anxious to make her aware of this intolerable injustice. 'You do see?' he shouted, 'she didn't want her but she took her to hurt me. Get it?' The 'get it' came out as an ironical sob. Then he faltered and looked around; he seemed dazed by the journey back to the present. He was embarrassed and looked down at his hands still gripping the table to see if they could offer him a distraction. They did. He grabbed the wrist of his bandaged hand. 'God, it's sore, I must re-bandage it. Come on, you can do it for me.' His tone was quite altered and recovered; he walked up and down the room cradling the hand and issuing orders. 'Get that enamel bowl from the bathroom and you'll find some Dettol up there, too.' Lydia hurried, trying to get the orders right, thinking of blood-poisoning, gangrene, amputation. 'No, no, blast you. Rinse the bowl with boiling water. Don't you know anything about hygiene?' The moment of the unwrapping came. 'Ah, careful. God, you're clumsy, Lyd. I'll do it myself.' He raised the hand high and started to unwind the bandage letting it fall inch by inch to the floor. 'You can't imagine the pain. The throbbing in my arm is terrible ...'

Lydia stood on tiptoe, wetting and biting her lips, preparing not to show shock at the green pus, the torn flesh. Each time she was near enough to see the wound, not yet exposed, Ben would turn away as if even her sight of it might hurt him. Finally, the last inch of bandage dropped to the floor, a piece of antiseptic-sodden cotton-wool with it. The two of them stared at a whitish patch on his hand and a thin red line where the skin had been parted on the surface. Lydia looked from Ben's hand to his face and back to his hand, puzzled. There was really nothing to be seen.

'What are you smiling at? It's not funny, Lyd. It's bloody painful. It might not look much but it sure as hell hurts. Go on, you push off and do something else. I don't mind, I'm used to being alone. I can perfectly well do my own bandage.' And he could, too, beautifully.

'Is there anything I can put on; boots, a mac or something?' she asked.

There were several serious-looking garments hanging from the pegs by the door but she did not feel she could quite help herself. And again her instinct had been right because Ben came over, walking almost backwards in order to protect his hand. He sorted carefully among the coats with his good hand, pulling out a shoulder here, a cuff there, to identify each one. At last he took down a short tartan jacket made from blanketing with a diagonal zip across the front and one or two elsewhere on obscure pockets. He looked at it for some time before handing it to Lydia with a shrug and saying, 'You might as well have that, I suppose.' She felt she should demur, the offer was so reluctant, but at the first breath of protest he became irritated. '... Go on. Go on. And there are smallish boots too, if you look for them.' He returned to his bandaging.

Lydia put on the jacket which was only a little large and really very chic; she found the boots. They were new.

'Ben?'

'What is it?'

'Were you expecting me to come yesterday? And to come here? These things: coat, boots and stuff ...'

'There's a hat there too. Try it, it should be all right.'

'They all seem to be so right. Were you? Expecting me?'

'I don't know. I knew if you heard me ring you'd come;' and softening the arrogance he added, 'I suppose: I hoped you'd come ... God, God it's painful.' He fell about cradling his hand again, clearly not prepared to continue the conversation. Lydia made a rush for the outdoors with Ben calling after her, 'Don't think I can't see you laughing, because I can. You're a heartless cow. And don't get lost.'

She sat down on the path which ran between the two sandy patches of garden and started to put on the boots. The air was biting and laced with the smell of salt and seaweed. The path which was concrete, only wide enough for one car, was raised above the ground by about four inches and ran away a few hundred yards to where thick scrub grew. There was a cluster of cottages and a little beyond that, judging by television aerials reaching hysterically above stunted, wind-battered trees, a village.

She went to the gate which screeched painfully as it rubbed in salt-rotted hinges, and there was another noise too. Lydia looked back towards the cottage. The sound was quite clear: a telephone was ringing and then stopped abruptly. It was answered. Of course it would be. Ben would have rushed to it, wound or no wound. She went off towards the shore.

The tide was out and it was a long way to where the sea really began. Once or twice Lydia thought she had come to it and found that the water was only a huge and shallow pool which she waded through, arriving at another expanse of soggy sand. Brilliant bursts of winter sun would pick out the sea proper in sparkling relief until the clouds closed and the scene again became one multi-toned grey. She sat down and pushed her fingers into the muddy sand. Who was it who was always butting in, breaking their world with that tinnish sound? Of course, there was no reason to assume it was the same person ringing all the time, it was probably business or old friends. But there was something about that ringing that made her feel cut off, alone; as if people she did not know, could not see, were laughing at her. She looked at her shadow spread for a moment on the sand and saw a little head poking out of sagging shoulders. But if you're spineless doesn't it follow that your shoulders sag?

There was a shout. Over the dunes strode Ben's great figure, his gleaming bandaged hand held aloft like an olympic torch. He was running now, he was so fine. And how could they not laugh?

When he reached Lydia it was all right again and she forgot about the unseen people, the unheard laughter. He lifted her through the air and let her fall towards him, encompassing her skull with his hands.

'Thank God for you, Lyd.' He froze suddenly, still holding her close. Again he was listening. Please, no, not the telephone, it's not possible. Her explosion of happiness dimmed.

'Listen, listen.' Ben let his hands fall to her shoulders and the wind wrapped her hair around the contours of her face while she

stared up at him. 'It's a curlew. That sad, sad cry is a curlew.'
He looked down at her.

'... Because your cry brings to my mind
Passion-dimmed eyes and long heavy hair
That was shaken out over my breast ...'

'That's Yeats on the curlew, you know.' He lifted her hair from
her face and let it fly in the wind. 'Only yours isn't heavy.'
There was disappointment in his voice.

* * *

'... Do you remember once that I told you I was desolate, and
you saved me from it? Well desolation is mine again, Lyd.
Please, please save me again.

'It took some days for me to gather the courage to go and
see her. If the man had not been there it would have been
different but by the time I crossed the road, rang the bell and
heard her voice, distorted through the entry-phone, I was well
armed with information about her life: what time she took the
child for a walk in the Luxembourg Gardens, the fact that he
was always there; I was familiar with the faces of the inner
circle of their friends who seemed to come and go at all hours
of night and day. I knew that when I entered there would be no
one but her and the man there, and of course the boy.

'She wasn't surprised to see me, she said. She said they had
both been expecting me. They were welcoming, to a point, they
didn't seem to want to rush me away. The man, Laurent,
stayed, always a little apart, using on me the conscientious and
cold courtesy that Europeans are so good at. I felt uneasy with
the child and stayed as far from it as I could, but he had, then,
an alarming habit of standing in front of me and staring; if I
went to another part of the room and stood (to be out of his
reach as well as his gaze), he followed me. Laurent never left
the room all the time I was there, but at the moments when he
was not actually looking at the two of us, she gave me strange,
appealing glances. I couldn't understand their meaning, for
having done that she would be extravagantly affectionate to
Laurent.

'I went back several times; sometimes they were alone with
the child, and other times some of those friends, whose faces I

knew, were there. I ingratiated myself by producing some
Columbian Gold. That impressed them because it obviously
didn't fit with their idea of me. She wasn't surprised. There was
no sign of the Fraternité or the Maître, although some of them
talked about him. They seemed an affluent little crowd and
there was little accent on work of an obvious kind. Laurent
appeared the most affluent of the lot, judging by the gold
smattered around his neck and wrists and an unmistakable
manner he had; in no way was he intimidated by me; in no way
that I could see, that is. It was so like her to choose a man who
was her equal, not only physically but financially. She was too
emotionally insecure to do otherwise, and it is for that reason
that, in the end, I was the only one for her.

'Things changed subtly after the first few visits and rather
than being the subject of interest, the outsider, I was accepted;
never by Laurent but by the others, and it was he who became
the observed and the subject of interest. Perhaps it seemed
strange to them that he received me there at all, but he wasn't a
man who invited comment. Still, however, I had not been
alone with her, not for a second, and I knew that if I was ever
to take her away with me I would first have to get her alone.
She knew that and seemed to avoid it as strenuously as I sought
the opportunity; but all the time she looked at me when no
one else could see. I believed she was imploring me not to give
up.

'Finally, when I thought I would go mad at always being
with her in a crowd, I struck on the way to see her alone and on
my own ground.

'Do I sound ruthless, Lyd? Do you think I should have left
her and come back to you then, avoiding the pain and
disaster? Perhaps I should; at least then I would not have lost
my hair, my heart; even my sanity remains only in patches. But
would you have taken me again? Will you take me again? At
least meet me. Just to have you talk to me.'

'It's better we don't meet. We mustn't. You understand. Are
you so very changed? I'm sure, however much, I'd see you as
the same. Go away, please. Don't come back to my street.'

7

Some weeks passed at Coalbarn in perfect peace. When Lydia had looked back on that interlude it now seemed a little lifetime and no time at all. She and Ben played out the pantomimes that become dear to people living together: she would interrupt his exercises every morning to see his puffing, straining body fighting insidious age, and every morning when she did he would shout, 'Shove off.' In fact, she would walk away consoled, reminded that the man under whom she trembled; the man who by his touch would remove all barriers of inhibition in her, the man who could make her rise gloriously from her silly body and emerge as a woman, passionate and complete, was, in fact, no God but just a chap, fifty-ish and vain. She mocked him mutely about his wound until, to her disappointment, Ben decided it was better; but then he replaced that, to her delight, with a sprained shoulder. A clever choice, because she could not mock a wound she could not see. But she did, anyway, because he would be disappointed if she did not.

Their days became neatly arranged; nearly always Ben remained behind in the morning and while Lydia walked and explored he would do some business on the telephone. Later he would join her and complain how the man taking over his position in his company would not do things quite his way but anyway why should he care? He had made his fortune, on their own heads be it, etcetera, etcetera; and Lydia would console, placate, only to find that the next morning he was frantic again, bullying and insulting his office staff, then charming, flattering, amusing, having obtained his own way. His sway, in spite of semi-retirement, still appeared to be considerable. Lydia would listen to the beginning of these calls, but the fear of hearing the beginning of the business drama which finally would lure him back was too much and soon she would leave him walking up and down the room holding the telephone and waving his free hand. Sometimes, if she appeared not to be going, Ben would gesture to the outside and, holding the receiver between his shoulder and jaw, would help her with her jacket, never ceasing his conversation; and rain or shine she went.

Lydia stopped expecting clarification of her situation; she was old enough to know what she was doing. Ben negated Eric's existence by never referring to him and in this landscape, quite unlike one she had ever seen before, it was easy to believe that her leaving had done Eric no real harm: the consequence of her behaviour were so out of context to this new life of hers. But 'life', that was not the word; for although time was passing, wonderfully full and slow, these days seemed, nevertheless, transient and she felt that a misplaced gesture, a word too true, could end them in a breath. That thought made Eric seem a little more real. She tried to imagine him, but Eric doing what? Eric sitting? Eric teaching? Eric alone? She tried to telephone him, once, from a call-box on the edge of the village and was relieved when it rang and rang about those familiar rooms she could see, so clearly, as she waited, as empty. And what would she have said? 'I'm sorry, please make your life without me,' or, 'wait, do; I know this will pass although I dread that passing.' Could she have said, to practise Ben's endearing arrogance, 'I still love you too and I will be back when ... when ...' that was when she thought of life without Ben and the horror of contemplating that made her run from the call-box through a high hedged lane, through scrub, some mud, dunes and back; back to Ben. And as Lydia, breathing hard after the long run, watched him calmly examining his latest purchase, five volumes of Gould's Birds of Great Britain, unaware of her vile infidelity: (ringing her loved; her once loved) she tried to imagine what it would mean if there was no longer Ben, but it was hard because it would mean nothing, it would mean there was no more of her to be of any significance. It would be the end of her. In this errand of taking him back to happiness, of showing him the door, she had, herself, become lost.

There was one day which marked clearly the end of the peaceful ones. It was particularly dark, even at midday, when the sky dragged a tortured belly across the nervous earth, and Lydia had helped Ben put two large planks over the ground-floor windows in preparation for the massive storm promised. They jammed the planks into position with poles, hoping that they would act as shutters, for even with the stove burning at one end of the room and the fire at the other, the wind still whistled through the windows and made the room cold. Their defences worked and they lay in front of the fire after lunch, warm and slightly drunk from the wine in Ben's cellar, which was an outside lavatory. Ben was in the womb of the sofa reading and Lydia lay on the cushions on the floor. She rearranged herself to study his face better. She loved to look at his face and could do so in peace as he was engrossed in what he was reading. After some time he came to a juncture that let his attention wander. He noticed Lydia stared at him reading him as intently as he read his book. He looked back at her and she waited; any moment now he would reach down, caress her and say, 'Do you remember when ...' or 'Thank God for you now, Lyd ...'; he would say something gentle. But this time he did not reach down, simply smiled apologetically. Lydia frowned at him wondering at the unvoiced apology. She did not want to destroy this world created by the murmuring fire and the stifled storm outside with the noise of words. The smile faded from his face leaving the apology.

'Antediluvian?' he asked, trying for a grin.

'What?'

'Me. Is that what you were thinking? S'pose I must be in your eyes. More so when I look at you through mine, I can tell you. Only Lyd, don't pity me. I don't mind my old face too much, you know. I've seen it from boyish fat to maturity; subtler; leaner; lined; collapsing. I've watched it every day for years and it doesn't matter to me.'

'Pity, Ben, pity? Oh how wrong. I was just loving your face; that's all. Do you mind?' He shook his head with only a little embarrassment. 'But I must admit ...' Lydia began, putting this frank moment to use, 'I do wonder what would have happened if we'd met in your younger years.' Ben smiled at her careful selection of words. She meant 'At the height of his maleness', but could not say it. Of course she had met him then, but she was only a child and had not noticed, or maybe she had, just enough to carry in memory. 'Do you think if we had met as equals, the same age, the same set, you would have noticed me? I don't. Some friend of yours would have said, "I say, Ben old thing, do pop over and shake a leg with poor old Lydia. That one standing there under the potted palm, she hasn't danced with a soul all evening." And you would have, because you are a polite sort of chap, but there would have been nothing more because you wouldn't have needed me then, when everyone wanted you.'

Ben drew her hand onto his knee and stroked her hair. 'So you look into the past when you watch my face, but I, when I watch yours, look into the future. I try to see what would be there if we got together, I mean if we really got together. Now I look into your face and see hope and love and caring; but in some years' time ... and not so many at that, it would not be you who stares, with love, at me, but me trying to see into your averted eyes; and I would persist. At last you would give in and I would see impatience, revulsion and the shadow of some younger man ...'

Just then there was a crash and the window banged open, letting the wind burst in upon them with an 'AHHHH' like the villain in a Victorian melodrama. They jumped to their feet and Lydia clutched Ben.

'It's all right,' Ben said. 'It's only the plank being wrenched away from the window by the gale. You stay inside and pull the window shut and I'll go out and try to get it back in place.' Ben took down an oilskin from beside the door, a large hammer hanging from the ceiling and sorted some nails. 'I shall try to nail it in place and see if that's any better. Bet it won't work.' The front door slammed behind him and Lydia went to close the window. She put some coal and logs on the fire and started to tidy about, thinking of the interrupted scene.

While she was reaching to hang up a saucepan the telephone rang and it shook her rigid. It occurred to Lydia, as she stood watching the telephone, that whenever it had rung she had always been outside; Ben had made calls in the morning to his secretary, she supposed, business connections, but it had never interrupted their hours alone before; it had played no part in their life together. But now it was sounding away, eroding what was left of the dazed peace of their afternoon with Ben outside, this time, and no chance of him hearing it above the gale.

Lydia felt she was about to meet the truth, the mocking crowd, the present world of which Ben never spoke. It was all there waiting to tumble down the line at her. Should she just let it ring, or call Ben? But there was a compulsion to discover a fragment of Ben's life beyond her, so that she might, by the sound of a voice, by a word, discover where she fitted, what she meant.

Lydia raised the receiver and listened.

'My love, I'm sorry. I simply couldn't ring this morning. I hope you didn't wait in.' It was a woman's voice, deep, strong and seductive. It went on without pausing. 'Now, sweetie, stand by for bullying: you've been down there far too long on your own, no more excuses, I'm going to … Ben? Who is that?'

A supremely confident woman this; it did not seem to occur to her that she might have dialled the wrong number. Lydia felt that she was the one in the wrong. The voice went on, but now it was a little less sure, as if it was beginning to see the scene to which it was talking.

'I want Ben Wavell. Is he there?'

Lydia did not speak and after a moment the receiver at the other end was replaced. Ben came in and the storm tried to push through with him, but he kicked the door shut at the same time as wiping his feet.

'Well, I've done it. I feel rather pleased about that.' He went over to the fire and rearranged the logs Lydia had placed. 'I thought I heard the telephone ringing when I was out there;' he crossed to Lydia and with one hand on his hip and the other lifting strands of hair from her eyes, he continued; 'if it ever did when I wasn't here you wouldn't answer it, would you?' He did not look into her eyes but at her hair which he was still placing. 'I don't think it would do really. I mean private lives and all that. I'm sure you agree?'

Lydia turned away. Well, she had not answered, had she? And if silence made her a liar then he was one already.

What remained of the afternoon melted into evening. Only the clock distinguished the two. Ben showed her how to make

Moules Marinière from the mussels they had collected that morning on the shore. She was given the laborious task of scrubbing and trimming them – 'No, that's not enough, Lyd, you filthy thing. Look at all that mud, that must come off.'

They drank more wine while they cooked and became freshly intoxicated, having recovered from the afternoon bout.

'Lyd, to trim them you hold the knife like this – not like that.'

Lydia turned, hands on hips. 'Do you ever get tired of bossing people around?' The question came casually ironic, certainly without rancour, and inwardly she was laughing at the predictability of his response as she went on, her voice in a pale imitation of his, 'It's not that I wish to …' she fished around for his word, '… to pry or anything, I just wondered; I mean, I get vaguely cheesed-off with being bossed and … please don't think the troops are rebelling or anything but …'

'LYD.'

'What?' She had been enjoying her speech, walking up and down, slicing words from the air the way he did.

'You're making fun of me.'

'Am I?'

'Do I really boss?' He stepped towards her.

'Yes.' She moved away.

'Am I really very arrogant?' He stepped again.

'Terribly.' She moved further, putting the table safely between them.

'Inconsiderate?' His hands upon the table leaning towards her.

'Oh, yes.'

'Nothing to recommend me?' He edged his way round the table.

Elaborately crossing her arms she turned her back on him to hide her laughter that was nearer all the time. 'Nope. You whine, criticize and dismiss.'

He reached her and slipped his arms around her waist from behind, 'So I'm done for. No appeal court, naturally. There's nothing I can say?'

'Not a word.' She remained rigid, turning her head away from his mouth that sought her neck.

'What about …' (and here his bantering tone fell away) '… I love you, Lyd, you're my happiness. Please don't ever leave me.'

'That'll do nicely, thank you.' She turned round and threw herself into his arms, 'At last you've said it.'

He gripped her to him, 'So I have. So I have.'

Then quite illogically Lydia set against the almost insupportable happiness of the moment the memory of that morning's telephone call, and she was filled with misery. All spontaneity was gone, she felt heavy, joyless, jealous.

As they ate he chatted and joked, unaware of the change in her. Afterwards they settled in front of the fire and Ben sank in the sofa contented, eyes shut, moving his finger in time to Mozart on the record player.

The woman had said she was sorry she had not rung in the morning, she hoped he had not waited in. Well, he had. Just as he had every other morning while Lydia walked alone on the mud flats with the sea a mile away. How easily he had formed that habit for her. But that woman, whoever she was, thought he was alone. Ben was the only one, Ben lounging there on the sofa; Ben happy, happy, was the only one who knew what was going on. But now there was something he did not know: these two women had found out about each other simultaneously and Lydia wondered, as she sat with her back to the fire plaiting a piece of marram grass, what would happen when he found out about that.

She did not have to wait for long. The next morning, in fact, a calm brilliant morning brought another kind of storm.

'What the bloody hell do you mean by not telling me she had rung? And what were you doing answering my telephone anyway. I told you never to do that. For Chrissake, Lyd, you're intolerable.'

Ben had come rushing over the dunes while Lydia had been dutifully walking and waiting, knowing that whoever that woman was she would be ringing again, almost certainly when Lydia was out. She had seen his figure coming from a mile away, just a dot at first, and then she could hear a smacking sound as his feet hit the wet sands long before what he was shouting became audible. He seemed to be spreading his anger all over the shore and now he was before her, outraged and panting.

'And of course you know what is going to happen now, don't you? She's coming up here. So that's it. That's our little world finished. By tomorrow night the whole bloody world will know about us and I'm going to look pretty foolish.'

Now she regretted deeply not having asked questions before, for they were coming upon her all at once.

'Well, why is that woman so important? Why? ...' Her breath came in gasps. '... And why shouldn't the world know about us?' Each shouted question she reinforced by thrusting her shoulders as she spoke, her fists pounding at her sides. 'You must know I'm committed to you. Just by leaving Eric the way I did committed me to you. He exists, you know, even if you choose to pretend he doesn't ...'

'Oh, Bloody Eric,' Ben said, as though it were a title.

'Yes, Bloody Eric. He was all I lived for until you. And why, tell me this, why would you look so foolish? ... Unless,' her tone now suddenly altered, 'unless what you said, at last, yesterday, isn't true.'

He was saying something now, possibly it was reassuring, but really she was beyond hearing anything. The only thing she knew was she was totally, irredeemably in love with him and that every word he said, every movement he made re-inforced that love. She knew how he was. She had instinctively understood him since she was a child and that was where her weakness lay, in that and in their mutual knowledge of her understanding. He could be himself with her, did not have to apologize for the arrogance, because she knew what went with it, and it was all right, everything was all right. If his words were harsh they only served to make the gentle ones, which always followed, seem dearer and more glowing for their stony setting.

Ben held her shoulders between his hands. She tried to pull away from his grasp and could not; at least she could turn her head so he could not see her crying.

'No, Lyd. Don't do that. Please, please.' He released her and she sank to the ground.

He walked up and down beside Lydia's crouched and sobbing figure with his hands in his pockets, looking about him, embarrassed, as if he was with someone who had stopped to relieve himself in the middle of a public park. Finally he stood beside her and looking down, said in a quiet, pleading voice, giving in to the inevitability of explaining himself,

'Listen to me, Lyd. It's just that it's too soon. I'm not prepared yet to explain to others about us when I hardly know myself what I am doing.' He knelt beside her and put his hands on the back of her bending neck. 'This woman, Lyd, is a friend. She's called Millie. She has given me a lot of companionship and she stood by me when a lot of people dropped me because of ... of unpleasant gossip.' He flinched at the memory. 'She's not a lover, although she has given me tenderness when I have needed it. She's one of the most generous and kind women I've ever met, but she's a "situation" of her own, grown-up children, amiable, alcoholic "Old Man", etc.' He seemed to have an aversion to the words "marriage" and "husband". 'She was a girlfriend once years ago, long before Viola. She was the first girl I ever kissed. We were at a dance and I said, "Can I kiss you?" and she said, "All right." So I did and she said, "No, that's wrong. You're supposed to use your tongue, like this." And she showed me how. I thought she was frightfully daring and although we're exactly the same age I've always thought of her as the older woman because of that. So if she is a little possessive, protective, maybe time has given her the right.'

He turned Lydia's head towards him. There was sand on her lips and grains of it perilously near one eye, clinging to where the tears had been. He removed them with his middle finger and held her face between his hands. She looked back at him, trusting him implicitly, loving him for all he told her and for all he did not. He held her head tighter and it began to hurt.

'Trust me, please trust me,' and then so quietly that Lydia could not be sure whether the whispering sea coming fast towards them confused his words, 'I won't let them take you away this time.' She looked hard into his eyes trying to understand what he had said but the only thing that became clear was that, as he looked sadly, lovingly, intently, at her face between his hands, he did not see her at all.

The bright morning had dimmed and a wind was getting up. They walked slowly. All the way Ben held her close, his arm heavy on her shoulders.

The day passed with a feeling of intimacy between them, as if a common enemy was drawing them together. Ben's manner was softer, with less bravado. She caught him looking at her as if her presence was a surprise to him, but not an unpleasant

one. He asked, as he had never done before, what she wanted
to do, eat, listen to and waited for her answer as though it
would be a revelation to him.

They tried to calculate how long it would take Millie to reach
them as she had assured Ben she was going to. They decided it
would not be until early evening, but evening came and went
with no sign of her. Eventually they went to bed, exhausted by
the waiting.

When Lydia opened her eyes the next morning she could not
remember where she was. She had been dreaming she was in a
desert being chased by a girl with very long, dark hair. The girl
was furious with Lydia about something and Lydia was
frightened; she hid from the girl behind a giant armchair and
watched the girl run past with her hair floating behind. Sitting
amidst that mass of hair was Lydia's father who looked straight
at her wagging that nicotine-stained finger she hated so much.
The finger grew larger and larger until it was battering her into
the sand with the grains filtering into her nostrils. It was then
she woke. Ben was leaning on one arm studying her face.

'Hello,' he whispered. 'I've been watching you sleeping. You
must have been dreaming about something awful. You
seemed frightened but I didn't want to wake you because you
looked so lovely.' He pulled back the covers and looked at
Lydia's body limp from sleep, wearing only the shrunken blue
pullover that she wore in bed.

'You're so fair. It's strange, because if I had been asked
before this morning what your skin colour was I would have
said darkish, sort of olive but that couldn't be more wrong.
You're white, white; almost bluey white.'

He put his large tanned hand on her stomach and compared
flesh. Lydia raised her arm to caress him but he caught her
wrist in mid-air pushing it back onto the pillow, his weight
upon it and brought his head close to hers. He put his lips to
her neck and spoke. It was something he did often; he would
place his mouth to some part of her body and speak quietly so
that she would feel his lips moving. The speech would go on
and on, rising and falling, and little by little he would move to
other parts of her body, conversing with her flesh all the time.
It put her into an ecstatic inertia, her limbs heavy with desire,
her pulse pounding so hard in her ears that she never heard his

words. But this time she did, 'Not now, Lyd. Not now, because she's coming. But when she's gone, then ...' and he talked on some more, words she did not hear.

As she dressed and went downstairs Lydia felt an increasing strength inside. It seemed that Millie, far from separating them, was bringing them together. Ever since she and Ben had arrived at the cottage, although he had been amusing and entertaining and certainly passionate, he seemed to have been removed from her, as if something about her had disappointed him. She now had his new attitude as a guide; at last he seemed to know she was there and it was her he saw and not some illusive image.

Ben was downstairs before her and already preparing breakfast. He had opened the front door to let out the smell of burnt bacon and was letting in a fine misty rain. Lydia began to plump up cushions and replace books on their shelves.

'That's marvellous, Lyd. Keep it up. The place should look faintly respectable.'

They both heard the car at the same time. Ben rushed to the window and Lydia stood by the table, last night's dirty plates in her hands. He turned to Lydia, 'She's here. She's here. She's getting out.' Panicked. He was definitely panicked.

Ben shook himself, braced himself and quite suddenly he was changed again. He was loose, confident, disarmingly charming once more. He winked at Lydia, grinned and did a few steps of his Charlie Chaplin walk just to show that he thought the part he was about to play was pretty silly too. He went to open the door.

'Hel-*lo*! I thought you'd never get here.'

'Oh, didn't you, well, tough luck, I did.' It was the same seductive voice, richer and deeper for not being on the telephone. There was also a breathlessness about the voice sounding as if it would break into laughter at any moment. 'Aren't you going to help me get this lot out?'

'Sorry, Millie, coming,' Ben said as he moved out of the doorway towards the car. Lydia saw Ben approach the woman, but still could not see her, his broad back blocked her view. She watched his hands on her shoulders as he bent to kiss her. Lydia envied the woman his proximity, the touch of his hands.

'God, what is all this stuff?' Ben asked, as they came back to the cottage bearing boxes.

'Just things I know you need here. You've no idea how to make a place … Oh, hello.'

The woman spotted Lydia who had retreated deep into the room as they had advanced.

'I'm Millie. Who are you?'

'This is Lydia, Millie,' said Ben. He looked anxiously at them both, frightened of a scene.

'Hello, Lydia. It's very nice to meet you.'

There was nothing sarcastic in her voice, but something odd about the way she glanced at Ben as she spoke.

Millie was tall and very slender; she was wearing immaculately tailored trousers and a loose cashmere pullover, all beige; a silk scarf was tied around her shoulders. Her gold chains, bracelets and rings chinked together as she moved. She smelt expensive; everything about her was soft and sensuous. Her face was not hard as Lydia had imagined, hoped; it was gentle, tired and a little care-worn, with a fading sun-tan. She had made-up carefully and recently. Her hair was a rich red-brown and short: a fuller female version of Ben's. She must have been in her early fifties but looked younger.

All of Ben's 'She's a good old thing', 'a mate', 'a loyal old stick', had not prepared Lydia for this Millie at all.

'Well, Ben. Coffee?' Millie said. Her tone with him was ironic but kind. She obviously knew Ben very well. She knew how he was going to react to the embarrassing situation and was prepared to sit back and be amused. The only time she seemed to be uneasy was when she looked at Lydia and then she screwed up her eyes as if trying to remember something.

'Moules Marinière I see. And delicious too.' She examined the debris of last night's meal. 'One of Ben's specialities, Lydia, but I'm sure you know that. I'll bet you don't know it was me who taught him how to cook it. You are mucky, Ben, leaving the washing-up until morning.'

'Now stop, Millie. Here's your coffee. Sit down and drink it.'

Ben handed her the cup to stop her sidling round the room. 'Where did you stay last night? We waited up …' he faltered, 'I stayed up for ages.'

'My dear, how thoughtful of you, but I, too, was being thoughtful and I thought, well, two's company and three's a crowd, even if one of them is as small and as young ...' she lingered over the words, 'as Lydia.'

'Oh, God. Here we go,' said Ben.

'So I stayed in the pub in the village. Funny place,' she started to talk fast. 'I had a meal in the bar last night; a lot of characters straight out of Cold Comfort Farm all staring at me with their cross-eyes and droopy lips; dim-witted and suspicious. It comes from in-breeding, you know, there's a lot of it in this part of the world, but of course you don't mind that sort of thing do you, Ben?'

Ben slammed his cup down so violently that it shattered, spilling coffee everywhere. He took a step towards Millie and brought his arm across himself as if he was going to strike her. Millie sat on the sofa looking up at him, her face pale. Ben turned and went to the window. Lydia could see from the movements he made with his shoulders that he was recomposing himself. He pushed his hands through his hair and pulled them down over his face. From the corner of her eye Lydia also saw that at that very moment Millie was making exactly the same gesture. She did not pull her hands over her face but pushed one hand through her short, glossy hair, smoothing her thoughts. She smiled at Lydia. Clearly she had said something she regretted and wanted to start afresh.

'Do you like it here, Lydia? I must say I love it, but Ben won't think of the comforts, so I brought a few things.' Millie went over to the boxes brought from the car. 'I have a little electric grill for when that bloody stove is out and you are starving, and I have the most wonderful thing for drying the inside of Wellingtons; you know how impossible they are to dry inside. And you'll never guess, I've brought an electric blanket.' As she spoke she looked over to Ben once or twice to see if he had had enough time to calm himself. 'I mean, it's hell getting into a damp bed, isn't it?' she continued. Her head was bent over the knotted string of one of the boxes, but her eyes travelled over to Lydia. And what would Lydia say to that? Would she say, "Oh Ben and I don't mind" or would she say, "Ben's my electric blanket" or would she say, "when you've got what we've got you don't need heat." No she would not, she would quietly go over and mop up the spilt coffee.

How could this woman be so cool? How could she talk

about grills and gumboots and damp beds when she saw that Lydia was here with him? Lydia felt that Millie should either be openly angry and jealous or not be there at all, not to come along like an electric Lady Bountiful making oblique references that infuriated Ben and which she did not understand.

It was not going right. She did not feel so strong. She wished her hair shone and her jeans fitted. She wished her nails were clean and that tears were not so dangerously near. Lydia rubbed the floor ferociously. Millie knelt down beside her; she took the cloth from Lydia's hand and removed a piece of broken china from beside Lydia's bare foot.

'Why don't you go and put some shoes on,' Millie said quietly, 'your feet must be terribly cold and you could cut yourself. I'll clear this up.'

Lydia could see in the sad, tired face why she was a "mate", "a good old thing", and tender too. Lydia rose and went towards the door that closed off the stairs. Ben had turned and was looking at them both.

Lydia was halfway up the stairs when the door at the bottom was slammed and she was left in total darkness because the three doors upstairs were also shut. Two strides would have brought her to the top, she could then feel for the latch on any of the three doors, the landing was so confined, but so incapacitating was her fear of the dark that she simply froze and stared down towards the door she could not see below. She could have shouted, "Hey, I can't see" or "open the door", but she did not. A few seconds later the door started to swing open again of its own accord, as it always did when slammed too hard, and a bluish half-light roamed through to the first stair. Lydia breathed again and was about to turn and go upstairs when she saw Ben's hand reach towards the latch on the other side of the door. He closed it firmly, purposefully. He had shut her out. They did not want her there; they did not want her to hear; so she sat down with her feet pressed against the wall (to prevent the feeling of falling in an endless void that darkness produced in her) and stared at the offending door. To her relief the bluish light was again, like a friend, seeking a way through, this time by a crack beneath the door. Amidst the smell of stale biscuits, creosote and damp Lydia listened.

Ben spoke immediately with disgust. 'Never would I have believed that you could say such a thing, such a dirty, cheap thing. You have been the one who ...'

'Please, Ben, don't. I'm dreadfully sorry and you know that is not my way, but I was shocked.' Millie's voice then started to rise in the same way that it had when she described the pub. 'That girl, Ben. Didn't it occur to you it would be a shock for me? She's just a child, and after all that happened. Do you realize that if you appear with her in front of people that know you, even if they doubted the gossip before, that would confirm it in their minds? I stood by you, Ben. It wasn't all that nice for me and, as you know, defending you caused trouble between Charlie and me at the time. And I stayed with "Her" right through until she was ready to leave England, and what do I get for all that? You marching off with a girl so young it's disgusting; making everybody believe those terrible things they said at the time must have been true.'

'Firstly, she's not a child, she's nineteen plus ...'

'Oh, I see. So that makes it all right, I suppose?'

'Let me finish and stop, Millie, stop bitching. I hate it. I was going to say: secondly ...' he paused, he had no "secondly". 'Oh, there's nothing to add except that really for this little while that Lydia and I have been here together I have been happier than I have been for years. It's peaceful with her. There's none of that silly nonsense you get from those marriage-hungry divorcees; thirties and frightened. I know what people would say, but just because of that should I let her go and return myself to that insufferable loneliness?'

There was a silence, then Millie spoke as if the pieces of a jigsaw were laid before her and she was examining each one individually, holding them up to him.

'You talk of loneliness, Ben. In a way, my dear, you've brought it upon yourself. I can think of women who are eating their hearts out right now for you and they are attractive, intelligent, and young enough, goodness knows.'

'They bore me. They are all the things you say, but they are interchangeable and unspecial. I'd rather be alone than with any of them.'

Millie gave a controlled sigh and continued, 'Viola leaving you and taking Nathalie, and then Nathalie returning, and ...'

Millie selected her words, '... doing what she did, would be terrible for any man, but you of all people should be able to rise above it and start again. It's been three years since that awful time. Get on your feet again before it's too late. You don't have time to waste on little affairs that will get you nowhere. If you want to settle, Ben, find someone suitable soon before you're too old.'

'I'm trying to settle, but it's not easy to find someone compatible, and you make it a damned sight harder coming down here and telling me that the one lady who makes me most happy at the moment is too young.'

'It's not that at all.' Millie began to speak unnaturally, slowly enunciating each word with care. 'It is that she does look much younger than she is. She could be, with her peculiar build and her childishly fair colouring, seventeen.' She waited for a response from Ben and since there was none she said again, 'Mmmmm, Ben? Seventeen.'

'I don't want to remember all that,' Ben said almost inaudibly but in the broken voice which once spoke of his 'desolation'.

Millie said, 'I recognize her, you know. Lydia, I mean; I didn't at first and it bothered me but then when she was wiping the floor she suddenly looked up and it was as if not a moment had passed since that Summer before Viola left. Nathalie was eleven then, wasn't she? And that little girl was there.'

Neither of them spoke. A log collapsed in the fire setting it into animated chatter. A wind groaned tediously, pulling at the windows and at the door that separated Lydia from Ben and Millie. Then Ben must have risen because there was a sound of a chair grazing its legs on the flagstone floor; the rough sort of movement Millie would never have made. Ben was crossing to the window. He always turned to the open-air when cornered in conversation. He would be pushing his hands through his hair and rubbing his neck as he drew them down. His head would fall for a moment on his forearms, meeting on his chest. Now. Now he would turn refreshed, collected. Speak, Ben, please speak.

'Millie,' his voice was strong again, 'thank you for your solicitude. You are a dear, kind friend. Haven't I always said you were a dear, kind friend? But let me work it out in my own time and I promise I will bear your advice in mind.'

'No, Ben. You won't push me away with your "politesse". I know you and you are heading for a muddle and you know it too or you would not have hidden yourself away here.'

'Good. All right, Millie.' Ben was brisk and business-like. 'Now then, what are you going to do? Presumably you don't want to stay here, but at least come for a walk on the shore before you leave. I'll call Lyd. Why not stay for lunch and go home after? If you're not too pissed. I know you, old girl. Come on, we'll all have fun.'

Millie spoke again, frostily resolved to keep to her subject. 'She's here, Ben. She's come back. She's in London now.' Silence. 'Do you hear me?' Millie repeated, 'She's here.'

'I heard. I heard.' Ben sounded impatient, frightened. 'Have you seen her?'

'Yes.'

'Is she ... is she ... How is she?'

'Lovely, Ben. Quite lovely, as ever.'

The chair scraped again. He was sitting. His voice came muffled as if he spoke with his head pressed into his arms.

'I miss her, Millie. You can't know how much I miss her.'

'All right, all right,' her voice was near to his. She was leaning over him, consoling him, 'but I thought you'd like to know. Better to hear from me than anyone else.' Her voice was gentle and sympathetic, but it had about it the hint of victory. 'Now then,' she continued, taking up his brisk and business-like tone, 'you will use the things I brought, won't you? They will make life here so much more comfortable. I'll be off now. Shall we call little, er, what's her name? I'll say goodbye to her.' Nothing happened. 'Ben?' Millie said, 'Come on, sweetie, everything will be all right.'

Lydia had had enough. She had listened to the conversation like a blind man studying a wrestling match, but now to hear her side being brought to his feet by the victor who kicked him down was too much for even her, whose chosen role was that of passive observer.

When she 'came to', as it were, and decided on action she found that in her intent upon hearing every detail of conversation she had forced herself into the door-frame with her ear pressed against the door and in order to walk through she had first to disengage her imagination from the other side. She went in.

'Lydia, there you are,' said Millie, as if the one thing she had been longing for was Lydia's presence. Millie no longer looked or sounded beige and seductive. She looked short, ruffled and very fifty. The only lines on her face that showed were those of determination; years of getting her own way.

Ben was sitting with his elbows on the table, his head sunk into his arms. Lydia walked over to him with an authority not usual with her and put her arm across his shoulders without her old fear that he might throw it off. She stood protectively over him as if he were something she had created and had seen vandalized quite enough. Millie moved swiftly about the room collecting her belongings: 'Good, well I'll be off then and leave you to it.'

There was something in the way she said that, that made Ben leap up, almost pushing Lydia over in his eagerness to appear enthusiastic.

'O.K., Millie. Off you go then.' He handed her her scarf. 'You're a good old thing. Didn't I tell you she was a good old thing, Lydia?' Lydia nodded. 'Give us a kiss then.' Ben placed his hands on Millie's shoulders and she looked smaller still. They exchanged noisy, social kisses. Lydia stood in the doorway watching Millie getting into the car and arranging herself, while Ben fussed uselessly about her. The engine started, and already Ben was loosening himself, rearranging his shoulders and stretching his back when Millie put her head out of the car window.

'I shan't leave it like this. You know that, don't you, Ben? I can't, for your own sake.'

* * *

'... My patience brought her back to me, Lyd, can it do the same with you? Is there anything in your life that needs you as badly as I do? I would ask you for myself alone, but there's someone else in my life who needs you as much. Will you, Lyd, meet? At least please meet?'

'What was I telling you? Ah yes, how my mind does wander now. That's because these recollections hurt and if it weren't that you should know, then I would close down my mind for good and remember no more. By then you see, Lyd, I'd been hanging around Paris for nearly six weeks.

'The plan to get her alone: I had made an arrangement to go and see them yet again, but half an hour before I was due to arrive I telephoned and said I was ill, that the doctor had been to see me in my hotel and that I was not to leave my bed. I made it sound serious and that hospital could be necessary. Right away she said she wanted to come, but I told her that I wasn't strong enough to have visitors, so, of course, she said she would come alone. It was as if she had been waiting for me to do that very thing and I cursed myself for not thinking of it sooner.

'An hour later she came to my room, my bedside, my bed. As easy as that. And to this day I won't understand why she ever had to make a show of anyone else mattering to her. Unless she guessed then how it would end, for perhaps, like our effect on each other, our love for each other, our end, too, was inevitable.

'After that afternoon I never went back to her apartment, she always came to my suite at the hotel, almost every day. It would only be a matter of time before she capitulated and agreed to come away with me. I planned travel for us, seduced her with descriptions of the South of France, which she had always loved, the Italian Lakes, the hills of Tuscany and more. She was on the brink and the final push (odd I should put it like that, come to think of it) came with a car, but not just any car.

'Well, you know us, Lyd, we were luxury lovers (although we'd play at simplicity just for the pleasure of the contrast) and during the hours of my wandering around Paris, while waiting, longing to see her after a separation of sometimes as long as twelve hours, I found a gleaming white 1957 drophead Jaguar Continental. I bought some scarves for her and put them on the passenger seat. When she came to me that afternoon I took her down to the street where it was parked. When she saw it she was ecstatic, like a child again, and for a moment the fierceness that had settled in her eyes during the previous years left them. When she found the scarves she laughed more than ever and rubbed the glossy hair cropped against her head. I don't know what I can have been thinking of when I bought them except that I had a picture of her driving away in an open-top car and she needed a scarf, her long hair was flying all about her in my vision. It was a shock, really, to see her standing laughing and rubbing her little boy-cut head, as if after all I had been pursuing the wrong girl. She had changed in many ways.

'Have you changed? You were the gentlest woman I have ever known. Has anything happened to harden your eyes, to make them fierce like hers? Would I see a difference? Will you give me the chance? I have to see you, Lyd. Is that man I have seen your husband? Is it the man you lived with before? I went to your old address, that place off Baker Street. I remembered you had said you lived in the top flat and I walked all the way up. The people there did not know your name at all, but as I was leaving I passed a man on the stairs who looked at me curiously and asked if he could help me. I said I was looking for you and he asked me if my name was Ben, when I said 'yes' he smiled and gave me your address. When I asked how he knew he smiled again and said someone described me once. I didn't like him, he had red hair and beard. But he brought me back to you, Lyd, and I won't go now until at least you have met me. I believe I've spoken enough like this. Do you want to meet me? Please let me understand. Say once more that you want me to leave you alone forever and it'll be for the last time. I have pride left. I'll do as you ask.'

Lydia tried to speak, was shaking her head to free it from confusion, trepidation. Moments passed, she said nothing. 'I understand,' he said. The line disconnected.

8

With Millie's departure the intimate peace and happiness that had promised just before her arrival increased. It grew steady, real, and Lydia could see how before Ben had been ill at ease and surly, even his love-making had had a furtiveness about it that made it piquant but with short-lived satisfaction. His of touch needing constant reiteration, to feel again what was so nearly said, so secretly said, but after ... imagined?

Now he was changed, as if before he had doubted how he could face the world and how he could explain himself to it; but when it appeared to him in the guise of Millie he had decided that he did not care anyway, he had affection for the world but could do without its approval.

Ben spent the rest of "Millie's Day" (as they referred to it in the period of their happiness that followed) on the beach and when he returned he came alone: somewhere on that desolate shore he left the ghost that had lurked between him and Lydia. The image that clouded his eyes and her face; the voice he sometimes answered at night; the form he sometimes aproached and touched, to find Lydia, her hurt face trying to divine the reason for his bitter, betrayed expression: these were gone, he had come back free.

The door slammed behind him as usual when he entered the house again at the end of that afternoon.

'Lyd, Lyd,' he shouted up the stairs. She rose from a chair by the fire. 'Oh, sorry. I didn't see you there. Listen, Lyd' he went to her and took her hands in his, 'we're going back. We can't go on hiding ourselves down here. It's peaceful, it's perfect, but it's not real life. No, don't look like that.' He put his hands on her arms, on her shoulders and drew her into him. 'Stop trembling, my love. You misunderstand me. I'm not going to

leave you. I mean, we're going back together, we'll start life
again together, although sometimes I can't help thinking you
haven't ever really started it at all. And in some time, if it
works, and it must, Lydia,' he turned her head up to his, 'it
must because I can't stand any more breaks, pain; then we'll
marry, if that is what you want. I can't say I want it exactly,
because I don't have much respect for that cold little corner
that is English middle-class marriage but you might make me
change my mind and you probably will because I am fairly
conventional when it comes down to it, although people will
try to tell you that I'm not.'

He spoke fast, not allowing Lydia to interrupt and she was
amused that all he said seemed to be mildly off the point; but
she liked the proposal, which was no proposal at all, and she
liked the cockeyed confession when it came, although that, too,
was no confession at all. 'That's another thing,' Ben went on,
'people will try to tell you all sorts of things about me; you
must not necessarily believe them. They may say that ... well,
things that might seem that I like women too much, perhaps in
a wrong sort of way, from their view anyway. If I am different
from the majority of my contemporaries it is because I like the
society of women, their talk, the way their minds work, their
reactions. Oh, yes and more too, much more. And from what I
gather from my women friends I'm moderately unusual in that
respect; it would seem that when it comes to love-making in
general the Englishman would rather hold his nose and read
"The Sporting Life". But that's all off the point. What I want
to say is: we stay here a few more days, say a week, or rather:
please, Lyd, will you stay here with me? And then we return to
London and live together, or rather: please, Lyd, will you
return with me and live with me? Me and nobody else?'

So at last it was set. They were to be together and the nearest
Lydia came to remose was when the irony bred from her
actions struck her: the love she shared with Ben, that had
become so sensitive, was precisely the thing that enabled her to
bear the thought of Eric. Now he would be merely a man she
had once loved and would soon slip into painless past. Yet
there were times she would imagine she could see him,
standing just there, in the corner of the room, his arms spread

in a gesture of acceptance, looking directly at her, his eyes bewildered, hurt. She would want then to speak to that figment but could only stare until it faded, until the corner where he had seemed to be was again no more than the meeting of two whitewashed walls. Then Lydia would go to Ben, take his hands and search his face for some reassurance that it was all right, that their love did justify her and he would touch her hair, her features with his fingertips. 'There, there, don't think. It is all right. Everything is all right.' And they would draw too close for ghosts.

The intention had been to leave quite soon, but there was a burst of fine, mild weather which delayed them '... and anyway,' Ben had said, 'life is as real here as it is anywhere else.' And Lydia went along happily with his inconsistencies. But finally they did make the decision to leave after 'just one more week-end.'

It was the Sunday of that last week-end and dark outside, for the weather had closed cold and thunderous about them once more. Ben and Lydia had spent the day preparing the cottage for its desertion. This was not really a big task, but they did it reluctantly and therefore slowly. Odd pictures and little insignificant prints had to be removed from the walls to prevent the damp from foxing them; anything that might be spoilt by heatless weeks would be wrapped carefully in polythene and packed away. Ben was playing through the records and packing each one as it finished. He had started on the books, wrapping and placing them in a tea-chest, but paused to study again the "Gould's". 'I must see if that was an avocet we saw this morning or a ...' he rustled through the pages, 'or it could have been a stilt, but its bill was too short. It did have black markings, Lyd, didn't it? God, I wish my eyes were better. I'll have to think of glasses, you know. Anyway, it's far too early for either of them. You saw the markings better than I, Lyd, what do you think? Darling, you're not listening.'

In fact she had not heard him. The music from the record player was loud but what had distracted her, as she stood on a chair removing old packets of forgotten food from a top shelf, was a light she had seen. A sudden yellow-white beam had swept across the window and disappeared. Ben came across to her and with his large arm about her hips he followed the direction of her attention.

Still the music played loud, a sonorous cello. The light came again, it swung before them and was joined by another, parallel in the dark. The lights stopped still and steady. Headlights. No movement. Ben went uneasily to the door. They both heard, even through the music, a short unmistakable sound; the oily interlocking of metal parts when a car door is closed.

Lydia was remembering Millie's parting words: 'I shan't leave it like this. You know that, don't you Ben? I can't for your own sake.' Words she had not thought about until this moment.

Ben reached for the latch and looked back at Lydia. It was the last time they possessed each other; that look held every plan, every promise, every touch that had passed between them.

Ben opened the door and let his hand fall to his side, the door continued to swing open on its sloping hinges.

The room suddenly seemed warmer and more vivid than ever before. The colours were all just right, reflections of the world outside: grey, pale violet and deep misty blue, all there unintentionally in the flagstones, in a piece of driftwood (Ben and Lydia had retrieved it from the shore because it looked so much like a small horse struggling in sinking sands) and in the shadowy reaches of the room where light and heat hardly touched. The fire was given an extra pulse in pans hanging from the ceiling, in the shabby red cover of the sofa, in the rugs around it. Reminders of hours passing softly in pointless occupation littered the room: a collection of oyster shells baring iridescent bellies, a fishing net they had tried to mend and failed because the instructions in a seafarers' manual had confused them. Everything begun, nothing finished.

These things Lydia saw, felt, absorbed in a fraction of a second, but the impact was so strong that if she had been asked to recall that evening, all that happened and was said, she could only have been clear about the room and above all the warmth. And what disturbed her was that the warmth was going. The atmosphere was changing. Someone was entering. It was Millie. She came forward, cheek proffered, and positioned herself close to Ben so that her cheek-bone touched his chin awaiting his kiss.

'Ben, dear, I would have called but, I don't know, everything was such a rush.' She was excited.

Ben placed his hands on her shoulders, an automatic gesture, for he was not looking at her and hardly seemed to know she was there; he was looking past her through the open door into the darkness outside. Ben pushed Millie gently, decisively away and took a step to the door. She did not appear to mind being rejected in this way, for she stood with hands clasped low in front of her smiling proudly at Lydia. Her eyes said, 'My scene, little girl, you watch.'

There was someone else outside the door and Ben's demeanour had changed. The moment he had looked over Millie's shoulder he had softened, his body became somehow humbled, but his expression was ecstatic. First two hands appeared, held wide in greeting; beautiful, unfriendly hands with long fingers and almond-shaped nails. Ben started to reach out slowly, too slowly for the hands, because they closed fingers onto palms once or twice in impatient invitation.

A thin, young woman stepped into the room and Ben's arms, still holding her own aloft. She was nearly as tall as him and, but for a certain throb, a radiance, a tremor that was unquestionably female, she could have been mistaken for a young man. She wore tight jeans, tucked at the knees into flat beige leather boots, and a bomber jacket of the same stuff, jingling with buckles. Her little skull (that Ben now encompassed in his hands) was close-cropped and dark.

Ben wrapped one arm around her and placed her head in the hollow of his shoulder, locking it there with his own head as if returning some lost part of himself to its place; still holding her body close he drew her head back and kissed her face. Her arms hung limp now, but there was a yielding in her posture more eloquent than gesture. She moved her head from side to side slowly, letting it fall forward to his shoulder again, on the way brushing her lips past his.

'I didn't think I would ever see you again. My darling, I've missed you. I've been so lonely.' Ben spoke indistinctly into her shoulder.

'Poor Daddy. Poor Daddy,' Nathalie said into his.

Ben began to ask questions but they were audible notes to be
answered by himself as he observed; Nathalie understood and
did not attempt to speak.

'But how are you, how are you really? Does Paris like you as
I love you? It's been so long, Natta. Are you happy? Do you
know how to be again? You were so bitter, I didn't think you
would ever return.'

He stopped to pull her to him again to confirm her
presence: not another illusive image this time, and withdrew
her to ask some more. 'Are you really here? I can't believe it;
I've pretended so often. There, there, let's see you. Let's see.'
He gripped her at two arms' length and she stood casual,
amused, affectionate. 'Natta. At last.' Overcome he gathered
her again.

Millie's smile had faded as she watched them. This scene, the
one she had manoeuvred and had expected to control, had
taken off on a life of its own. She had wanted to cope with
embarrassment and hasty, unrehearsed explanations, steer
them round to show Ben in front of his daughter what a fool
he was making of himself with that girl, that 'what's-her-
name'; but as she watched something began to dawn on her
and she was disturbed although she did not quite know why.

Nathalie withdrew from Ben's grasp quickly, deftly but to
sustain his trance she touched him; for the first time she let her
hand touch his. Her body still facing Ben she suddenly turned
her face upon Lydia and Millie with the challenging, defiant
look of an actress to an exacting director when she had
achieved what they both sought.

'And Lydia,' Nathalie said, 'more than anything I want to
see you.' Her voice was a collection of accents from her
international schooling since the age of twelve; even her
appearance had an un-English impeccability about it. Nathalie
went over to Lydia and started to arrange her hair in the same
absent-minded way that Ben sometimes had; talking to her
while never actually looking at her.

Lydia swept Nathalie's interfering hand away, resenting the
supposition that things would return to what they always had
been between them: Lydia the Side-Kick, the Fall-Guy, Lydia
the Admiring, who would fall in with whatever would happen.
But Nathalie smiled disarmingly, knowingly, at Lydia's

impatience, reducing it to petulance. 'Millie said you were here,' Nathalie said, nodding, with her head on one side, an eyebrow raised, the tail end of a bow; concession: "This battle I give you; the war's not won," and still she smiled, the corners of her wide, witty mouth turned down.

'Yes, I suppose it must be nearly two months,' Lydia said. 'Have you been here before? I mean, I do know it's a long time since you have seen your father.' Suddenly "Ben" was hard, after all, last time Nathalie saw her she was still stammering "Mr Wavell", "Sir", and once more she felt reduced, or perhaps just reminded of that status.

'Has a lot happened in your life, Lydia?' Nathalie said, ignoring Lydia's question. 'I long to hear about you. Do you work? Are you married? How are those parents?'

Lydia flinched at the questions and gave herself time to see Nathalie's face before she answered: long, hazel eyes, sincere now; face relaxed, she really wanted to know the answers to her questions, there was no trick; they were, after all, friends.

'No. No. No. And dead,' Lydia said.

Nathalie took a deep breath and held it while her face gathered delightfully, deliciously for laughter; those fine brows, fine features, that mouth with the sensitivity of an electric wire, all dissolved asymmetrically and simultaneously with the release of that laughter. 'Oh, Lydia, Lydia, I'm so glad to see you;' and Nathalie threw herself into Lydia's arms, 'and if I'd only thought of you I'd have missed you ... desperately.'

While Nathalie focused her attention on Lydia, Ben and Millie came together and started a quiet conversation under the strains of the music still playing.

'Were you packing to leave, Ben?'

'Yes. I was planning to be off tomorrow or the next day.'

'Does that mean it is all over with her, or does it mean something else?'

He ignored her question. 'This is very unexpected, Millie ... I find it hard to understand how you managed ...'

'Oh, that was quite easy really. I just told her how lonely you were and that perhaps you were about to do something very silly that you might regret later.'

Ben's attention had wandered back to Nathalie and only having half-heard he answered, 'Suicide is not my kind of thing, Millie, you should know that.'

'Ben, really! I didn't mean that.' She regarded him carefully for a moment as he watched Nathalie, then leant forward and patted his arm. 'So, you're not cross with me?'

'Cross? *Cross?* Why? Because you brought my child to me? Don't be silly, it was very kind of you to give her a lift. I'm sure she would have come anyway this time, but you know how lazy she can be.'

'I don't think that is quite fair, Ben.' Millie tried to regain his full attention in undertones. 'It took a lot of persuasion. If someone like me had not tried to make her see you again it might never have happened. I'm sure she would never have done it on her own.'

'She does exactly what she wants, nobody makes her do anything. But, Millie, you mustn't think I don't appreciate your helping, you're very thoughtful.'

Millie was annoyed. He was so confident so quickly, when she had expected him to be confused and overcome.

The record finished, a silence fell. Nathalie looked around the room with her fingers hitched in her back pockets.

'It's nice here, Dad.' She spotted a bottle of red wine and in two graceful strides reached it. She poured herself a glass unperturbed by the eyes that now watched her every move. No one could think of anything to say and her effect was magnetic. She took a sip, then wiped her nose with the back of her hand making the vulgar gesture entirely acceptable and even seductive by the relaxed and amused manner in which she did it.

'There's a funny smell in here. Hair oil, Dad?'

'Yes. I mean, no, it's creosote. This was used as a boat-house before and the smell won't leave.'

'Do you know what I really want?' She put the glass down and banged her fists emphatically on her knees.

'No, no, what? Tell me.' Ben sprang to life. 'Are you cold? Would you like …?'

'I want,' she interrupted, 'to go to the beach. I want to see the sea at night. There's a bright, bright moon, it's like day out there. Will you take me? Please, please, take me, Dad.'

'Of course, fool, of course I'll take you.'

'O.K. idiot, take me and I don't want that thing.' She threw down a coat he had just handed her. 'I never feel the cold. Not any more.'

Ben and Millie glanced at her and at each other quickly and began to speak at once.

'I will cook a little …'

'Millie, would you …' They laughed nervously.

'Yes, well, same thought anyway,' Millie continued. 'I will prepare something to eat while you two go out, and I do think you are a silly girl not to wrap up, Nathalie, you don't look well as it is. Does she, Ben?'

'She's perfect, she looks fine. Let her do as she likes. Come on, Natta.'

Ben held the door wide and let the cold gush in again. Nathalie winked at Lydia as she passed to go under his arm but Ben did not look back at all.

'You're fatter, Dad.' She ran her fingertips inside his waistband.

'Oh, yes, Skinny? And what happened to your hair? It's cut to show your scrawny little neck.' He grabbed the scrawny neck and kissed below the ear.

'Oh, Lord,' she said with mock tedium, 'here we go: nag, nag, nag.'

The door closed behind them. First their laughter could be heard then just the wind. Lydia suddenly felt very sick. She leant against the beam set into the wall above the fire and stared at the flames. Millie was moving about the room behind her, tidying no doubt; touching things.

Although Millie remained silent as she prepared the food and the table, Lydia knew very well her eyes were upon her, assessing her defeat, wondering if it was indeed a sob that shook her back.

Was it possible she could be done for so quickly? In the face of Nathalie, so strong, such fun, so much her father's daughter, Lydia felt invisible. From the instant Ben saw Nathalie he had not looked at or spoken to Lydia. She had ceased to exist.

Millie made small warning noises, coughs and clearings to show she was about to speak and give Lydia time to control herself.

'Well, what a pair they are, eh?'

Lydia turned slowly. Their eyes met. Lydia's face was without colour in spite of the fire.

Millie had intended a little conversation, light and insignificant but when she saw Lydia's face she was disconcerted, for although bewildered and pathetic, it had a serenity unexpected. She sank onto a chair beside the table (prepared and cosied to a degree Lydia had never managed; check cloth, candlesticks, napkins in rings, place mats, things from cupboards Lydia had never opened, it had not seemed important) and laid her hands slowly, emphatically upon it smoothing the cloth. She was like Ben when, having tried to avoid an issue, he would look at Lydia and realise he had failed, rendering himself to the inevitable, he would settle and take a prop to ease his explanation. Lydia wondered if everyone who had spent any time with Ben became infected with his likeness; perhaps she now was a mime of his gestures, like Millie.

'Lydia, you don't understand why I have returned, do you? Did you really think I would leave you alone with him, allow him to commit himself to you irrevocably?' Millie stopped her smoothing for a moment and studied Lydia. 'You are not as young as I first thought.' She paused, then added quickly, 'But still too young for him; the age gap is not the point exactly. There is nothing so odd in old man-young girl, it's happened for centuries. But it's not right for him. There are reasons.' Millie rose and folded her arms, her hands nervously massaging where they touched. Head down she started to pace the floor. 'I've been loved by him too, you know.' She glanced quickly at Lydia to see if she did, then down again. 'I know what it's like. It's like a beam of light suddenly cast upon you. Most people have a capacity for love but I have never known a man able to give it so completely. There ceases to be a part of your being that is private. He invades it all with the music he likes, his silly jokes, his reason, his body; and when he withdraws that love life is bleached, like the forsaken shores around here.' She waved her hand impatiently towards the window. 'Even to see something new is deadly without his eyes to share and introduce it his way.' She looked at Lydia briefly again but her eyes were now vague with remembering. Staring into the fire she continued; 'I'd known him years before when we were both very young and I thought him faintly ridiculous then. I only met again when he married Viola who was a great friend of mine at that time. When Viola left him to marry Erik, we came together as friends but it turned into more ... much more. No one knew. We were very discreet. I didn't tell my husband because it never really got to that, but he guessed. It lasted until Nathalie came back to live with him. He just switched off then and was totally taken up with her, almost as though he had never loved me, but I was able to stay near him by being a good friend and goodness knows he needed one. She was a handful.' Snapping back to the present she said, 'I wonder if he told you about all that?' She turned upon Lydia. 'Did he tell you how Viola took her away for four years? How he was stopped from seeing her and how, finally, Viola having started another family, two more children, at her age too, packed Nathalie off back to her father, spoilt, neurotic and promiscuous.' She was watching Lydia carefully now. 'They say there's no bond stronger than that of father and daughter. I wouldn't know. Charlie and I only have sons. What about you, Lydia? Are you very close to your father ...? Mmm, Lydia? ... Close?'

Lydia descended upon the present. She had been remembering all her hours with Ben, trying to disentangle fragments of memory from the future they had planned. And what was Millie saying? 'Mmm, Ben ... seventeen?' 'Mmm, Lydia ... close?' Still she talked. 'Really, the answer was that poor Ben had no time for himself. It was quite impossible for him to have a private life with Nathalie about. But years are a strong bond too, and since Viola had given up on Nathalie, I stood in for her as best I could.' Millie was proud of her efforts. She reflected for a moment. 'But that wasn't until later. At first he saw no one. He and Nathalie stayed cloistered in that London house of his and only after a long time did they begin to appear in public; restaurants, clubs and things, the odd dinner party; sophisticated stuff for a young girl, all very wrong. He was very jealous of her; well, fathers are, aren't they? And I think also it was his way of trying to keep her under control. They had a lot of 'in' jokes which no one else understood. Very rude and most annoying.' She shuddered as she remembered her embarrassment, resentment. She had always hated not being in on jokes. 'They would go off into gales of laughter at some word. One of their silly jokes was to pretend that she was not his daughter but that she was his … well, … lover. Really, a stupid, tasteless thing to do. A mistake. Most people knew who she was because a lot of them were friends with Viola too, and indeed had known Nathalie since she was a child, but some didn't know and fell for it.

'Needless to say Nathalie started to break free when she became bored with those games. He dealt with her very badly. If you try to curtail a young person's freedom too much … well …' She shrugged her shoulders and raised her eyebrows to show the result must be obvious. 'He tried to keep her in or with him all the time and had terrible furies when she escaped him and went out alone. Not surprisingly, with no mother to advise her, she became pregnant and that was when she turned on him: she said the baby was his. She said it to everybody. Poor Ben was devastated but he never spoke of it to anyone, not even me. He didn't even try to deny it, not that that was necessary, but, you see, some people took their vicious pleasure in believing it.

'After that his character totally altered and he became quite withdrawn, almost reclusive. I took Nathalie to my house and looked after her throughout the pregnancy. She altered a little too and became quite sweet, very vulnerable, except if anyone mentioned her father, and if it was suggested that they should meet, she became almost hysterical. All acting, of course. She always was very dramatic, even as a child. I tried to talk her into getting rid of the baby, but she would not hear of that, not until it was too late to be without great risk. She then became very bitter and harder to handle. The baby was taken away for adoption as soon as it was born, little mite. I rang Viola, of course, several times but she was not interested. I think she was afraid the situation could spoil her happiness. Ben asked about Nathalie often, but stopped trying to see her, accepting the situation.

'When it was all over the only request she made of her father was to have enough money to go and live in Paris, where it seems she had friends. Even that she asked through me. He was so anxious to do anything for her that he set up accounts and made far too much money available. Men can be so naive when dealing with children. He even bought an apartment for her, which she refused to live in. So at seventeen she was rich and alone in Paris, quite relinquished by her parents. Ben's behaviour was extraordinary; he treated her just as one would a grown woman. He seemed to have forgotten that she was his daughter. Of course, she had been so difficult, and the vile slander she started ... he never stopped loving her, naturally, but he did not seem to think she needed him, even as a distant protector. I, of course, sustained a relationship with her, which was not easy but we had grown close in an odd way and I persisted. Someone had to.'

Millie rounded on Lydia again, hands clasped, and a tight, self-satisfied smile. 'And now I have the fruits of my labours; I have brought father and daughter together once more, and there is no doubt that they are happier with each other than with anyone else. I'm sure I could have brought this about at any time, but it never seemed necessary before. I shall always be about to be of assistance. They are like a couple of children together.

'But you see, my dear, what I am trying to tell you is that he obviously saw his daughter in you, though goodness knows the likeness escapes me, but she is back now and, I am sure, much wiser and regrets deeply her silly lies. So you are not needed here any more. Do you take my point, Lydia?'

Neither of them spoke for some time. Lydia stood with head bowed, glad she was unable to examine her feelings because of Millie still standing in front of her watching for a reaction. They looked towards the window. With the groaning of the wind was the sound of two voices in unharmonious unison:

'... a-roving, a-roving,
I'll go no more a ro-ow-ving,
For roving's been my roo-i-ane,
La la la laaaaa ...'

'They're back, they're back.' Millie's face softened and she went quickly to the door, straightening cushions and chairs on her way. She opened it just as they arrived on the step.

'Great timing, Millie,' Ben said loudly. He advanced into the room, an arm slung around Nathalie's shoulders swinging his pullover from one finger, his shirt open to the waist.

'What the devil happened, Ben, you're soaked through?' Millie said.

'That girl,' he said beaming and pointing at Nathalie's stomach, 'pushed me into the sea.'

'Well, if you will dance about in front of the waves like some faggot, what do you expect, Dad?'

'We don't have faggots in England, Natta, we have queers.'

'You should know. Go on, Zorba, get some dry clothes on,' Nathalie said.

'Bring them, Slave, I'll change in front of the fire.' He pulled off his shirt and dropped it to the floor starting to undo his trousers.

'Oh, no you won't,' Millie said, laughing. 'Go on upstairs.' She picked up the shirt and handed it to him. Only then did Ben look at Lydia, a little surprised as if she was an unexpected, but not totally unwelcome guest. 'Oh, hello.' He hesitated. 'Well, maybe I had better change upstairs.'

When the door slammed behind him Nathalie stood and stretched before the stove, fingers touching the ceiling, her long neck and limbs taut and boyish. She relaxed, pushed both hands through her hair and started to slide her bottom over the warm stove.

'You are unruly, Nathalie. Imagine doing such a thing to your father. He's not a young man, you know, and he could catch a terrible chill.'

Nathalie put her arms around Millie's neck from behind and laughed.

'Oh, unruly me, Millie. Smack me, go on, smack me.' She pointed her bottom at Millie who was taking plates from the oven. 'But, anyway, chills don't come from the elements, they come from the heart.'

'Don't philosophize with me, young lady, and move out of the way, will you. I hope you're hungry.'

'No, I am not hungry, but I'll sit with you while you all eat. I'm hungry for talk. Lydia, have you ever been to Paris?'

Nathalie pulled Lydia onto the sofa, her long eyes flicking over Lydia's features like one who has taken a fast reading course; from temple to chin, hairline to corner of mouth; take in the pallor, the shadows, the twitches, they will tell the story. Never mind the words. '... and the area is called Montparnasse. I live there with ...' she stopped to decide on her words and chose "friends". 'You'd love it there, Lydia, and they'd like you. Why don't you come?'

'I haven't got any money ... and ... and I can't speak French.' Lydia was quite aware of the banality of her remarks, but it was Nathalie's own fault. There was something so absorbing about Nathalie, there were so many dimensions, that when asked to participate instead of observe, Lydia blanched, forgot who she was, what she had to say.

'But none of that matters. We all speak English and all sorts of other languages. Once you're there you don't need money and I'll pay your fare.'

'This is silly talk, Nathalie,' Millie interrupted. 'Lydia can't possibly go to Paris with you, I'm sure she has someone of her own and I'm sure that poor little man must be sitting at home now wondering about his dinner.'

'Well then, that poof has been sitting there for two months wondering about his dinner so by now he'll be dead and Lydia can do as she likes. And anyway, Millie, is it possible for you to approach a relationship on any other level than a gastronomic one?'

Millie was impervious to this kind of onslaught, the words sailed like so much flak about her, and she continued, 'Nathalie, are you really happy there? Would you not consider coming back to England to live?'

Nathalie smiled slowly and said, 'I don't know yet. It depends on what I find here. Would you like me to, Millie?' As she asked the question she looked at Lydia.

'My dear child, of course I would.' Millie came over, squeezed in between them on the sofa and took Nathalie's hand. 'Why don't you consider it? Good lord, I could arrange everything for you. You wouldn't even have to go back there.'

'How kind you are to me,' Nathalie said coldly. 'Is there any more wine?'

Ben burst into the room looking unusually tidy and smelling shop-bought. Now the clean shirt was unbuttoned to his waist.

'Fixed your toupee, Dad? Millie says you are too old to push into the sea. Might kill you off.'

'I'm not bloody well old.'

'Bloody well are.'

'I say, look at the table,' he changed the subject. 'It's like a restaurant. No, Millie, it's nice really. Reminds me of that week-end in the S. of F. If you hang on I'll get the wine.'

'Where do you keep it, Dad?'

'In the lav. outside.'

'Since when did boat-houses have outside loos, or loos at all?'

'Since I came here, Natta. In a small house like this it is essential to evacuate to evacuate. Get me?'

'Gotcha.'

Ben, who had been putting on his gumboots, stopped and smiled at Nathalie. She did not smile, but looked at him, also remembering. Millie had noticed the little re-play of the past and completed the scene.

'Not that awful slang again, please.'

Their heads turned towards Millie, mildly shocked at having their rosary completed by an outsider. She did not notice.

When Ben returned, cradling bottles, Millie said, 'Now then, Nathalie, why don't you sit there next to your father and I'll go here next to you.'

'No, I want Lydia next to me,' Nathalie said.

'Oh, very well, if you insist. Lydia, go over there then.'

But Ben became impatient. 'Silly woman, you'd think we were at the Lord Mayor's banquet the way you're carrying on.'

Nathalie sat down and began tilting back her chair. 'No thanks, not for me.' She waved away the steaks and salad. 'I'm not hungry, and I don't eat meat.'

'That's your friends, Nathalie,' Millie said impatiently. 'I know that sort. All prunes and wholemeal minds.'

'Leave it alone, Millie,' Ben said.

Millie changed tack. 'Ben, you'll never guess. Nathalie says she is going to come back and live here.'

Ben dropped his fork and pushed his chair back. 'Is it true, Natta, really?'

'I didn't say that. But I might.'

Ben turned in his chair and reached towards her neck, thin and very white in the candlelight. He touched lightly where the tendons stood out, but she was looking away from him, at Lydia.

'Darling, it would be all right if you did,' he spoke as if he was alone with Nathalie. 'It would be wonderful … again. Do you remember?'

Nathalie put her hand on the back of Lydia's chair, let it rest, then placed it on her shoulder, on the dark side of Lydia's head beyond the candlelight. Nathalie caressed her hair.

'Lydia looks very sad, I think. Does anyone know why Lydia looks sad?' Nathalie asked quietly.

'I don't know, I'm sure, but listen to what your father is saying. Come home, Nathalie.'

'Lydia would like it, wouldn't you, Lydia?' It was Ben. He had spoken to her at last. Maybe nothing had changed after all, but if she said "yes", would he think she had relinquished the plans for their life together? How could she say "no", and anyway Nathalie was her friend. Above all, that seemed, still, to be true.

'Well, Lydia, would you?' Nathalie said.

'Of course … well of course, but, but …' there was no need to pretend, after all, they knew why she was there. If only she could talk alone with Ben, why hadn't he helped her to do that? 'What about …' She tried to continue.

'There. There, you see. Lyd wants you to stay too.'

'Oh, Dad, you're impossible,' Nathalie said in affectionate exasperation, 'you didn't give her a chance to speak.' She brought her hand back from the darkness to her wine glass, tipped it, drained it and brought one long leg close up to her body. 'You are a horrid old man. Loathsome really.'

'I wasn't before you were born.'

'Probably not, Dad, probably not.' She turned her head sharply towards him, the nature of her smile masked in the half-light.

'Now, come on you two, that's enough. Tell us about your life in Paris, Nathalie,' Millie said.

'I will, but I must have a cigarette.'

Nathalie stood up to release a crushed pack of cigarettes from her back pocket. Still standing, she lit one, cupping her hands and jutting her jaw. Millie was eating, but Ben watched minutely. She settled again and rolled her shirt-sleeves prior to explanation: 'You see, I live among a fraternité. We are taught by the Maitre, who lives part of the time with us and the rest in seclusion.'

'My dear,' Millie said, 'how "libre". Is he something like a male mistress, not the head kind but the heart kind?'

Nathalie tapped her cigarette impatiently. 'I don't think I can discuss it.'

'Natta,' Ben tried to draw her attention away from Millie's shallow talk, 'what exactly is this man teaching you, the Maitre?'

'To put it simply: how to exist on planes other than the physical, the emotional. Few of us venture further than that but we are taught that we have the astral, mental, causal and buddhic bodies. The personality we all have prevents the individuality from manifesting itself completely and these bodies I mentioned require centuries to develop; but the day they do, our mental body will become so fine, so sharp, intense, that it will understand and know all; our astral body at that same time will reflect only noble feeling and our physical body will be free, strong and always healthy.'

'You seem to have it all very pat, Nathalie. Are you sure you haven't been brainwashed? Next they will want all your money. Oh my God, they haven't got it already, have they?'

'Oh, Millie.' Nathalie sunk her head into her hands. 'You make me feel sick.'

'Come on, Natta.' Ben ran his hand over the contours of her defiant little head; (how fortunate that Millie should offend Nathalie and give him another excuse to touch her.) 'But hey? How does smoking fit in with all that?'

Lydia saw his smile upon Nathalie. Dear face; strong face; windburnt; used. He knew Nathalie would latch on to conciliation. Nathalie smiled back.

'You're right, Dad. It doesn't, but I can't not. Get me?'

'Gotcha.'

Ben pushed aside his plate and took a cigarette from Nathalie's pack drawing her hand towards him to light from hers. He examined the hand and put it to his cheek. She withdrew it. He poured more wine all round and settled with his forearms on the table.

'Would I gain from this "fraternité"?'

'Well, you should try to open your mind to it. If by the time you are ready to pass out of this life you have no understanding it doesn't matter, it won't change anything, any truth about eternity, but it will take you longer to become complete and until you do, you will keep coming back.'

'But I like it here. I don't mind coming back.'

'You have a lot to learn. You have a very young spirit … in a very old body.' She bit her lip and grinned.

'Thanks. That had to come, didn't it? So I'd have to sit around having a whole bunch of puppies telling me how old I am?'

When it came to his age his sense of humour was fragile – subject to failure.

'Of course not. I'll take you though, Dad, because I know you're lost.'

'It's true, Natta, I am.' Quietly he said it, and the three women watched him.

Smoke idled above the table as they sat for a while locked apart by silence; each one pursuing a separate path of recollection and meeting again at Eden in a summer, summers before.

Millie was the first to speak, but her voice was no intrusion.

'Do you remember the waltzing, Ben?'

'Yes, the Viennese waltzing. That silly evening, no one could do it, well only a few. Most of the people crashed into each other and fell flat. I had never laughed so much, none of us had. I don't think it was quite what Viola had had in mind but it was a success. Blasted dance. I couldn't do it then and I can't do it now. Are you any better, Millie, or were you good then? I don't remember. Why don't we try now? I've got Strauss.' He sprang up, rocking the table.

'Brilliant idea, Dad. Do you remember, Lydia? They wouldn't let us go and you wanted to so much. You even cried at lunch.'

It was not worth contesting. The current of the inevitable was now far too strong.

They moved the table and chairs to one side and Ben put on a record.

'Mademoiselle, may I have the honour of this dance?' He bowed low before Nathalie.

'Why, Sir, if you think your poor old legs can stand it.'

'Brat.'

They positioned themselves, Nathalie's back a fluent arch under his hand.

'Nothing's happened, Dad, the record's stuck.'

'Shhh. It's the quiet bit before.'

The music filtered in.

'Louder, Millie. Turn it louder,' Ben shouted, and Millie rushed to turn the volume right up, then stood at the side of the space fluttering a little, girlish and expectant. How ready she was to be transported; for her it was Paris 1900s, a ballroom lit with a thousand candles instead of a smelly, converted coalbarn, boat-house.

'Our turns are good, aren't they, Natta? But don't do that. You keep leading me, I'm leading you.'

'Astray. Astray.'

'No, come on. The man leads.'

'Yes, but you're not. You're flabby, fishlike.'

'Right, my girl, I'll show you.'

He held her tighter and she flinched. The wallflowers watched. Millie smiled and said something to Lydia who did not hear.

'No, Dad, don't. Stop. You're hurting.' She pushed him away and he almost fell, but at that moment he was so pleased with himself and the music that he turned to Millie, who slid into his arms, all grace.

Nathalie came over to where Lydia stood and dug into her back pocket again. She lit a cigarette and leant against the wall, her profile suffused in smoke, then turned her head sharply towards Lydia. Her face was pale and her eyes darkly shadowed.

'Why are you here, Lydia? Can't you see you're not strong enough for him, in any way? He'll hurt you, Lydia. I swear to God he will hurt you.'

'No, Nathalie, you're wrong. I love him. We love each other and we're going to live together, then get married. It's very simple and it will happen …' Lydia reeled from her own candour. Nathalie did not speak and Lydia thought "Battle to me".

The music stopped.

'Lovely, Ben, quite wonderful,' Millie said. 'I haven't danced like that for years. Why, I was …' Ben did not wait for her to finish but went straight to Nathalie.

'Darling, I'm sorry I hurt you. I didn't mean to. You're angry, I can tell.'

'S'all right, Dad.' Quite removed from the place, the time, saying anything to keep them all quiet, 'but I'm terribly tired. I want to rest.' She leant on Ben heavily as he guided her to the sofa. It looked strange: someone so young, vivacious, suddenly needing physical support.

'Nathalie, dear, you look very pale.' Millie bent over her. 'It's the excitement, I feel just the same. We'll go back to the pub and sleep there tonight, then pop back here before we drive on home in the morning.'

'What's this, Millie? Pub? Home? Natta's not leaving. Do you understand? You're not taking her.' Ben's voice gathered intensity.

'Calmly, Ben, calmly. What about …?' She nodded towards Lydia. 'And we have to look for a flat in London, don't we, Nathalie?'

'Say you're staying, Natta. Say it to her. *Say it*,' Ben shouted.

Nathalie closed her eyes, sighed and nodded, 'I'm staying, Millie, I'm staying.'

*   *   *

Lydia remained, receiver in hand, from time to time murmuring, 'Ben … Ben?' knowing full well he was not there. At last, with reluctance, she replaced it and rose, smoothing her hair, her dress, sloughing-off those recollections. No more of this, she thought, no more of them. What was it she had been going to do? Ah yes, the adoption people. But not now; another day. She went listless towards the kitchen, she would cook, that was a pleasure and solace to her, but before she let the door close behind her she turned to the telephone, alert. She had felt it was going to ring, but it did not.

Shut in the kitchen all morning she emerged composed and went to the front garden to gather lilies and roses to arrange throughout her house.

Outside the heat was exasperating. No need to even see the road, she thought, as she bent low, cutting. Finally she gave in to herself and went to the gate to look, just once. He was there.

She withdrew behind the hedge, breathless, head back, eyes screwed shut. Placing her flowers on the path, she walked to the gate, into the street, began to approach that corner. Her tiger-striped cat accompanied her for a house or two, insinuating itself in and out of the wooden palings. Unaccustomed to such weather the residents had withdrawn to the cool of the deep-walled Victorian houses. There was barely a movement anywhere; the cat had settled to wash. No sound at all but the flap-flap of Lydia's sandals on the pavement which altered to a duller note as she stepped onto the melting tarmac.

She halted halfway across, between her house and the tree. Her slight body in the cotton shift made ethereal by vaporous heat rising from the road.

'Go; please do.' Her words echoed blunt in the stillness. Curtains twitched at the windows about.

Ben Wavell leaned his head away and down as if he had been struck. Lydia turned while his head was thus averted, started to walk away.

'Lyd? Please? Listen to me.'

She stopped, closed her eyes, then wheeled round. It seemed as first she would shout, but as he stepped towards her she hesitated.

'All right. I'll listen.'

He walked away, glancing back to see that she followed and she did. As the two figures, drawing closer with each step, disappeared round the corner, the curtains were parted with frank curiosity.

Lydia came to Ben's side as they walked towards his car, low, crouching, almost predatory, parked out of sight of her street.

'Why did you come back?' she asked.

'Because you said nothing. Is there a child in your life, Lyd?'

'No.'

'Would you like there to be?'

'Finish. Tell me what happened. I can't stay.'

'They weren't a family and I didn't take Natta away from her child, because I offered to take him with us; but she didn't want that, nor did she want to leave him at her apartment. Through some friends of mine in Paris we found a nanny and installed her in a suite in the hotel where I was. We took the child, Christian, there a week before we left so that the nanny and he could become accustomed to each other. It all went so smoothly and if Natta seemed a little solemn I knew that when we were alone, I mean really alone, away from Paris and anyone we knew, I could dispel that solemnity. It's true that our relationship always depended on our isolation and she said that was because the relationship was wrong, but I wouldn't agree and said if she thought it was wrong she should go. And then she would give me that look, the one she threw at me in her apartment; a look that combined loving and loathing, a look which seemed to suggest that whatever happened between us was up to me. But that wasn't true, it was all up to her; I was her slave and always had been, and she knew it. I wonder now if she felt a slave to me.

'The morning we were leaving the hotel Laurent came. It wasn't a surprise; we had been expecting him. She never told me what she'd said to him about her departure, but I suspect it was very little, if anything. Her relationship with Laurent did not have much to do with words and her relationship with me didn't either. Oh yes, we teased each other and joked when we were happy, but we rarely talked. She is still a stranger to me.

'Laurent simply stood in the middle of the large sitting-room of my suite, his hands in the pockets of his long, black coat, his dignity making the fake Louis furniture look more vulgar still. None of us spoke; we must have looked ridiculous standing there watching one another. Finally he said to her in French, "Are you coming, or not?" And she didn't answer. She turned away from him and shrugged, as though the matter was between him and me. Laurent and I watched each other, and since I was the victor I could afford to realise that I liked him. When he turned to go the red scarf, the one he was wearing when I first saw him, bothered me. It was not wound about his neck this time but trailing at eccentric length behind him; it was made of a silk jersey material, like men's evening scarves in the days of Jack Buchanan and Fred Astaire; but the length, colour and fabric made it look like a stream of blood pouring from him as he left the room. I watched him go quite slowly down the wide passage and when he came to the door of Christian and his nanny's suite he stopped. The door must have been open, although I couldn't see that from where I stood. If I had known I would have gone ahead to close it; I had no wish to cause him more pain, for I already knew what it was like to lose Natta. But the next moment he had entered the room and when I went to look he was kneeling with Christian held tightly against him and the nanny protesting at his side. When Laurent rose to go the child merely studied the three of us with just Natta's expression, as if to say, "this is to do with you and not me."

'But Lyd: when we drove away through Paris with the sun, the air, our freedom and each other, we were so happy and I was utterly sure I had done the right thing. Within an hour we were shouting, singing and speeding through the country; she threw her arms around my neck many times, ridiculously dangerous and wonderful. At last, at last, she was my own child again. I would swerve just to frighten her and she would curse me, loving being frightened.

'You remember how we were together? She always used to tease me, didn't she? I think you loved her as much as I did. How could anyone not have loved her? Lyd, you were part of Natta and me as well.'

Ben flung wide the passenger door of a dark blue Aston Martin Lagonda. Lydia held back.

'I don't want to go anywhere. You understand that, don't you?' He nodded, closing the door after her. Lydia leant forward, forehead on knees. 'Please God, please God' she whispered, unpractised in prayer.

9

Lydia went upstairs. For once she did not bother to press every light switch her fingers reached in the darkness. She groped behind the bedroom door for her dressing-gown but could not find it; she took off her jeans and reached under the pillows for the long woollen socks she wore in bed and could not find them either. She turned on the light. There was the room: same as ever; the wind blowing through the open window swinging the unshaded ceiling bulb letting its light reveal first one corner then another, searching with Lydia for what it was about the sameness that was different. The room was unusually neat, Ben must have tidied; but something had gone; little things had gone: her dressing-gown, her socks, her clothes that were always strewn over the only chair, her sketch-pad and the silver pencil Ben had bought her on a visit to a nearby town. To pass the time while the shop engraved it (MY DARLING LYD. ALWAYS. BEN) they went to the museum, where, in the Egyptology section, they were fascinated by a fervent and inaudible conversation between a sallow-skinned man with sweat in the dark rings under his eyes (the humourless light of the museum made him look as if he was crying) who twisted the fingertips of one hand into the palm of the other as he talked to a young man, very blond, not English, who made petulant shows of departing, but stayed.

Lydia went into the other room where Ben did his exercises. One bed was made up freshly with the sheets turned down. The other one, the little one in the corner, was made up too but the fresh sheets had been disturbed and the blankets cast back to look as though someone had slept there; her socks lay among the sheets and her dressing-gown at its foot. On the chair beside it were her clothes and her sketch-pad. The pencil was not there. His capacity for deceit was extraordinary and it hurt. It hurt.

Lydia pulled on her socks and lay face down in the pillow, breathing the scent of damp feathers. Soon she heard Millie's voice outside.

'Don't come out, Nathalie, it's terribly cold. I'll collect you first thing. Will you see me to the car, Ben?'

Footsteps and Millie's voice again. 'I think it's all gone very well, don't you? But she does look tired so don't keep her up too long, will you? I know what you two are when you get talking.'

The car door closed, then her voice came back muffled, 'Ben, you won't ...' Hesitation.

'I won't what? What, Millie?' He was challenging.

'You won't do anything ... oh, never mind. I'll be back in the morning early and we'll do as agreed.'

Lydia must have slept then, because when the door to her room banged open she was aware of having had some short release from pain, confusion.

'You're in here with Lyd. Is it all right for you?' There was a silence as Ben and Nathalie looked at Lydia still face down in the pillow. They knew she was not asleep.

'Goodnight then, my darling,' Ben whispered. There was a rustling and the buckles on Nathalie's jacket jingled.

'I still can't believe it, Natta. My only, my lovely, Natta.'

''Night, Dad,' she said, unmoved.

Ben came over to Lydia and flicked her hair.

''Night, Lyd,' he said brightly.

Sleep again, more release.

It seemed she had been asleep for hours when Lydia awoke next, but it was still dark outside. A sound had woken her.

It was a cry, anguished but complete like the gasp of the freed. It must have been her own cry and she lay in the first silence of waking listening to its echo, although it had seemed not to be part of her. At first she could not look towards Nathalie's bed in case it had been herself that had cried out, so Nathalie would be lying there awake, waiting to talk, ask questions. But when she did look the bed was empty.

Lydia stood by the window watching a slow, cold light in the East. This night was over; one less eternity to endure.

Nathalie came in and shut the door. She was naked and her

skin shone white in the paling darkness. As she leant against the closed door, one arm covering her head, she did not look the boy, the gamine she was in public. The line of her hip was a soft curve; one thigh fell gently against the other throwing a shadow, making the black triangle of hair a vast, dark swelling area. The round of her stomach gleamed moist, pearly. She dropped her arm to her side and let her head fall hard against the door. A little hysteria seeped out with each breath, a laugh, a sob. She saw Lydia. 'So you've been awake,' she said, without changing her dejected posture. 'You look like a white mouse in this light.' Lydia moved back to the safety of her bed from their confronted nakedness. 'And you move like one too.'

Stretched under her bedclothes Lydia heard Nathalie lighting a cigarette. She sat up. 'Where have you been, Nathalie? Did you go downstairs?'

With a T-crossing, i-dotting sigh Nathalie said, 'You know where I have been, Lydia.'

After a silence so long that it made her remark a non sequitur Lydia said, 'Yes, I suppose I do.'

A while after Lydia assumed that Nathalie must be sleeping and wondered if ever she would sleep again. Then, very close to her head, she heard Nathalie's voice. 'Lydia, Lydia … don't be asleep. Please don't be asleep.' She was crouched and crying beside Lydia's bed. 'Please hear me, I don't mean to hurt. I didn't ever think I would come back to England and I never wanted to return to him, but when Millie told me about you and him I couldn't believe it. She seems to think you will do him some harm, stupid woman. It's you, Lydia, who will be hurt; he can't be satisfied until every part of your body and soul is tainted his shade.'

'But I don't mind that. I love his shade, there is nowhere else I want to be.'

'Oh yes there is, Lydia, there must be.' Nathalie pleaded, shapeless tears on her lower lids. 'He's a destroyer. I'm sure if you looked at your life now, the life you have left to be with him, you will see something of value has been destroyed. He can't help it, he doesn't want to do it, it is an inheritance of evil from some other life of his.'

'Really, Nathalie, that's just talk,' Lydia said, disbelieving, unimpressed, 'and any destruction in my own life I take the blame for, it's nothing to do with Ben.'

Nathalie seemed to collapse forward, her close-cropped head drawing one cheek then the other across the sheet with even repetition like that of the insane. 'No, it's true. It's true, because I'm the same, it's inherited. I got it from him. I've wanted to put everything right in the muddle of my life, but I don't seem to have the strength for anything but destruction.' She looked and pulled at the sheets about Lydia. 'But there is something, Lydia, something Daddy and Millie don't know: I have Christian, my little boy, my son. Millie made me give him away when he was born; I did. I did what I was told. But I got him back. Millie never told me there was time to change my mind and suddenly someone else told me; and I did: I went and got him.' There was a wild look of incredulity in Nathalie's own eyes as she said this and Lydia did not know whether to believe her or not. Nathalie turned her head back upon the bed again, stroking it backwards, forwards, over and over. 'And I love Christian. He is all I live for.' She suddenly looked up again, 'and I can't not love Ben; he and I are made of the same awful stuff …' Her voice trailed away to an undertone in her search for reasons to love him, '… and he's getting old … and he's our father … Gemme?' Nathalie smiled up at Lydia, who frowned and touched the trembling mouth and wet eyes.

'Gotcha,' Lydia said.

Nathalie climbed onto the bed and put herself into Lydia's arms. They lay down together, Nathalie's despair subsiding in small convulsions that shook her shoulders.

'It was all good then, wasn't it, Lydia, and fun? You know, Eden …?' Nathalie raised her head from the shallow area between Lydia's breast and shoulder, the part that Lydia herself sought so often on Ben. Her eyes scanned Lydia's anxiously; confirmation was essential to her.

Lydia smiled for the first time at Nathalie. 'Yes, yes, of course it was. You don't really need to ask,' she said.

Ben was telling Millie what a good night they had all spent when Lydia came down. Nathalie was already there dunking a roll in her coffee.

'Oh, hello, Lyd. Help yourself to some coffee, it's over there.' He pointed to the stove. As if she didn't bloody well know where it was.

'Morning,' Millie sang, 'and did you sleep well? Have a roll, I bought some this morning. Nathalie, drink up and we'll be off. Sorry to rush,' she turned to Ben, 'but I think we could catch a 'plane to Paris today to tie up loose ends there and be back in London in a few days, not long after you.'

Nathalie put on her jacket, avoiding all eyes and speaking to no one. Millie opened the door; for once no wind blew in, the day was still.

'I'll go on to the car. 'Bye for now, Ben.' Ben ignored her kiss, he was looking at Nathalie. 'Oh errm ... goodbye ... er ... Lydia.' Millie remembered. The door closed.

'You don't have to go if you don't want to, Natta.' Ben held Nathalie by the shoulders. 'It seems crazy to me, you've only just come. We could go back together, even to Paris, if that's what you want.' He turned her averted head towards him. 'Do you hear me, Natta?'

Suddenly she put her arms around his neck, the force of her embrace made him stoop. His surprise at first paralysed his arms, they continued to hang, fists clenched, at his side. He then took her to him fiercely and they stayed like that until Nathalie said, 'You hurt, Dad. Stop.'

She released herself and opened the door; turning she raised her hand in an hieratic gesture, first to Lydia and transferring the blessing without lowering her hand to Ben who, unable to bear her departure, had withdrawn to the far end of the room. She brought her hand back to Lydia again, conjuring an invisible hand between them, uniting them. She smiled broadly, amazingly, a blithesome smile which said, "Well, was I good? Do you get the joke?"

She whistled 'I'll go no more-a-roving' as she went to the gate. Ben was motionless, his face struck, mouth open, in an expression of disbelief.

'Hey, Dad,' Nathalie shouted over the roof of the car, 'I'll bring you a toupee from Paris.'

The car roared away. Ben, his shoulders sagging, his face agonized but hopeful, pathetic, looked at Lydia. He gave a silly, excited laugh.

'It's all right, Lyd, she's coming back. Did you hear? She said she'd bring me a toupee.' He heard no satire; just a promise to return.

As soon as he said it the stupidity of his remark slapped him. Hands in pockets he walked to the window, his shoulders expanding with regained composure. He pushed one hand slowly through his hair.

'Here, you know, she's right, I am thinning a bit.'

He started to touch things about the room: straightening fire-tongs, flipping open books still waiting to be packed, picking up a shell and contemplating it.

It was quiet, very quiet; no wind, no fire, no talk.

'Lyd,' he said at last, the firm voice that was her safety, 'I'm going to …' He stopped to study her face. Was she ready for what he had to say? 'I'm going … out.'

Lydia watched him disappear over the first dune and shut herself inside.

And what now? Now, she thought, to clean this ghosted room. Furiously she began to scrub the floor, the muddy suds making pools in the worn flagstones. Without pushing the furniture aside she knelt, forcing the brush along the floor with her weight behind it.

'No … no … no,' but the word came more as a grunt with the vehemence of her efforts, 'they won't take it away from me. I'm allowed happiness too. I can have it. I can …' She talked on as she worked, protesting the inevitable, insisting on the improbable. 'See if they can get me out. He wants me. He loves me too. I'm here, I'll always be here and she's gone, they've both gone.'

The dirt redistributed about the floor, she began to wash up, remembering which plate was Nathalie's, which was Millie's, which cup, which glass; and Millie's broke with the vigour of her rubbing. That must be a good sign. Her hatred was all for Millie. It was not possible to hate Nathalie, whose ambivalent expression seemed still to be upon her; and besides, there was something about that wayward girl, a shadow in her eye: the compliance of defeat.

She put the rubbish of their visit in a black plastic bag, bits of food, cigarette ends, some crushed, lipstick-marked tissues of Millie's, and she dropped the electric boot dryers in for good measure. There was a scarf, too, silk, pink and brown (perfectly pink and brown) that went in. Fanatically she tied the bag with wire. Suffocate it all.

She was panting as she went upstairs. Pushing open the door to the room where she had slept she wondered which phantom would greet her: Ben's red and white striped bottom, the slack muscles gathering at the top of his face as he bent double, or Nathalie half in shadow leaning lubricious, despairing against the wall.

The phantom that came, however, was not a vision, but a sound: the cry she had heard last night and thought to be her own. In the silence of the empty house she could hear again quite clearly what had died upon the air hours before. She knew now that the cry of submission, ecstatic delirium, had not been her own but Nathalie's. She tore the sheets from both beds and went into the other room, their room, and tore those off too.

Each bed, before Lydia had ripped it apart, reflected the night passed by its occupant: Lydia's was crumpled in the modest oval where she had lain; Ben's was a turmoil, a storm of sheets and blankets, fat, pubescent pillows (feathers curling through the ticking where the case sagged open) sat upon the heaped covers like jovial Buddhas. Nathalie's bed alone was without disturbance, a soft indentation where her gentle weight had briefly rested.

When Lydia took the pillow from that inscrutable bed to strip it of its case, something small and hard fell to the floor. She bent, searched and found it under the bed on the far side. It was a rectangle of rich, dark red enamel with gold edges and a band of gold down the centre. It was no more than one and a half inches square. Lydia's fingers pressed it and eased it, for it was surely a case of some sort; then, under those various pressures of her eager fingers, it gave, revealing a centre panel between the two red sides. Lydia pulled them fully apart and there was a small photograph inside. She carried it over to the window to see clearly. It was then she felt cold and bereft; not a feeling comparable with what she had suffered and was still suffering, this was a basic thing, uncomplicated, inarticulatable; for the face that stared at her from the little frame was the same boy-child's face that had watched her and faded from the cradle one night in her flat. She snapped the case shut and put it in her pocket.

Having gathered the sheets Lydia could not think what to do with them. She dragged them downstairs with some vague intention of burning them, but knew already her waning venom would not sustain her through the long process of pushing them through the little door of the stove, section by section; or through the business of lighting the fire for that purpose. So she dragged them back up again, making a second trip to collect escaped pillow-slips. Her burden was becoming a bore. She decided to push the whole lot under the bed in which Nathalie had slept.

She remade her bed, her real bed; her's and Ben's bed; their bed; our bed – with fresh sheets and care. She collected her clothes from the chair where Ben had put them and tossed them back on the chair from which he had taken them, the sketch-pad too. Still she could not find the silver pencil. (My darling Lyd. Always. Ben.) Yes always. She stuffed her socks under the pillow and re-hung her dressing-gown on the back of the door.

Quickly she checked around the house. All seemed to be restored. No signs. Nothing left. So, commencing on herself she bathed, washed her hair and brushed her teeth violently (the toothbrush slipped and she cut her gum), put on different clothes. All this she did with almost pre-natal fervour.

She went outside and there found herself unprepared for the stillness and the peace. Indoors fury and frustration had clamoured in her head but having spent these there was ... well, she could walk; walk and find out what was left.

Wide shore, broad shore, sea just visible a mile away and no one to be seen. The wetter sands nearer the breast of the sea sucked lasciviously at her gumboots. Impossible to sustain any violent feeling out there, the tenderness and turbulence of the land and sea was all too powerful, blotting out imported emotion. Her attention was rapt by the flight of the curlew, the oyster-catcher and the deceptively muddled formation of brent geese. The wind was lost around the corner of the world so visible on the horizon and although Lydia did not know it, as she walked she smiled. She knew the weak sun well enough by now to tell it was afternoon. Very soon the sky would trouble itself grey and the ceiling of the world would drop.

As far as the 'Holes' she would go, a treacherous, be-creeked area far up the shore, by which time the tide would be turning so she would have to skirt it and come back across the shoulders of the dunes.

It took a long time to reach the 'Holes' and when she was absorbed in crushing the sharp ridges peeked in the quilted sands, Ben came up behind her.

His appearance was so unexpected that at first she could not think how or why he belonged and even felt disappointment at being disturbed; until she remembered fragmented scenes and that it was because of him, thanks to him really, that she was driven outside to relish all this loneliness.

She let him drop his heavy arm over her shoulder and they walked on. At one point, without slackening his pace, Ben pulled her head onto his chest, covering it with his other hand, then let it go again.

By the time the gate creaked shut behind them it was evening. The fire was dead, the stove was out (Lydia had intended to stoke it) and neither of them had the heart to warm the place and shut out the night.

The room felt and smelt unexpectedly all right to Lydia, but dead now. No more cries, phantoms.

'I tell you what, Lyd,' Ben said, 'let's go to the pub. Let's eat there tonight.'

The idea was different enough from their normal routine (what they did all that time ago before Millie and Nathalie arrived, all that time ago yesterday) to be acceptable. But it was still a frightening one for if they did not start to play life the way it was, it might never be the same again.

They went to the pub.

When Lydia made herself forget that the heartlessly haunted house was still there to return to, to be dealt with, she quite enjoyed the idea. They had never been out together, only the odd shopping trip, nothing like this; they had not needed or wanted to.

The inn sign, slung in a bracket at the top of a post, creaking in the wind, looked promisingly authentic and inside was polished wood and brass.

They sat at a round table in the corner. Ben went over to the bar, asked to order a meal and returned with two whiskies. He sat with his forearms on his knees, hands clasped. Twice he looked at Lydia without turning his head and when she noticed he averted his eyes. There was a cluster of country colonels who sustained a loud conversation about fishing and a mutual interest in Ben and Lydia. A group of young marrieds came in, the men gathering round the bar and the women at a table while they shouted their preferences to each other. Four motorcyclists also entered, black leather, studs and tinted helmets, but one look at the horse brasses and the hostile faces of the landlord and his large, hennaed wife and they backed out, pushing over their female versions who were coming in behind.

'Yeah?'

A gum-chewing waitress came over; pencil poised on pad she checked over Ben and Lydia.

'I'd like to know,' Ben said, leaning over to her, intimate, 'what you would choose.'

'Who, me?' She hung her mouth open and pushed the grey blob of chewing-gum round her teeth, even teeth; a pretty girl, dark.

'Yes, you,' he said without actually adding 'you who must be so renowned for good taste'. 'You don't have to eat it. Just tell me what you think is the best and I know I'd want that.' He fixed his eyes on hers and she was mesmerised, like a rabbit with a snake, tongue and chewing-gum at a standstill, both protruding slightly.

'Well … Chicken in Basket's nice. You get them little plastic gloves wiv that.'

'What, to eat?' Ben grinned.

'Na, stupid, to wear. No knives and forks. Saves washin' up, see?'

She grinned back and massaging the chewing-gum briskly between her front teeth she travelled her eyes over Ben; interested.

'Then that is what we'll have,' Ben said, accepting more than chicken and plastic gloves.

'Right,' she sniffed and started to write laboriously, 'so that's two c-h-i-c-k-e-n in b-a-s-k-e-t-s.'

Her eyes went over him again as she pocketed the chewing-gum in her cheek and turned to go. Ben half rose and touched her tight, pneumatic, black-clad rear with one finger. He spoke low and slow, 'And two whiskies. Soon.' (There could be no end to his demands.)

'And two more whiskies,' she repeated just as slowly (anything is possible).

'I say,' he called after her.

'Yeah?'

'With water.'

Her eyes turned heavenwards in mock desperation as she articulated her bottom towards the bar.

Ben sat back pleased with himself until he looked at Lydia, when he rearranged his pose more modestly. He fiddled with mats and ashtray on the table, lit a cigarette and said, 'I think tomorrow might be as good a day as any to leave, don't you?' He did not look at her face; not to see the fear there. He did not want to see that at all. He rolled his glass between his fingertips staring into the golden pool, reflecting light from the noisier and crowding bar-room.

'There's no reason why we should change our plans.' He was uncertain and nervous; it showed horribly clearly that he was frightened of her reaction, any reaction she would have, 'but perhaps we should move a little more slowly. After all, it will be forever, won't it?' He finished brightly, with the unconvinced finality of a restless reader to the child. He saw from a glimpse of her hand moving towards him that it would not do. Details. He'd add some details, but he wasn't going to touch that hand, not now. 'Better for us too, in the long run. Instead of coming to my house right away I think you should return to your "situation", you know, brave it out. Then when the position is clearer you can move in with me, and Natta, of course. By then she will have settled in. Because she is coming back, you know.' His eyes challenged Lydia briefly, defying her to contradict. 'But she and I are hopeless at looking after ourselves for any amount of time, whereas you can be quite efficient when you want to be. It could be fun. The three of us.'

'She won't come back, Ben. You must see that. She would never have come in the first place unless Millie had bullied her.'

'That's not true. It's not true. She loves me, we belong together; we're not like other people. You don't understand at all. She was coming back to me anyway. She told me so.'

'Well, if that really was true it's the end of me, isn't it? Where could I fit in? You didn't talk to me last night, or this morning. It's just like the past, at Eden, I don't really exist if she's there.'

'This is intolerable,' Ben noted aloud to himself, but when he turned to speak to her it was with genuine concern, an

anxiousness to make her understand. 'Lyd, you mustn't
think ...'

Back came the waitress with the food, make-up refreshed,
ready for another round. She gave Lydia hers first and
ponderously dangled the other in front of Ben, who had by
now focused his whole body upon Lydia.

'Oh thanks, thanks,' he said, impatient; glancing briefly and
hardly noticing the girl. With a malevolent suck on her
chewing-gum she spun the basket at him, shedding chips, and
tap-tapped away. 'Lyd. Look at me. I am talking to you. You
mustn't think I am trying to end anything, on the contrary, it's
just that I think we've been a little selfish. She is my daughter. I
owe her something. Everything. But I'm sure Natta would like
the idea of us all living together. She's a very sophisticated girl.
Very original.' He paused and frowned, remembering
something with faint distaste. 'Very original.' He gulped his
whisky. Re-enthused, he added, 'It could all work out very
nicely. For all of us.'

The waitress returned with more drinks and downcast eyes.
'Why, thank you, thank you,' Ben gushed, prizing under her
lids with his smile. 'You're very kind.' With a sulky nod she
walked away, delighted.

Now he was breezy and confident, gentleness gone, although
as he talked, still without looking at her, he reached for Lydia's
hand and held it tightly for a moment. The touch said, 'Bear
with me. It will pass. Please be patient.' and reminded her of
the real promise of how their life would be. It was still possible
to believe it. They were happier together not speaking; a look,
contact, these they understood. Things went wrong with words.

They ate their chicken, which tasted of fish. After a while
Ben's expression became withdrawn, sad. He kept shaking his
head and frowning, pushing back some advancing thought. As
Lydia looked at him she thought how there were aspects of
aging that made the sexes one; for instance, the corner of his
mouth, where it sagged down with the deep line traversing it,
could have been that of an old woman, the pale, soft weakness
of it. But he is tired; be fair. He's very tired.

Suddenly he said, as if he had been rehearsing it for some
time, 'We have been living in a sort of capsule down here; a
little bubble of existence where only we have been important.

How we react in the real world will tell our feelings for each other. A great test for us will be when real life touches us, as it started to yesterday.'

Lydia waited for him to explain about the beds and her clothes, but he just said, 'And I think we did well. No scenes or anything. You know, tempers.'

So now she told herself that what he had done was reasonable, that he had been showing some delicacy, even consideration for her feelings. Anything would she forgive him, credit him, to be back where they were before.

They finished their drinks and sat on, but nothing seemed right any more; finally Ben said, 'I'll go to the bar and settle up, then we'll go home.'

He did say "home". That was important. So he thought of Coalbarn as their home. Maybe. Maybe still …

Lydia watched Ben move through the crowd, head and shoulders above it and helplessly loved what she saw. Several people he passed looked at him and then over to Lydia, matching them, adding them.

Ben was away some time and Lydia started to peer into the throng of people; she saw through a brief space left by a departing group that the "colonels" had cornered him. One was slapping him on the back and gesticulating with a gin and tonic. The crowd seeped in again and her view was lost. He had seemed to be enjoying the conversation. Lydia stood up to go and join them, but as she did another clearing formed, Ben and the "colonels" were looking at her. Half sitting on the bar stool Ben was leaning incredulously towards one of the men who was standing (even as he sat Ben was taller than them). Ben pointed towards Lydia and looked hard at the man.

'Do you mean *her?*' he was saying. 'Good God, no. *That*'s not my daughter. My daughter is …'

A wave of laughter from somewhere drowned what he said but his eloquent hands went on to slice out of the air someone gay, magical, expansive, slender, crazy; someone altogether unreal and obviously Nathalie. The man looked a little embarrassed at Ben's enthusiasm and gave a loud, false laugh, closing with a little cough into his fist: of course, of course, how silly of him; anyone can see that's not his daughter. The other "colonels" were busy with nods and nudges. 'Obviously quite a fellow, eh?' One of them reached round and gave an impression of a punch on Ben's arm.

'Have another, old boy. It's my round,' Lydia heard the man say.

She could not hear Ben's reply but in the fraction of a second that she saw his face he looked eager and relieved to be in light company.

Lydia pushed her way through the people to the door and outside.

She started down the lane, the high, sparse hedges of daytime made solid by the night, but long before she reached the end, where the hedges fragmented and the road became a track, she could hear Ben running after her.

'Wait, wait. For God's sake slow down.' He was shouting.

She went faster, but even as she did it struck her as futile because she only had one place to go. Nevertheless, she went on and turned right where the track ended; in daytime a little beaten path would have been visible through the marram grass leading across the marshes to Coalbarn, but at night there was no sign of it and she took her own way, stumbling in the tufted ground riven with creeks. With each fall she let herself be still for long enough to hear that he was still following, calling.

'Please wait. Don't go.' Breathless and desperate. But he was following, seeking her, the man who referred to her as 'that' was still prepared to seek her. Not a 'she'; not even a "what's her name", but this is what she had come to be for him: a "that".

Exhausted, with lungs burning and panting, she sank down by the door of Coalbarn. No key. Ben had it. So now having run from him she would wait for him. Farcical really, but there didn't seem to be much sense left in anything.

He appeared as a black shape still running, which was curious because he knew where she was and that she could go no further, but when he started to speak she knew once more that there was something beyond her.

He leant against the gate gasping. As he drew in air there was a constricted whine from deep in his throat.

'Never ... never ... do,' he paused between each word to drag in more air, 'that ... to me again. Do you hear?'

He came through the gate breathing more easily but his shoulders were still heaving. He opened the door and pushed

Lydia through into the unlit house. Holding her by the arms he started to shake her violently.

'Never, never leave me like that again.'

Letting go of one arm he held her away from him pushing her shoulders up with the force of his grasp. The door was still open allowing the moonlight to fall upon his distorted features. The tone of his voice altered, he was losing control.

'Do you know what it's like to be left? To think you have someone with you but you turn and they are gone and you don't know why? Do you, blast you? No, you don't because you've been too safe, too protected, no one has ever left you. It's my fault you are the way you are, I spoilt you, but you won't do it to me again. I won't let you. I didn't mean to let you go but you would never speak to me, wouldn't see me. You could have kept it and it would be ours. That's not wrong, not evil. Love justifies everything, doesn't it? I was always careful, careful; miserably restrained and controlled, except only once and you know why. Why, why did you make me jealous? Did you really need more confirmation of my love?' His voice changed again; shaking his head slowly, pleadingly, he said, 'I've watched you go before, I let you. Please, please, my darling, not again. I can't bear it again.'

He paused, studied Lydia's face and then looked beside her at something only he could see. Slowly he raised his hand to her cheek and touched it lightly as if she would disappear on contact. His confused eyes searched her face like a landscape upon which something of value to him lay hidden. At last he whispered, 'It's you, Lyd, isn't it? After all, it's you. Do you know I thought it was … that it was someone else.' Lydia led him over to the sofa and he obediently sat letting her raise his feet and lay him down. After closing the door and turning on a light at the other end of the room, so he was still shaded, she started to make coffee, but heard him say, 'If that's for me, Lyd; nothing for me, but please be here near me.' She went and looked down at him lying foetal, he raised a hesitant hand, she took it and sat down placing his head onto her lap. He settled so he could see her face above his. 'Thank God for you now, Lyd.' He laughed gently. 'I suppose I always say that but I can't remember ever before feeling the peace I've found with you.' He lifted his head and looked at the room. 'The house has gone dead around us. Can you feel it? No fire, no warmth. It's all dead.' He stood up, 'Come and sleep with me and we'll shut out this life for a bit.' He put Lydia's hands to his mouth, 'You will always be there for me, won't you, Lyd.' It came not as a request but as an observation of a certainty, and she believed with him in that certainty. He held her tightly against him. 'Oh, God, what a mess. I'm not a happy man.'

They turned on no lights upstairs, something to do with their mutual desire not to prolong that day. As Lydia prepared for bed she felt security returning, that is until, sitting up in bed clasping her knees to her under the covers, she saw Ben was putting on pyjamas; peacock blue silk. It had always amused her that for all his liking of the simple life everything he touched and that touched him had to be of the best: cashmere, silk, mohair and hand-made shoes. But this was not amusing; for Ben to wear pyjamas as armour against the touch of her own skin was appalling. He found them in a drawer after some fumbling and obviously had not used them for a long time, if ever. He then started a silly charade, removing his clothes and donning the pyjamas while trying to expose as little of himself as possible. It was not because of the cold; he never minded that, in fact one of his pleasures was to be naked in the unheated bedroom for some time then rush to the warmth of the bed and Lydia's body.

Was this man in the corner with his back to her, tripping as he tried to put a bare leg into pyjamas while the other still wore trousers, the same one who was going to undress in front of the fire and three women the night before? Then Lydia remembered that it had been the sight of her that had stopped him in his striptease. The security ebbed. She lay down but faced inwards to show that she was available for conversation, or anything, if he wanted it; but when he came to bed he faced away from her and said nothing, though the blue silk shoulders were tentative and not ready for sleep; they exuded a nervousness: they were preparing.

Lydia turned onto her back with her hands under her head. It was one of those cluttered silences where everything and nothing is said and misunderstood. After some time during which they lay both aware they were far from sleep, Lydia reached out and touched a blue shoulder. As soon as she did she recoiled, appalled that without a twitch, a wince, a breath from him, she could receive a signal of such force: don't touch me.

She reflected on their relationship, on how little she understood him, on how she had the ability to lift him from black moods but not to understand the reasons for them. She thought that even now they had not come very far: she made him happy when he let her, they were going to get married – at some point – he had said so and he had not changed that. But he still seemed to be able to reduce their union to a triviality; by hiding as he undressed it was as if they had been together for one harried night and now he was overcome by the wrongness of his choice.

She thought of how many times it had seemed to be finished with him but that each time his love had come back stronger. And that was the thought upon which to sleep. There now, there now; it'll be all right in daylight.

But the blue shoulders spoke. The cowardly blue shoulders.

'I can't go through with it, Lyd. Us, I mean. The only way I can help myself, the only way I can stop going mad and the only way I can make things right is to play my part and that is Father to Natta. To think it would work with you there is only dreaming – you must have known that when I said it. We have had happiness and it's time to go back where we belong, you in your corner, me in mine.' His voice was very calm and emphatic. He did not speak again.

The last clear thought Lydia had was that she could have been asleep and never heard him; that she could bluff it out and that in the end he would have to say it again to her face and without the blue pyjamas. Surely without the blue pyjamas he could not say it.

But she knew he meant it. That this was the end. And now thank God for night.

The next morning Lydia stood at the bottom of the stairs. She was wearing the skirt Ben had discarded for her, the one she wore the day she had left with him and had never worn since. Round the half-open door came the smell of breakfast cooking, coffee and the smoke from the fire. That meant the wind was in the East. Ben must have been up for a long time.

He was moving about the room; clumsy noises, and she knew which part of him had caused each noise: pushing a chair out of his way with his thigh; his foot slamming the door of the stove; crashing down the frying-pan with his hand and swearing as the fat spat at him. She could see, without seeing, his broad back and feel under her fingers the roughness of the navy-blue jersey he would be wearing over the soft one against his skin. The clothes he always wore at Coalbarn. How could she ever live without him?

She wanted to rush in and beg him not to finish with her, to say that without him part of her was, and always would be, dead. But although she did not know him entirely she knew enough to know begging would only entrench his decision.

She entered the room and stood nervously. Ben turned and grinned.

'Hello, I've got breakfast ready. You look very smart. I haven't seen you in that before.'

She sat down at that table.

'Here, I've got everything. Tomatoes, mushrooms, scrambled egg, and it's not rubbery, even fried bread.' His public voice. Always his public voice. He put the plate in front of her. Lydia went over to the stove and helped herself to coffee; the only thing she wanted.

'Oh, sorry, I forgot, let me do it. You sit down.'

The telephone rang and he pounced upon it.

'Millie? Hello … Yes, my dear. How are things going?' He twiddled with the wire. 'Good. Good. That's fantastic. I say, how lucky. So you'll both be back when? – When? Sorry, it's a bad line. Oh dear, not 'till then.' His voice dropped and sprang back again. 'No, I suppose it's not long really and it will give me a chance to catch up at the office. Actually all sorts of things have blown up, they've been on three times this morning already. Shows I've been away too long. Listen, is she there? Can I talk to her? Oh,' his voice fell, 'O.K. then. Bye Millie … Millie?' He held the dead receiver towards Lydia and shrugged. 'I was going to say thank you.'

He replaced the receiver but before he reached the table it was ringing again.

'Yeah? Ben Wavell. Hello.' He was talking to a man; he had to be: his tone was so different, mock masculine.

'Yes, well telex them not to meet and not to sign. There's a clause that must be changed. Tell them, too, I'll be there myself 19.30 their time today. Hold everything 'till I arrive ... Fine, fine. See you later.'

So life continued in the outside world and he was still part of it, while Lydia was doubting not only her part but her existence.

He sat down opposite her and lit a cigarette.

'You haven't eaten a thing. Oh, Lyd, really.'

Nearly, nearly she struck him, but even now she could not be sure if it was over; and it was, after all, her serenity he had seemed to love so, if she gave in now to the protests inside, if she lashed out with her hand and word, that might seal it for Ben and she would never know, then, if simply and suddenly betraying her image in his mind had brought the affair to a close. She was still prepared to play any game, act any part. Anything, anything, not to have the lights go down on her.

Ben knew she had only just restrained herself. He went on in a quieter voice, 'I'm sorry I'm being a bully. I suppose I don't really know what to say.' He watched her for a moment, marvelling that she was not hysterical or even abusive. 'Look, ermm ... I've asked Miss Light to come and collect you. You know old Violet Light; come to think of it you probably don't. Isn't that some name? Very imaginative parents, especially for this part of the world. She's seventy and she's the only taxi driver in the village – but don't worry, her driving belies her name.' He grinned at Lydia for a moment but gave up and let his face fall serious. 'Look, I just thought it was better if you take a train; there's one at midday. You see I've got to go to Rabat and I can go straight to the airport if I don't have to drop you.' He added as if it would help, 'Miss Light will be here soon.'

There was nothing she had to collect, nothing to be seen to, nothing to be said. And Miss Light did come soon: her 1950's Ford Anglia sat steaming at the end of the concrete ridge barely half an hour later.

Ben held the door open and Lydia passed under his arm. Suddenly he grabbed her and turned her to face him. He looked anxiously into her eyes.

'Lyd.' It was his own voice, at last it was him who was speaking. 'Lyd, if I've been insincere it was accidental. O.K.? Accidentally insincere.' He gave her a little shake with each syllable to drive his words home.

She looked hard at him for a moment trying to understand, but even as she looked he receded again behind his mask and the public voice. He was pressing something into her hand and she felt a surge of hope. It could be the silver pencil, or a note to say it was not really over. Maybe for now, but not forever.

'If ever I can be of any help you will get in touch, won't you? I mean if you need anything.'

She walked towards the car.

'Lyd ...' he was shouting as she opened the door. 'I say, Lyd ... Lyd,' as she sat down in the front seat and slammed the door. As Miss Light drove away he was shouting again from the doorway, Lydia could see him and not hear him. But it was all right, he only wanted to say thank you.

The note, the promise that was pressed into Lydia's hand turned out to be fifty pounds and Lydia's beaten senses were further bruised; not because he had given her money, she had none so that was practical and permissible, but because it was such a careful sum. Ben must have sat down and counted the fivers and tenners and judged what she needed. He must have thought about what she was going to do: take a taxi, take a train and perhaps another taxi to arrive at the place which had been home until the moment she re-met him; he must have thought of her doing these things and still been able to let her go. If he had given her far too little or much, much more, something at either extreme which was out of all proportion to what she needed, it would have proved that his senses, if not bruised like hers, were at least too shaken and distracted to be precise.

Miss Light (a bundle of khaki raincoat with a beret on top) made detailed checks of the gauges and mirrors as she drove sitting well forward in the seat and peering over the wheel. Not until Coalbarn, the sea and the marshes were behind them and they had passed through the far end of the village did she say, 'So it's the station then? London train?' in a sing-song accent, leaving the words "then" and "train" dangling on a high note.

When Lydia did not answer she looked to see why by turning her head but keeping her eyes on the road then quickly switching them to Lydia and back again. That gave her just enough time to see Lydia, her head against the window, her fist pressed to her forehead and her mouth contorted in a controlling effort.

Miss Light nodded and repeated what she had said, this time as a statement, 'So it'll be the station then. London train.' Now those two words dropped a note below the others with heavy finality: as if between the two statements a whole drama had been acted and what had been the prologue was now the epilogue.

When they reached the station Miss Light parked carefully; after switching off the ignition she sat tense, gripping the wheel and scanning the dashboard; if the car had any tricks to play she was ready for it. Satisfied that the engine was at peace she turned in her seat, with difficulty because of layers of clothes, and looked at Lydia.

'Station,' she said, and turned the other way. After considering the knobs on the inside of the door for a bit, she pulled one and looked quietly surprised when the door opened. She walked around the car but before opening Lydia's door she paused, hand on handle, then opened it with a flourish, taking it by surprise. Although as familiar as a grease monkey with the engine of her car, Miss Light had never quite brought herself to believe in the motorcar as a machine, to her it was a living thing that might do anything, any time.

The stocky figure in man's clothes guided Lydia firmly by the elbow across the station yard to the ticket office, where she released her.

'That'll be one-fifty.'

Lydia fumbled with the money and dropped some. Miss Light gathered it up, selected a five-pound note and returned the rest.

'Now wait you. Wait you. There be change.' Miss Light arched her back, paused, swung her bottom to one side and reached behind, lifting the flap of her raincoat and exposing the back pocket of her old, dirty cavalry twills. If the manoeuvre had been carried out by a big-breasted girl in feathers and a G-string, the effect would have been erotic. She delved and counted, while staring into the middle distance, not withdrawing her hand or the money until she had felt the right amount. She handed it to Lydia, now more composed, and patted her arm.

'There then,' she said, and swung away shaking her head and tutting. Before she crossed the yard to her car she stood, arms folded, legs apart, looking at it, watching what it was doing without her.

* * *

'Thank you for coming. Please believe I don't want to hurt you. Face me, won't you, Lyd?'

Lydia remained head down taking in the scent of nicotine and limes that came to her when Ben had entered the car. 'That's not my name.'

'What do you mean? Don't say that to me. I know who you are.' There was panic in his voice.

'I only mean my name is Lydia, not Lyd.'

'But I always called you Lyd.'

'It's just that I never really liked it. It doesn't matter.'

'You never said.' His eyes wandered; he dropped his head to the crook of his arm. Patches of his thick, curling hair were missing: a neurasthenic balding-by-the handful. Lydia wished she had not mentioned it. 'It doesn't matter, really,' she repeated, riffling years and dates in her mind to arrive at his age, fifty-eight or nine, no more.

He raised his face, wearied to collapse with suffering, deep lines around his slack mouth; hollow, drug-dimmed eyes. He grasped unsteadily at the air as though to clutch her words, studied his empty palm.

'... They told me in the sanatorium that I was suffering from guilt, that I would never be better, that there would be more breakdowns unless I cleared my mind of guilt. But, you see, they didn't understand; they didn't know. And could I have risked telling them that I knew what I was doing when I let her go? That was when I started to think about you. You were always there at moments of crisis, Lyd. Do you remember the last summer at Eden? How Viola took Natta to Paris and met that man, Erik, who even then was her lover? I never guessed. They left us alone in the house, do you remember? And when I met you all those years later it was like a miracle, because I thought I'd never see anything to do with my past again. But you brought it all back.

'At first the trip with Natta through the South of France was like crossing the frontier of a dream, we were so idyllically happy, but after some days she became tense and difficult. She made me crazy by kneeling on the passenger seat and scanning the road behind as we drove. I decided she was bored of moving all the time and we settled in a hotel in Monte Carlo. I loathe that place, but she seemed fairly happy at the idea of stopping for a while. At least: the odd smile she gave when I suggested it was better than I had had in two days. She raced about the hotel on her own like a twelve-year-old; she would say she was going to the lifts or to the arcade; she liked to go to the bar fifteen minutes or so before I was ready and then pretend to meet as strangers. I liked that too. But I never let her go out of the hotel without me. Does that sound silly? I was afraid for her; she was very young, after all. Well, at least, that was a mistake I kept making: I kept thinking she was twelve, and at twelve you don't rush about with no one to look after you, do you, Lyd? She should have listened to her father, she really should. We had some bad rows there, but then suddenly she changed and was sweet again. For seven whole days she was kind to me, oddly kind, not her usual bantering self; it was a new side to her. We stayed there long enough to gather a little crowd of hangers-on. You know those Monte Carlo types: defunct royalty, gamblers, life's rich losers, but it was all colourful and amusing for a while.

'When I felt I could stand it no longer I started to suggest new places, but that made her unhappy again. She would dash off to the lifts, sometimes for an hour. You see, she was a child, don't you? Would a mature woman play in lifts because she was unhappy? I followed her once and I saw her disappear into one lift, so I got into another; there was a bank of five of them. Up and down I went for nearly twenty minutes, getting glimpses of her boot or hearing the jingle of that bloody jacket. When I heard her laugh once I stopped following: she returned quite a long time after that, but her mood was so altered that it dissolved my anger. You see, I was desperate to have her happy; to keep her near me. I didn't understand that her happiness was, by then, quite beyond my control. She said, if we were to go, she wanted to go to Russia, that, after all, she was half-Russian and she wanted to see the land of her

ancestors. That sort of nonsense. It was the last place I wanted
to go: filthy food and rotten service, and it would be too
complicated to take the car. By then I was devoted to the car; it
was so admired everywhere we went. She liked all that, of
course. But the car was also a kind of base for me, like my own
home between all the hotels. I even went to sit in it sometimes
in the underground garage of the hotel if Natta had made me
particularly unhappy; it gave me solace.

'Well, off we went to Russia, anyway. It took a while to
organise and I garaged my beautiful car, making damned sure
it was with no crook or anyone who would use it in my
absence. We left without a word to the motley crowd we had
gathered about us during our stay; Natta and I had no
affection for them and we decided not to say Goodbye. It
seemed a suitably theatrical disappearance in the circum-
stances and would give those poor stateless souls something to
talk about for a few days.

'Russia was when I became really unhappy; and it was when
I began to suspect. Do you know how to deceive, Lyd? I can't
believe you do. I'm sure you have always been straight with
that round-shouldered man you live with.

'But you've come to me now, Lyd. I knew you'd come to me.'

'I only came to hear what you want to tell me and ...
besides ...' She faced away, ashamed of "besides".

'Besides what?' He moved his hands towards hers, hesitated,
withdrew before touching.

'Besides, we never said "goodbye", but that was then. Too
late now for "goodbye".'

The blue alley of sky between the houses deadened, there
would be thunder; rain soon, thank God.

10

The train was the slow one, due to stop at every station; the blessing being that it would be hours before Lydia reached London. So long as she was slung in this brown, smelly anonymity nothing had happened, nothing was past. Shortly after it left the station the train was rattling gently over a track beside the dunes. Lydia was dully amazed to have the sea spread before her again; she had thought, after the drive with Miss Light, that it was miles behind her and had been regretting not securing one last image of it to carry away. Now here it was, but too calm, too sparkling, smiling as she left.

The train stopped and started, people entered the carriage and left it, but these were real life people, busy people with things to do, places to go, nothing to do with her. Encased in herself and her misery she mused. Like an awful wound she dared herself to look closer and closer at the past two months and in this private state she was able to do so without tears. She could cry when life was happening to her, and although her tears were spontaneous and genuine they were still a statement for observers, a primeval expression supplanting words; alone, unknown, they did not come. Like anyone else passing time on a train she took out her work and attended to it, a patchwork no one else could see: pieces of elation made from the times he said 'Thank God for you now, Lyd', big dark pieces when he expected someone else and saw Lydia before him; confused pieces made of Millie, Nathalie and Eric and hundreds of dread blank pieces of life without Ben. She would sort the pieces and make sense of this mess, a consoling pattern to alleviate her. She had left one man to live with another, unasked; she had bet on knowing the man's silent voice, his real voice, but now he had asked her to go. He preferred to live with his daughter. How despicably simple. She shuddered and looked quickly to see if anyone had heard her thoughts, but the carriage was empty. Although people had been there, settling briefly between stations and they had seen clearly that the girl in the corner staring blindly through the grimy windows, knees crossed, ankles crossed, cradling her shoulders, who now and again gave her face a moidered swipe, pushed her hand through her hair and clutched again at her lichen-green coat, was anguished; but unlike dogs human beings rarely sniff about one another uninvited. If you want the solace of another you raise your hand and say, "I'm in pain. I need", and if you are lucky they will say, with a diffident sniff, "Oh, really, what is it?", but not much more because losers contaminate.

A pirate waiter from the buffet car sold her some coffee in a paper cup which spilt when the train juddered to a long stop between stations. Some soldiers came in and tried to chat her up by talking to each other about her.

'Think she's English?'

'Naa. Swedish.'

'Never. Not with skin like that. Nice though, isn't she?'

'Mmm. Think she'll talk to us? Think she's got a boyfriend? How old, sixteen?'

'Go on, twenty-three if she's a day.'

In the end they gave up and went to another carriage and more responsive quarry. She slept spasmodically.

Otherwise nothing else happened and when the train drew into the huge, darkly shadowed, dinning London station Lydia's anaesthetic of anonymity was done. She knew quite well where she was, how she was placed but as she stepped down from the train she found herself a reason to hope. Youth's capacity for casting around and finding a hope like a stepping-stone to place beneath its feet and carry on to middle-age using ever diminishing hopes, ever decreasing stones, came to Lydia now: maybe Ben would be there. He would want her back and drive wildly to meet the train; so she stood looking up and down the windy platform. Any moment Ben's figure would materialize from the thinning cloud. But the crowd went and only a porter came towards her slamming the carriage doors.

'End of the line, Ducky.'

She sat opposite the barrier to see if Ben went there, perhaps the drive had taken longer than she reckoned. But he did not come. Of course he didn't.

A fresh crowd started to form about the barrier, eager and ready for their journey. One or two of the last lot, the travel-weary ones had hung about near Lydia, but even they now had been met or had trudged off purposefully. Cold, clangorous and dirty though this haughty Victorian station was, it was not hostile, merely unconcerned and she could have stayed there, preferring that to action. But she was cold and knew she would have to sleep somewhere. It was still only six o'clock but night had begun.

She walked outside the telephone kiosks trying to think how she could announce herself to Eric when he answered and what she would say, "I want to see you." "May we talk?" "I'd like you to understand", or nearer the truth, "I don't want to come but I've nowhere else to go." Finally, after no decision she dialled; nothing. She dialled again, still nothing. She asked the operator to check the number.

'Sorry, Love. Out of order.'

That helped. It gave her somewhere to go. She could stand outside and see if lights were on in the windows of the apartment. Of course there was another house she could go to and stand outside, where the lights might be glowing soft amber through the curtains and she might hear, faintly, lute music and probably a telephone ringing.

Then she remembered Ben was abroad. A plane to catch, "19.30 their time". He could not have come.

It'll be some days yet. Then he'll come.

She took a taxi to a few streets from the flat and walked. Slowly she rounded the corner; no one about, a door banging, someone shouting. The street had settled for the evening: lights on, a television flickering. Carefully she walked past some houses ready to pretend she was entering one in case Eric appeared; but when she counted along the windows, the right building, the right floor, there was no light. Nothing.

She began to walk away but something made her look back. Something had moved in the window; but no, nothing anywhere. She looked again. There seemed to be a very dim, faltering light but it was only the reflection from the opposite window. She looked at the opposite window and those near it, there were no lights in them. It could not be a reflection. There was a candle burning somewhere in the flat.

Under the basement steps where the dustbins were housed she and Eric kept spare keys and now in the crumbling brickwork beneath her fingers she felt them.

The street door clicked shut behind her. Inside was the same light, same smell, same hall. Same, same, all hopelessly same. Lydia pictured herself walking out again, without going upstairs at all and starting a nobly solitary life, but it was only a thought. She knew she had not the courage. Spineless. Who was it who had said that about her? It was a long time ago now, but it was accurate she thought and began to play with the seeds of self-hate. She had let Ben take her in, divert her, and she had let him push her out. Lydia, the Spineless, Lydia the Invertebrate, Lydia that little one over there.

Slowly she climbed up the stairs listening minutely every third step but there was no sound from anywhere in the house. Nevertheless she knew, beyond that door there was someone: Eric.

The key slotted nicely and turned. She went in, shut the door and instantly felt it was the wrong flat. It echoed; all around her the closing door, her footsteps, the jingling keys resounded. The flat was empty. She flicked the switch by the door but it gave no light. Bare floors, bare walls grey in the light of the London night and everything so still. In the bedroom a streetlight displayed the dusty boards. She remembered her vision of Eric bowing and receding. The door to the candle-lit sitting-room was wide open and standing there, blackly silhouetted, was a man. Not Eric.

Lydia gasped and struggled with the front door.

'Hey,' he said slowly, calmly. She knew the sardonic voice.

'Hey, Little Thing, don't rush away again.'

Lydia turned back and recognized the tall silhouette to be Greg.

In a flood of self-pity, exhaustion, fear and relief that he was not Eric, she rushed into his arms, clinging and crying she buried her head into the hairy garment he was wearing. His hands hovered over her back and rested reluctantly on her shoulders.

'Come then, come on. Tell all.' He was guarded.

Lydia tried to tell all, all that was important. About the pencil disappearing. And Millie, how determined she was; she wouldn't stay away. And Nathalie being so beautiful, so funny, and how Nathalie had teased him, how she always had, and he never minded but if anyone else tried he didn't like it at all. How, after Rabat, he'll come back, how he hasn't really left. Not forever. He couldn't. And about Miss Light. Oh, yes, and about the sea. How you walked and walked and couldn't find it and suddenly there it was like grey magic before you. And how he came up behind her when she thought she was alone. He held her then. He didn't say anything, but he held her and she thought it was going to be all right. Which it would be. It would be, really.

She made no sense at all.

Greg slapped her hard. 'Lydia, you're hysterical,' the expression on his ginger-haired face made it obvious he did not mind doing it.

Greg leant against the window-sill and studied Lydia who was now calm. With crossed arms he wrapped the heavy-knitted, roll-collared jacket around him against the bitter cold of the flat. White woollen socks peeped between the hem of his jeans and the heelless clogs he always wore. In the past Lydia had wondered how ever he managed to keep them on. "With bare feet they stick with the sweat," he had said, "but it's not so easy with socks."

'You can see Eric's gone, can't you?'

Lydia looked about the room. She had not registered the reason for the emptiness before but of course it was deserted, electricity off, heating off. Everything gone, only a mattress in the corner where obviously Greg slept.

'He went about a month ago. He got the job, the Boarding School.' Greg spoke bitterly as if he had more to say on that point but checked himself. 'And so since Vebeke's cleared off with that bloody, bi-sexual bassoon player, oh, of course you wouldn't know about him, would you? Well, I say "cleared off", what it means is, in fact, that I get out of that dump we called home because she paid the rent, Eric gave me the keys to this place so I could freeze quietly to death until the next tenants arrive, which, Little Thing, I warn you is the day after tomorrow, so don't think you can park your bony little arse here for long.

'Oh yes, life has carried on with out you, Lydia, and the gap made by your departure has closed; life sort of overlapped, healed over your bit.

'But you know something? I knew you'd be back. I knew if I stayed in this freezing, clunking, dead-switched place that one day the door would open and there would stand Little Thing, cast over. That's the only reason I stayed. There are better places.'

The light was behind him now so his face was invisible and there was something ambiguous about the way he spoke; Lydia did not know whether to take what he said as consolation (do not feel too guilty about what you have done) or accusation; whether he had stayed to take pleasure in her ignominious return or to console her. But she so much wanted a friend just now and after all he had always seemed to like her. Hadn't he?

Greg shook his head.

'God, Little Thing, you look awful. Like something the cat brought in. Come on,' he took her by the arm, 'I'll feed you. It's the least I can do.'

Greg took her to Rosa's, the Italian cafe where Lydia and Eric planned to have their little wedding reception. The place had been Eric's discovery because one day when Lydia had been in bed with a cold he took himself there to eat. Lydia and Greg maintained that it looked too dirty, that the yellowing festoon curtain set rigid with grease and the cockeyed notice hanging inside the door which always read 'Closed', did not bode well. The truth turned out to be that Rosa, the archetypal Italian Mamma, dark, voluptuous and vociferous, catered for the local Italian community who knew all about the excellence of her food and was not interested in other business. So when Eric braved the barrage of dubious smells mingling in the doorway he was not greeted with much warmth by the crowd of Italians on the humid inside, who regarded it as their private club. Eric returned frequently because the food was delicious and cheap; usually Lydia and Greg were with him. Rosa took a great shine to Eric and would ruffle his hair saying "Buono raggazzo" as he devoured the "piccola qualcosa" she gave him to sample. Greg called Eric "Mother bait" because of his ability to bring out the maternal qualities in most women.

A few of the regulars greeted Greg and Lydia now and Rosa shouted, 'Where's my Buono Raggazzo, issa not dais and dais I see him?' Greg nodded towards Lydia to supply the answer but she gave him an entreating grimace, so he said, 'Away, Rosa. Now what's good and the cheapest tonight?'

As usual that turned out to be spaghetti.

The only help that Rosa had was a thin, yellow-skinned girl, and that was not very often, so the regulars helped themselves to carafes of wine, glasses and bread from the counter which made the atmosphere that of a large family kitchen.

Greg brought a carafe of red and two glasses to the table. 'Go on, drink it up.'

Lydia did and wrinkled her nose at the vinegary taste before she could stop herself; she was surprised at how she had become accustomed to Ben's fine clarets without paying them much attention at the time.

'Not good enough for you? So sorry.' Again Greg checked himself and went on more gently, 'I hope the wine and food will help you to make a little more sense, I really would like to know what's been going on with you.'

Gradually Lydia told him about re-meeting Ben, how at first she had felt sorry for him and oddly responsible, but when she tried to explain the change from that to the irrepressible need to see him, touch him and be with him at any, but any, cost, she gave up, shrugged, shook her head and sucked hard inside her trembling, down-turning mouth to stop the tears. Greg filled her glass and coaxed more, but away from the hard part to the general, like where had she actually been? Then he found he had to draw her away from describing the sea, that too dried her of adjectives and brought about the quivering lip and shaking head. He tried the people, the names she had mentioned, 'Just how many women did he have down there anyway?' Slowly, slowly he unravelled the garble to something near the truth; but Lydia was sure Greg did not understand because if he did he would not just sit there detached but interested like a surgeon looking at someone's steaming intestines; and he did not see that somehow Ben would come back to her, that this was something that would never be over, and now Greg's expression was set, warning her not to try to explain more. He rose and picked up the empty carafe.

'Sounds like a right shit to me,' Greg said.

Lydia sank back in her chair dumbstruck and watched his athletic figure move across to the counter and pick up another carafe. What had he been listening to, what had she been saying that Greg could possibly think Ben was anything but tragic, a man trapped amidst desires and responsibilities?

'Hi, Gino, how's that lovely wife of yours?' he asked a man playing backgammon.

How could he talk to anyone else, how could he chat like that when he had just heard about her love, her passion, the greatness and the awfulness of what had happened to her? Remorse rushed in. In telling Greg she had cheapened her experience and not lessened the pain; he just saw it as a sordid and silly affair. Lydia felt no one except Ben would ever understand her again. Right then she started to nurture a conviction based on desperation that Ben would find her, sometime when he was ready he would find her. If she could not believe that there was nothing else to live for.

When Greg sat down she had decided to be dignified and reticent. He was not going to get anything else out of her. But it was too late. His pale blue eyes fixed her as she filled her own glass.

'I know passion, Little Thing, and it's a blind alley. No matter how many times you go up thrilled and hot, it's the same cool, dreary way back.'

She would not be drawn. He doesn't know. He doesn't understand.

Greg carefully studied the little balls of bread he had been rolling about under his fingers. He spoke slowly, 'You know, in everything you've said you have not once mentioned Eric: not that you worried about him, not that you thought of him at all. Yet now that this Ben chap has chucked you, you've come back quick enough.'

Lydia shut her eyes and her head reeled. She only opened them when she thought Greg had finished but as soon as she did he banged down his fingertips with the little pieces of bread still sticking to them and put his face close to hers.

'You're a cheat, Lydia. A first-rate bitch. I see now that you didn't think of Eric at all, all you thought about was your nasty little affair with an old man. And what can the attraction be, eh? Just want to be the most beautiful in the bed? Eric too much of a man for you? Well if he was then he wouldn't be now. I stayed with him and listened to the "She's just late", "She must have spent the night with a friend", "She must have had an accident." I listened to his excuses for you getting weaker and weaker. I went with him round the police stations and the hospitals, where the men we spoke to knew, just as I did and just as he did, that accident wasn't the answer but that his girl had simply left him. All of the second night after you left we trailed round the clanking corridors of those places waiting for the off-hand attendants to look up a name and, unasked, Eric would try to describe you; "She's beautiful, small, very fair. Quiet." He should have said, "skinny, mousy, deceptive". How long was it all going on before Eric knew? How many others have there been? Before he could bring himself to face what he knew all along was the truth we had to go through the business of getting a friend to print up some cheap stickers with your photograph. "Have you seen this girl?" He posted those about here until he was warned off by a policeman; "there were proper channels," they said. Doesn't sound like rational behaviour, does it? Well, it wasn't. He was crazy. Crazy for love of you, crazy for loss of you. Driven mad by your duplicity. I held his poor head while he cried and cried like a child. Yes, you picture it, his face contorted and swollen from misery caused by you.

'Little vulnerable Lydia, so kind, so quiet, so ... so ... so ... you make me sick. And do you want to know a strange reason why I care so much? Not only for what you did to my friend but because you smashed my dreams too. You and Eric represented something I didn't really believe existed, except that you were both there together to prove it: that a man and a woman can live together in kindness and peace. That is something I know I'll never have. I'm too randy, unreliable and irresponsible; that's why I only go for married women, far easier, they don't turn round and bite. But you and Eric seemed to prove me wrong, my contentment came from being near your lives. That marriage you so carelessly chucked was mine too, in a way. My fantasy; and there is something you don't seem to understand, you are, we all are, no more than the fantasies others project upon us and if you betray those fantasies you cease to exist. For Eric and for me, for the world you lived in two months ago, you are dead.

'It took a month before Eric could face the truth, that you had left of your own free will, that you were a two-timing liar, that you were not the little girl to whom things happened, but a subtle, deceitful schemer who made things happen; who picked her man, picked her moment and left.'

Nobody had ever spoken to Lydia like that. Most of the hard words she missed because she chose to and she was fascinated by Greg's reaction; he was physically upset and she was the one to have caused that. What she had vaguely heard him saying about Eric passed like third-hand gossip; she knew about Eric, what he had felt, even better than Greg the Witness; Eric's suffering was inside her with her own. Her capacity for pain was replete; there was nothing Greg could say or do to hurt her more and she found something to build upon from what he said: she was not the little girl to whom things happened, she made things happen. And if that was true she could do it again.

Greg was watching her, but instead of confused explanations, the excuses he expected, he saw only composure settling about her features. Good God, she was smiling. This Lydia was quite a different person from the one he had sat down with. Despite himself, Greg began to feel some admiration and curiosity about her.

'I've said too much, it's not my concern. And besides, what you did to disillusion Eric and me doesn't make you evil, it just makes you average.' He left the table to pay.

Lydia had drunk a lot and was feeling good, toying with the idea of being a manipulator; of the old Lydia being dead. She had never cared particularly for the old Lydia anyway. Suddenly life seemed funny and very easy. Seeing Greg leaning against the counter and talking to Rosa she thought that in spite of his red hair, never an attractive thing in a man, he was really quite sexy; it must have always been obvious but she had never thought of him like that before, she had always related to him as Eric's other half; this was like meeting a stranger.

Greg knew she was watching and opened himself to display. There he is, angular, hard-looking, all balls and blue jeans, worn white at the knees and on the mount to the left of his groin: now that, surely, had been helped with a little Ajax, just to discreetly advertise the scale of his imprisoned pudenda.

Lydia laughed to herself, finished her wine and let Greg see her studying, smiling. Yes, it felt very good to be dead, nothing to live up to. No allegiances. And she was not surprised when, as they walked back to the flat, he slipped his hand round the back of her neck. Anyway he had often put his arm around her, but when Eric had been there, this was different; the neck is a very private place. His long thin fingers moved on her throat, caressingly, the thumb pressing lightly on the deadly area, soft, penetrable, behind her ear. As they approached the house the gentle hand was also guiding her, surely, up the stairs, through the door.

Well, why not? Lydia the Manipulator. The old Lydia dead, long live Lydia.

Greg went straight into the bathroom; at least the water still worked. Standing in the shadowed sitting-room Lydia had moments of clarity mixed with the release of drunkenness. During the clarity she tried to decide whether to curl up in a corner with the pillow and one blanket or just to lie down on the mattress and pretend to be asleep; he couldn't really want to, could he? But in the warm, drifting euphoria that followed the clarity she thought why pretend anything? She'd show them. She'd surprise them. Who? Oh, all of them. One in the eye for Ben.

The noise of the flushing cistern exploded through the empty rooms. She would have to make up her mind quickly because Greg would soon be out and there would be no diversions like coffee, records, or talk even. They had nothing more to say to each other, that was certain. Therefore she couldn't possibly … in a wave of nausea she thought of that hard body against hers. She would leave, go anywhere. Go to Ben's house, maybe he would be back by now, waiting for her. Too late. There was a movement in the doorway behind her.

Lydia stood as firmly as the wine would let her, pretending to look at the blackened houses over the street. Nothing happened. All was quiet. So he had gone to the other room after all. Left her. Not even said 'goodnight'. Well, what did you expect? What makes you so suddenly desirable? Maybe the old Lydia is not so dead. Vaguely disappointed, depressed, she reached to pull the shutter and from the corner of her eye she saw she was not alone after all.

Greg stood naked in the doorway, his head and beard haloed gold by the lights of a passing car, with his arms stretched wide above him hanging onto the door-frame, one leg falling slightly over the other, he hung there like a ginger Jesus. He held the pose long enough to see Lydia rock back crashing the shutter and putting her hand to her mouth in prim amazement. Now everything she did was seductive. The way she pushed her hair from her face, pulled her coat around her and retreated blindly backwards into the corner; all seemed to be invitation. She tried to think of something mundane to say to break the silence, spoil the scene, but could only manage a cough and that came out as a quivering groan loaded with promise.

Greg brought his arms down and advanced, leonine, upon her; slowly, slowly, pausing in the parallels of light cast from street lamps, in order for her to see clearly, closer, how well he was made. The division of muscles on his stomach were as clearly defined as a Michelangelo anatomical study; his arms and legs the same. And gradually rising away from its fleshy couch with an intent of its own, his penis came first towards her.

Lydia felt earthbound and unequal to this kind of approach. She was clothed and should feel safe, but he was using his nakedness like a weapon. The whole pantomime was silly but frightening. Still she was thrashing about in her mind for some way she could leave. If only she could slip past and out of the door; leave him and his preposterous penis standing there.

Greg reached out one hand, touched her mouth at arm's length, went past her mouth, over her cheek and threaded his fingers through her hair. All very objective, very cool. An arm apart, side-stepping with ponderous grace he was guiding her again not towards him but towards the mattress; Greg's bare feet brushing the gritty floor, Lydia's shoes clonking and tripping.

It was not her, with the tatty green coat and pigeon toes, who was exciting him, it was his own nakedness before her. Lydia was no longer wondering how to leave, there was no way out, but how to equalize the situation and salvage a little dignity. If he was going to have her, she was going to have him, she was not just going to be the honoured vessel for this Narcissist. But thoughts were all very well, he had already eased her onto the mattress and was now kneeling astride her undoing buttons and zips and folding the clothes with fastidious concentration and a damnable I-knew-it smile.

Her humiliation by this one-sided disrobing, this passive rape, the way she kept snatching back clothes he had removed from her, which, shaking his head and tutting, Greg gently, firmly, took from her hands again and placed out of reach, was really quite delightful; and thank goodness she's not saying anything, they usually start to gabble at this point, trying to pretend it's not happening. How soon will she start to cry? Certainly after; maybe during.

But while he was removing her pullover and she was struggling with it over her arms and head, Lydia suddenly remembered who it was who had called her 'spineless'. She tore off the pullover and threw it away, narrowing her eyes on his pale blue ones. She undid her brassiere and threw that away too. Greg watched it sail through the air with his jaw sagging. When he looked back Lydia still fixed him with her eyes. She lay back, her arms above her head, and stretched sinuously. Blast him for his "spineless". Blast them all. Through half-closed eyes Lydia could see Greg still above her, but bewildered, unmoving; almost unmoving: that dreadful old cock of his was sinking.

From her lying position she reached out and took it into her palm. What was it Ben had said? "Not like that, it's not a cricket bat. Like that." Oh, yes, like that. Look at him. Greg was falling slowly into a crouching position, with head back, his fleshy lips parted in their gingery scrub as he breathed sharply in. Without releasing him Lydia raised herself and watched his hands on her forearms moving as if to stop her but unable to. He was tossing his head from side to side. How fascinating; he had become quite weak. Without the common commerce of love-making: kiss for kiss, touch for touch, a mutual advance on the erogenous zones, it was possible to see what was happening. All Lydia's previous experiences, even through the years with Eric had been muddled with emotions,

tenderness, concern. What she had done on those occasions, or
what had been done to her, was part of a maze, unseeing,
unthinking, just feeling. With almost childlike absorption (how
fast the fly walks without his wings) she guided him into her,
and it was her guiding hand this time, on his neck that drew
him down. He thrust only a couple of times before he came
and collapsed. No time to feel, to be transported. And *he* called
her spineless.

Greg moved off and lay on his stomach, facing away from
her; Lydia stayed stretched out with her arms under her head,
musing. Nothing seemed to hurt any more: she could see the
picture of herself leaving Coalbarn, with Ben standing by the
gate shouting something she could not hear; of him and
Nathalie talking and laughing, quietly, secretly. Hundreds of
little scenes conjured themselves and she thought possibly she
might have hurt the people in those scenes just a little bit,
made some impact. That was a comfort.

In silence Greg went to the bathroom from where Lydia
could hear the gurglings of his copious ablutions; the only
abuse he could think of. When he returned he lay down beside
her and, miraculously on that narrow mattress, allowed not the
merest whisper of flesh against hers.

'Well, Little Thing,' he said, 'well, well, well. Who'd have
thought it? Quite a little siren, aren't you? Bet you raised that
old man's blood pressure a notch or two. I wasn't at my best of
course. You probably couldn't tell, but it wasn't my usual
performance at all. I was a bit taken aback by your aggressive
approach. I'm going to sleep now, but I'll probably wake you
later.'

Finished, tired, lost, Lydia slept too; the deep, indulgent,
dreamless sleep of the hopeless for whom the last respite is a
snatch of oblivion.

Sun streamed through the tall window searching the room,
empty but for Lydia sitting wrapped in blankets with her back
against the wall, depressed by the joy of the bright day. No sign
of Greg. She shuffled round the flat and into those other three
rooms, which averted their familiar faces, showing only big,
bare proportions. No clothes for her in the bedroom, no
flannel or toothbrush in the bathroom. Everything that had

ever belonged to her was gone. She went back to the sitting-room and harvested her scattered clothes. When she picked up her knickers she found a ten-pound note and a scrap of paper inside. Scribbled on the paper was: "Knew you'd come to these first; they always do. Couldn't wait, got a lot of surviving to do. Hope the bread will help. Good luck ... Goodbye. P.S. If you *really* have nowhere to go then try the "Atlantic", 42 Spring Street, behind Victoria Station."

Greg's tenner compared very well with Ben's fifty pounds. It was an uncalculated extravagance. Lydia was moved and thought, only for a moment though, that they might have had something more to say to each other.

A waft of last night's bitter humour drifted through her and she laughed as she thought that all this washing after sex, and now money on departure from two men, was not really very flattering, but interesting. Her, a prostitute, of all people? Well, anything is possible.

She did not belong here any more. It was not hard to shut the door behind her on three years, Eric, and perhaps even more than that, on a whole way of life she had known. She was emotionally and materially destitute.

The bank clerk looked troubled when Lydia asked for a new cheque book. He looked through several lists and drawers, then excused himself from Lydia and the impatient queue rapidly forming behind her. Another man appeared on her side of the counter and ushered her into the Manager's office.

All smiles and conciliation, the Manager noted Lydia's scruffy appearance from his side of a wide desk. He half raised himself from his chair as she walked in, then decided any more effort would be wasted and directed her to a chair sufficiently far to give him a full view of her.

'Now then, the point is that your joint account with Mr Evans was closed down. Didn't he tell you?'

'No, he didn't. He couldn't. But some of that money was mine. I earned it.'

'Well, I'm afraid this is not the first time we have had this situation. The point is that you were jointly and severally responsible. Do you know what that means? It means it is quite possible for him to close the account without your signature. I did explain that when you both applied for the account.'

'Yes of course I know what it means but some of the money was mine. I earned it,' she said again in futile desperation.

'May I ask a personal question? ...Thank you. How can I put it? Are you both? ... That is to say ... Are you still living together? ... I thought that.' Lydia's head was shaking the negative but with a determination that made the Manager nervous. On and on she went shaking and shaking; her whole body taking up the rhythm of the endless "No". 'Of course there is nothing to stop you opening an account of your own.' His eyes scanned again the coat, the stockings laddered at the knees, the scuffed shoes. 'Do you, by any chance, have an income; a private one? Do you have a job? Well, where are you living at the moment? ...' Her body went on shaking the "No". 'I see, I see ...' And seeing a little more than "signatures" and "severally" he pushed a large silver cigarette box towards her, 'Would you like a ...?' She was tempted to take the box and leave him the cigarettes. 'Do you mind if I do?' he said. He seemed to relax with his cigarette and began to show a genuine concern. 'Now let's look at the situation carefully. Do you have relatives nearby? What about further afield? None?'

She was not going to tell him about Uncle Will and Aunt May at Hatch End and their dreary, bookish daughter who was a wizard at orienteering; she had not spoken to them since the disastrous time she spent with them after her parents were killed.

'Very well, then, what have we? No relatives, no job, no capital, no home ... Are you all right? You look very pale. You know your health is vital at this moment, it is the only thing ... Good grief.' The Manager strode to the door and flung it open.

'Mr Watkins. Come in here and bring Mrs Price. This lady has fainted.'

Lydia came to moments later cradled in blue pin-stripe smelling of nicotine. Gloriously for a second she thought it was Ben and looked up smiling, to be dashed by the kind, concerned face of the Bank Manager.

'Water, Mrs Price, the water ... There, there, my dear,' he said, and added as an aside to the others who had entered, 'By God, I'd like to get my hands on that young chap. She's no more than a child.' Shortly afterwards he was saying to Lydia, 'Well, if you're quite sure there is nothing more ... perhaps some hot, sweet tea before you leave ...? Or if there is any way I can be of assistance in the future ... You understand I can't take liberties with my position, but in some other way ... Go carefully then.'

* * *

A breeze drifted through the open window of the car. Ben's eyes travelled his palm as he spoke, following the path of some imaginary insect there, diffusing his words.

'... We flew to Moscow but straight away went by train to Leningrad. I was depressed from the first moment. I loathed the colour of the sky, the atmosphere. Actually, occasionally, late at night in some private corner of a public place you'd catch the true nature of the Russians, but the awful suppression was dominant, emphasized by sleeve pulling in the street, the whispered bargain at any corner. Natta was unperturbed by it all; she was radiant and enthusiastic and I tried to believe it was to do with being in the country of her ancestors. She was fascinated by the collection in the Winter Palace and wanted endlessly to return. Somehow, whenever we were there she'd be rooms ahead of me and instead of looking at the pictures I'd end up looking for her; then she would materialize behind me.

'I remember the whole of Russia as a search for Natta. She never seemed to be with me, always just ahead or just behind, but when she was no anger was possible because, more than ever before, she was my engaging, fascinating, only Natta.

'When we went back to Moscow we stayed in the Rossia. A truly horrific hotel with four Celcon block wings and something like four thousand rooms, I believe. Dragon-like women sat at desks at the beginning and end of each passage. Natta started the lift nonsense again, but this time I was more than angry. Those lifts often became stuck, sometimes for several hours before they were released; and what's more, it seemed that, in spite of the floor-dragons, loonies wandered the passages at will. We gave up eating out because the waiting in restaurants was intolerable. We bought food to eat in our room, but, no sooner than she'd finish, Natta would jump up and say, "See you in the Press Bar." I was so damned exhausted and depressed that I would sleep; keeping up with her was beginning to be too much for me. But while I slept I'd have terrible dreams of losing her, of seeing her with someone else and I'd wake in a rage. I'd make the trek to the Press Bar. There was a film festival going on at the time and the hotel had rigged up a nasty and comfortless bar in the hotel guessing, I suppose, that the flamboyant and arty Westerners, rather than enjoying what was to be enjoyed in Moscow, would tediously and incestuously seek their own company. Judging by the cramped conditions in the Press Bar the Russians were right in their assumption.

'I'd stand for ages at the doors to the small room watching the jostling, smoke-wrapped crowd, hoping she'd see me; I stood nearly head and shoulders above most of them. It didn't occur to me that that could be a disadvantage. Even moving through that crowd I never found her first, she always found me. She would grab my hand round the back of some verbose bulk and pull herself into my side, her bright eyes filled with pleasure. I'd ask her who she had been talking to, but she said no one. And when she put her head against my shoulder, as she always did at those moments, it was beyond me to enquire any further, though I was miserable past belief.

'The stay in Moscow seemed interminable and she was beginning to control our movements; I spent more and more time sulking and desperate in our room while she was off somewhere in the city. Blast my stupidity, but my mind has never functioned well in unhappiness. I couldn't think clearly. In the end it was her who decided to leave. That made me happy, but something about the decision put me on my guard. On the afternoon when we were passing time in the hotel waiting to leave for the airport she was bad tempered and impatient to go. Such a change. She went out of the room saying she wanted to see the floor-dragon who she'd been practising her Russian on. I gave her some minutes, then followed. I passed the favoured floor-dragon and there was no sign of Natta. I walked on down the still, airless, afternoon passage and at the corner I heard voices. There were two at first, then only Natta's. I didn't catch her last words, but she gave that cough of disgust. (You remember, Lyd, how she used to do it; a sort of guttural thing. In anyone else it would have been repulsive, but she'd an odd way of making funny habits like that seductive. Did you ever notice?) Just then I turned the corner and a door near to where she was standing slammed; just before it did, however, I swear to God I saw something black flap around the bottom of the door. But I was so tired, had had so many bad dreams, that I was beyond fighting her. She told me a stranger had been rude to her, but her manner was very bitter for such a trivial thing.

'I'd already started to plan a return to England, but she wouldn't hear of it, so we agreed on Italy. I'd wanted to go there from the start and it seemed that things were to be my way again.

'Where were you at that time, Lyd? Were you already in that comfortable little house; had you forgotten me so soon? Is that really where you want to be forever? ...'

An isolated raindrop plummeted against the windscreen; a long pause, then another followed, and another, until rain fell unceasing. Ben reached for the ignition.

'Don't move the car.' Lydia struggled for the door handle, he pulled at her arm.

'I only want to close the windows.' Without releasing her he pressed two buttons simultaneously, the windows rose with a whine, clamped shut. There was a finality in the sound, sealing them from the world misted to oblivion by rain. 'There,' he said, withdrawing his hand from her arm. 'Do you really want to go?'

11

Lydia walked away from the bank as quickly as her weak legs would let her and turned into a back street where, ejected from the back doors of several restaurants, rank garbage lay rotting. She counted the money left in her pocket: twenty-three pounds and some change; and the sun insisted on shining. In the air with the pungent smell of the refuse was something else. There now, it is not nonsense to talk of the scents of the changing seasons; this was spring, very early, very weak, but nevertheless ...

The need to go on and find somewhere to at least spend the night was a good thing; she understood what Greg had written about having a lot of surviving to do. It keeps your mind off the unalterable. But even just surviving has its quiet moments when thoughts insist on pushing through the cloudy mind; for instance, as she sat on the top of a bus going to Victoria Station in search of Spring Street, with a sort of gasp (nothing that showed, an inside thing from the part of her that watched the patterns her life made), she felt that she was free-falling through life: no aim, no place, no people of her own. It came in one of those fleeting moments of clarity when the reason, or lack of it, for existence seems obvious. But it passed, as it had to, because of the impossibility of living with that kind of understanding.

The area the bus brought her to was a running sore of architecture and mankind. The houses were mostly of two types; some temporarily constructed for the men who built the railway, but somehow, unlike those men, not discreetly disappearing in dust; others: the massive, blackened, barred and red-brick poor houses and asylums as dominant and permanent as the afflictions they were built to house.

It was near here Lydia found Spring Street, lapping at the hem of the suddenly silent streets of pied-à-terres, politicians and Parliament. The Atlantic Hotel was pressed between a greengrocer (still displaying his fruit in the old-fashioned way on a stall covered with green straw matting outside the shop) and a surgical stores as far from antiseptic as it is possible to be; the curious, various, pink shapes like tactile blancmanges in a rubbery sulk, crooking latex fingers through the window at the unmentionable desires of any furtive passer-by; and these things all hung about with faded leaflets bearing tiles like 'Catholicism and Contraception', 'God and Homosexuality'.

Several letters of the neon sign had failed leaving 'The A   ntic H el'. Lydia stood for a moment, assessing the remaining letters, smiled and thought, 'Well, of course ...'. She went up the single, steep step and inside, where it was dark, smelly and overpoweringly hot. The smell was nothing in particular: bodies and still air. When her eyes became accustomed Lydia saw a brown passage with several doors leading off it.

Someone walked in the room above her and instinctively she looked up to the ceiling with its sepia swirls left behind after a bath once overflowed.

When she looked down there was a fat man standing at the end of the passage who had probably been observing her from the moment she entered; he was no taller than she was, wearing a white, short-sleeved shirt and grey trousers caught by a thin belt high on the top slope of his massive belly. Without a word he approached her rocking his weight from side to side, his tiny feet encased in startlingly white socks and character shoes: soft, black shoes with a strap and button as worn by dancers and clowns. When the point of his belly was nearly touching Lydia he looked into her eyes, his head moving on his neck in the puppetish action of oriental dancers. His receding hair was cut to a close cap about his head; his lymphatic flesh betrayed no sign of age but his popping, hurt, brown eyes showed the infinite tolerance of the grotesqueries of mankind, learnt after many years.

'I've got one,' he said in a thin, castrated voice, 'a room. Come with me.' Lydia followed his surprisingly springing step up the stairs. On the second flight he began to slow and dragged air with difficulty through his slack throat.

'You see, I know you're not a visitor. No one has visitors here. There are customers for some of the rooms, but not visitors. Who told you? ... Oh, Greg ... Greg ...' he said, and coughed a little laugh turning round to look at her and draw a conclusion.

Two flights more brought them to the top floor and three more closed doors. Fat Man pushed the door at the back of the house and walked in letting the door close behind him. He re-opened the door to see Lydia still standing politely on the landing.

'Do you want it?' he said with his head on one side like a bird adjusting its view. Surely he did just mean the room?

He had already turned on the light which hung naked (inevitably) from centre ceiling. There was a low, narrow bed with a striped mattress and some grey blankets, ochre coloured lino and a cracked basin sagging away from the wall; a chair, a table, a small, filthy window, and a soot-caked skylight in the attic roof.

Fat Man walked around the room as though he had never seen it before. When he had finished he said, 'It's two pounds a night. Here's the key.' He took it from the hunched mantelpiece above the gas fire and handed it to Lydia. The people who came here were not ones who chose. His soft shoes hissing on the erupting lino, he crossed the room and said, before shutting the door behind him, 'I'm Glynne and it's all mine. This house. My Auntie left it ... to me.' His eyebrows flicked up convulsively as though still surprised by this truth.

Lydia lay down on the dirty bed and slept. Sometime during the afternoon she awoke and went to the cracked basin to be sick, but slept again afterwards. That day was over.

Other days came and went too; there was no pattern to them and yet no disorder. Lydia was living a step behind time, not eating, not washing; nothing took her attention; her only exercise was from her bed to the basin to drink from the trickling and coughing tap, or to the window, where, unsure of the time of day, she saw a senselessly busy world.

Once, however, something did take her attention: it could have been midnight or early evening when she heard heavy, loud footsteps coming up the stairs; for some reason they had woken her, it was certainly not Glynne. The footsteps came nearer until they stopped by her door, blocking the light shining through the crack into her darkened room. Lydia held her breath until they moved away and somewhere very near she heard a key slotted and turned.

When she next awoke she heard the gratey notes of sparrows and with difficulty opened the skylight. The sun that flooded in was stunning, and Lydia felt restored. Not restored to what she had been, but there seemed to be a little strength in her, some dismal determination, the flickering of continuity. She sat on the bed again trying to decide what to do; she had no other clothes and no money. Eric had taken all her possessions with him, including her pass-book for her Building Society savings, she had three hundred pounds there. She decided to go to the Building Society and explain that she had lost her book, and the procedure turned out to be quite easy; all they wanted was a few signatures from Lydia on several different pieces of paper, and time; 'Only ten days or so,' the woman told her, thanking God as she said it that she did not need money as badly as this sick-looking girl before her.

Back at the Antic Lydia ventured down the passage to find Glynne. At the end of the passage there was a door to the right with no number. She knocked softly, then a little harder; when she pushed it there was a rush of warm, damp air from the steps stretching downwards into pitch darkness. She was about to shut it when a light went on below.

'Yes?' It was Glynne's voice. His face appeared at the bottom of the stone steps with the glutinous quality of a maggot. 'It's you.' He said it as though she needed confirmation of who she was. 'Come on, then, come down,' he coaxed. She descended slowly while he moved about turning on lamps and electric fires. Corner by corner a large cellar was illuminated. It was crammed with furniture and had brilliant nylon rugs all over the concrete floor. It looked like a saleroom, except that everything was polished, cared for and arranged in some domestic order.

Glynne walked about the room with the same interest he had shown in Lydia's. A frown puckered his forehead and he said, 'This is where I live. I don't turn lights on unless I have something to do, or visitors. I'm not mean, I don't mind paying, but I don't like to see myself. If the light is on I keep seeing my hands.' He spread the fat little fingers in the air without looking at them as if the sight was enough to explain to Lydia, 'and other parts.' He flicked his hands impatiently downwards. 'But I keep it nice though and sometimes this room is full of visitors,' his anxiousness made it seem unlikely. 'But you're not visiting, what do you want?'

He was fascinated and enthused by the idea of Lydia cleaning her room; not a popular pastime with other tenants. He gathered a profusion of cleaning materials and said he would help her. He excused himself and went behind a curtain which billowed and bumped as he changed into huge overalls.

'I don't like to have my real clothes dirty.' But he had not removed the white socks and character shoes.

After an hour Lydia's room was greatly improved. The hardest and most effective part was cleaning the window: now daylight came in freely and the electric light could be switched off.

As he was leaving, puffed and flushed, Glynne looked at the bed. 'They don't all bother with sheets but I think you are the type who would like to. I know types. I was in the theatre once.' He considered for a while and said in a childish whine, 'I hate people in my sheets,' and then in a flurry of good nature, 'but I'll let you. They're percale, percale's nice. Very expensive.'

He brought the sheets up later in the day and found Lydia asleep. He covered her with the blankets and left the sheets on a chair. She did not even hear the door closing as his tiny feet tiptoed out under their fat load. She did wake up later, however, when the footsteps, those other footsteps, stopped again outside her room.

Curiously Lydia had never seen anyone else who lived in the house. She had heard them: someone below talking long and indistinctly into the night, apparently to himself because an answer never came; the slams, bangs and bumps of solitary people moving in solitary rooms. And those footsteps. The tenants went in and out at odd times. There was no 8 a.m. exodus to the rushing outside world; no 6 o'clock slamming as they returned; the people here had somehow slipped beyond the tracks trammelled by the busy, the belonging. When they

moved it was often during the night or in the too early morning
and always slowly, incurious about each other, worn down by
their own twilight destinies. She knew it was a woman in the
room one away from her own because Lydia had heard her
Glaswegian accent shouting down the stairs to Glynne, 'Jis tull
Tuoosday. Gimme tull then.'

After ten days Lydia returned to the Building Society and
collected her money. On the way back to her room she bought
herself a blue cotton dress printed with flowers, a plant and
some food, including a large quantity of corned beef; something she had always hated until now. She also bought an old
tea-set from a junk shop near the Antic.

She felt so happy at having possessions once more that when
she reached her room she stood on a chair under the skylight
and gave the sparrows an extravagant feast of bread and corned
beef.

Now there was only one excuse not to take a job and so admit
that this dismal world was the only one she had; only one
excuse, to wait for her past to reach out and touch her again, or
more precisely, Ben: she was becoming ill. The inside of the
cracked basin with its brownish-green gulleys below the ever-
dripping taps was now more familiar than her own face because
of the hours she had spent hanging her head over it. She hardly
knew the face she saw when she bothered to look in the mirror;
white and drawn from all the fainting and the weight loss.

Perhaps instead of thinking about a job, another sleep, just a
little one. She pushed the new dress onto the floor and lay on the
bed, cold but too weak to climb between the covers.

Some hours later in the evening her burning body woke her
up. The fever came over her in waves. She knew when it was
coming because her hearing and eyesight faded as she
descended into semi-consciousness. At moments she was like a
worm curled deep inside her sick body, she could see and touch
her scalding inside; at other times she would be looking down at
herself writhing on the bed. She was terribly cold and terribly
hot, quite delirious and then quite lucid. Nothing was constant
and the floor was not reliable, it kept falling away when she put
her feet towards it, and the cracked basin had retreated down the
suddenly elongated room. Everything was distant and dispro-
portioned.

Something was pulling her attention, however; something very far away on the other side of the room, on the other side of the door, was not right. As she stared at the crack along the bottom of the door the room concertinaed into its natural dimension. The rushing sound she was hearing subsided and she lay cold, wrung-out, listening to those footsteps coming up the stairs and stopping outside her door. There they were, shifting outside, listening to her inside.

Lydia staggered across the room and pressed her ear to the door. She heard cracking noises, unmistakably finger joints. She was going to end this menacing. She was going to face once and for all this probably violent lunatic inmate of the Antic. He might quite quickly, noiselessly finish her off; there could be some masochistic pleasure in it, and even if it was awful and did hurt; even if it was sordid and bloody he would be kind, relieving her of dreary survival.

She swung the door open, steadying herself on the door-handle dazed by the effort and what she saw: Eric, with hands clasped behind him and head hung. They stood for a long time, Lydia aghast and Eric quite still but for occasionally raising his eyes from the floor to Lydia and back. It had to be part of her delirium and when he said, stammering a little, 'Actually I didn't knock. How did you know ...?' She looked down at his offending feet, big with new brown brogue shoes and thought of course that that footfall would have woken her from any sleep; hadn't she, after all, been expecting it? This illusion of Eric looked down too. 'Oh I see ...' and rubbed clenched fists together, (isn't that just what he would have done?). 'Sorry. Noisy as ever,' (and said?). Lydia staggered backwards to her bed and fell upon it. Without her there to hold it open the door began to close. There was a shuffling outside the door and then a voice near her, 'Did you mean me to go away? I just thought we might talk ... but I do see I might be a bit of a shock for you ... sort of ...' He frowned and bit his lip as though considering whether describing himself as a "shock to her" might sound a little immodest. Lydia was fascinated. She tried to lift her arm to touch him but could no longer move and her vision was dimming. If he had been real he would have seen all this. He eased himself onto the edge of the seedy armchair facing Lydia's bed, hands forced between his knees, and looked about. 'I know it's not fair of me coming in like this but I wouldn't have if you hadn't opened the door. I wasn't going to knock. I've been watching you for a while ... not spying, honestly ...' Lydia felt another wave of nausea and fever coming, then she knew that this Eric was part of her delirium, how else, why else would he be here? It was the killer she had expected and her conscience had supplied the face of the one who would be justified in that act. And still he talked on, only now it was becoming a stranger's voice. Lydia said, 'If you're not going to kill me you might as well go,' but he didn't seem to hear and went on talking, '... and the first thing ... were singing ... you ... had to be ... each time to hear ...' The voice came and went without end. '... You're not, are you? What's the matter?' She felt his large, plump hand on her forehead. 'No, don't get up. You mustn't, you're not well. Oh, I see ... Sorry.'

Lydia reeled past him to the basin and while she was retching she felt the plump hand again on her forehead holding her just the way her mother had when she was very small and she leant against it in the way she used to then.

Lydia did not remember returning to the bed or that Eric was leaving, but in the brief moments that she was conscious he was always there, and once there was someone else: tall, distinguished-looking with a stethoscope round his neck.

'Awake now? That's better. Take this. Here, I'll help you.' The doctor held her in the crook of his arm while he pushed a pill between her dry lips and helped her to drink from a glass. Someone had given her more pillows. She imagined Glynne's voice saying, "I hate people in my pillows." The doctor turned and said to two figures standing in the shadows at the back of the room, 'Excuse me. Would you mind leaving us again, just for a few minutes. If you wait on the landing I'll call you.' The two figures jostled each other in their haste to leave.

'There,' the door shut behind them, 'I thought you would rather hear what I have to say in private.' He was placing instruments into a shabby brown case as he talked. 'Now then,' he snapped it shut and put it on the floor, 'you have not been at all well, but we will soon have it under control. A nasty virus, but in the course of examining you I did establish that you are pregnant, possibly three months. Did you know that? Of course I'll take a sample of your urine, but I'm pretty certain or I wouldn't mention it. I don't know if this is good news for you ...' He glanced at the room and doubted it. What a respectable, well-fed face he had, sun-tanned. Must have been on holiday recently or gardening at his cottage in the Home Counties. That kind of security seemed unreal now. '... so you will have to take good care of yourself. Eat more. What have you to eat?' He went over to the cupboard beside the gas ring. 'Plenty of corned beef and nothing else. Shall I ask one of those gentlemen if they will be kind enough to buy you some fruit and have this prescription made up? I expect they will, they seem very concerned. You're lucky.'

Yes, wasn't she?

'I'll come in and see you on my rounds tomorrow and I'll collect your sample then. After that you will be out of the woods and you can join the antenatal clinic at my surgery on Wednesday evenings. Thank goodness for the Welfare State, eh? It would be as well to have a thorough examination for the baby's sake as well as your own. Goodbye for now.'

He was not going to get involved, he was going to look on the bright side and not ask awkward questions, and the sooner his wife's father coughed up the rest of the money for that partnership in Wimpole Street, the sooner he could leave these back alleys and the deadbeats in them. It wasn't that he didn't care, he cared too much, was overwhelmed by the apparent futility of his efforts. Hopeless, hopeless humanity.

* * *

Ben sat, forehead in palms, fingers clutching his hair. Drawing one leg beneath her Lydia turned, reaching across the wide panel separating the seats, touched his arm. Very gently she said, 'I had unhappiness too, Ben.'

He snatched her hand kissing it fervently, saying, 'I'm so sorry, so sorry, so sorry. My fault. Forgive. Let me make it all right again. Make it how it was.' Unable to retrieve her hand she saw her other go forward, watched it as it made to touch his hair. He raised his head catching her in the birth of that tender act. 'So you do. We do still, don't we?' Ben said.

She snatched back that recalcitrant hand, biting it hard.

'Finish, please. What of Natta and ... and her little boy, little Christian?'

'Yes, I'll finish then, Lyd.' He opened his hold on her and looked ahead dreaming through the viewless grey of the rain.

'... Natta stuck close to me while we stayed for a while at Lake Garda and close to me in Milan. I bought her some expensive couture clothes there; that was the first time she let me buy clothes for her. She looked much older in them, I didn't like it. She looked a bit ridiculous, really, but her new appearance made something easier in me. Wearing the clothes that I'd chosen subdued her somehow, and in part I regretted her compliance. She did all I asked of her and was rarely out of my sight. In Venice she was almost considerate to me and sometimes when we were walking she'd take my hand. She'd always been physical with her attentions, she'd this way of pushing her shoulder into that hollow of mine, or bowing her head onto my chest in mock contrition, she'd fling her arms about my neck. But never before had she made such a quietly loving act as taking my hand as she walked with me. It was then I realised the extent of her unhappiness. My poor little overdressed girl in her inappropriate couture clothes had finally lost our bantering battle of years standing. I suggested she went back to her jeans and leather jacket, but she wouldn't, simply went on wearing the couture stuff which was a constant reminder of my lapse in taste and judgement. I despaired of her courteous consideration of me.

'We drove slowly down the spine of that beautiful country and she began again that maddening business of kneeling on the passenger seat and scanning the road behind. But I didn't say anything; I no longer had the heart to shout at her because she no longer shouted back, just obeyed me. We stopped at a small town and sat under faded blue canvas in the market-square having lunch; it was drowsy, hot and tempting to stay. Natta asked if I thought we should stay. Only a month before she would have slammed her hand down on the table and said, "Here we stay, like it or not"; her eyes would have flashed at me, with the corners of her mouth turned down trying to control her laugh at the certain outburst her adamance would have produced in me. Even if it was the one place in the world I wanted to stay I would have said "no", just for the joy of a row and for the pleasure of having her win and always, afterwards, the passion that seemed to produce in her. And here she was now politely asking whether or not I thought we should stay. I watched her and judged she wanted to stay, so I said "No" quite quietly, hoping to raise a spark, but she simply said, "All right", rose from the table and crossed the square to the shoddy hotel on the other side. I don't think she dared risk the lavatory in the restaurant where we were, although the food was wonderful. The two things rarely go together in Italy.

'But, Lyd, when she came back she had quite altered, was much more like her old self. I spotted the difference as soon as she emerged from the hotel, her walk was different; her whole manner. She made the most lewd gesture to some young man who stuck his tongue out at her; his face was a picture of horror. I began to laugh. As she loped her way across the square, you remember her walk, Lyd, that sort of challenging walk that on any other female would have looked masculine? Well, now the ridiculous couture clothes looked more preposterous still on her and when she got back to the table she started to complain about them. Naturally, I told her they were marvellous, that they'd cost a fortune and I was damned if she'd take them off. She set up a promising grumble and said she thought we should stay; I decided that if she went on like this, by the time we reached Rome that evening she would really be back to normal, with enough provocation. So I insisted we left, paid quickly, and shoved her into the car.

'Back on the road she began the kneeling again and I told her to, for Chrissake, sit down properly. She gave a healthily vulgar response and began to complain about the clothes, still kneeling of course. I told her she'd bloody well keep the clothes on. "Oh, will I?" she said; and damn me the next time I looked round at her she was stark-naked and still kneeling. I screeched the car to a dangerous stop, purposely terrifying her. Her skirt, blouse, jacket and underclothes lay scattered on the road behind us, her shoes and handbag too. I got out and started to retrieve them, with Natta standing on the passenger seat blaspheming at me. I saw a black car a way behind us draw into a layby and I assumed it was to watch our farce and see better Natta's lovely body now standing on the boot of the car lambasting me with some choice Italian words (amazing what she'd picked up in the time). When I walked back to the car with the retrieved garments she had her suitcase out and was casting stuff everywhere in her search for her jeans, etcetera. Out it all came, finally: the jeans, a cream silk shirt, the beige boots, and the bloody jingling jacket again. She knew that was driving me crazy by then, so she put it on. The temperature was ninety-five in the shade and she insisted on putting it on, would you believe? Thank God, she was quite back to normal.

'My plan had been to reach Rome, but by the late afternoon we came to a pleasant enough place called Caserta. I could see she was ready to stop by then, so I said we should press on and after a pleasantly animated row we looked for a hotel.

'Lyd, do you believe I was mad to think we could have gone on for ever like that? I wanted to be like that then; I don't any more ... I could be calm now but for one thing, and that is what the poet called The Hound of Heaven. He's after me, Lyd.

'Please will you save me from madness, and forgive me for what I did to Natta?'

Dreading the sound of her own voice, the question itself, Lydia said, 'Why me to forgive?'

'Because she loved you too and always said how she wanted you to meet Christian. You're her friend, Lyd.'

'And what to forgive? Must I really know that? Because I don't think ...'

'Yes, you have to know it. I have to tell.'

12

A baby. How long since she had stopped thinking of it, wanting even? So predictable that it should be now and yet she had never once thought of it through all the sickness, fainting. But no, not yet, before Ben comes back. Before what? Oh come on. The subsidence of the fever had left cool reason, or the birth of that reason had caused the fever; whichever way, the girl who had been merely treading water until Ben's return was a stranger, a dreamer to grips with nothing. Forget the 'not now' nonsense because there was no one to turn to, to listen, to help.

It was bitterly amusing to think that she must have conceived on that first night at Coalbarn and that Ben's punctilious efforts to control himself, until she acquired some contraceptive pills, were all in vain; she had been carrying his baby all this time.

Lydia looked about the room. Her clothes were hanging on the hooks provided to do the job of a wardrobe; three daffodils, heartlessly cheery, stood in a yoghurt carton on the mantelpiece; a dirty towel was spread on the floor beside her bed with a plastic bowl upon it and, reddening, Lydia realised she was in a nightdress, not her own. She did not have one.

She was standing wondering, when there was a knock and the door opened. Lydia moved towards the bed and staggered. It was Eric who entered.

'Golly, you shouldn't be out, you know.' He rushed to support her and guide her and fussily tuck her in; then he sat, fists on knees, toes on point.

Lydia lay weak, looking at him, while he looked at his fingers. There seemed to be too much to say; silence was, on the whole, safer. But not for a moment did Lydia let her eyes leave him in case, during that release, he might disappear; she was still sufficiently weak not to trust her senses. Eric began to talk to his hands, raising his eyebrows, cocking his head, working his face in the way he would to any enthusiastic listener.

'I hope you didn't mind me tidying your room, only I felt I had to sit in, sort of, and it was something to do.' He looked round the room and waved an arm. 'Ermmm … I'm the hanging and straightening and the daffs, but Glynne's the bowl and towel. Mustn't take all the glory must I?' He spluttered a giggle. 'Listen, I shall go out now and get your prescription and the doctor said about fruit. Would you like me to …?' He looked at Lydia and she looked away.

'Yes … yes please … that would be very kind. There's some money in the purse over there.'

'I say, lots,' he said as he looked into the purse, seeing what was left of the three hundred.

'It's the Building Society. You know …' Lydia leant forward anxiously in the bed.

'Yes, yes of course it is,' he said without sarcasm, 'now you have a little sleep or something and I'll, ermmm …' He made his exit still muttering then reopened the door and threw in an afterthought. 'Oh, I forgot. In case you wondered about the nightie, it was me. Glynne bought it actually (I don't think I would have chosen quite that pink for you, not with the green bits on it anyway), but I put it on; you see your other clothes were in a bit of a mess. It's been two days since you … Glynne said he'd put it on but I thought … ermm … Oh golly.' He shut the door quickly.

When Eric returned he used his five-pence coins in the gas meter and burnt his fingers as he lit the fire; split baked beans between the tin and the saucepan; spurted orange zest in his eyes as he peeled one for Lydia, and she watched those familiar rounded shoulders in the familiar whiskery jacket and questions began to seem safe, so long as he did not turn to face her when he answered them. He did just once, but so violently did Lydia turn her face away from him that he stood, wooden spoon and saucepan in hand, staring at her while the understanding dawned that her face could betray a wound she could not bear him to see. After that he conscientiously avoided looking at her when he spoke.

'Why are you here, Eric? How did you know I was here?'

'I know you won't believe it, but I didn't know. I came here because I've nowhere else in London, someone else has got the flat now, and Dad's not been well ... at all. He's had a stroke, so I had to come down to see him and Greg told me about this place.'

'He told me about it too,' Lydia said.

'Well, I guessed that actually ... when I saw you. I was a bit cross at first, but now I think he meant well. I got the job, you know ... Oh yes, you did know that, didn't you?' He frowned and stared, abstracted at the floor, until with an effort he pulled himself up and continued, 'Actually it's a nice, quiet place with Sports Days, Prizegivings and wah-wah parents. I've moved into the house, too. Well, sort of anyway. Still a frightful mess.' He asked Lydia no questions at all but gave details about himself to fill in silences that occurred. It was much later when Lydia was entirely exhausted and wondering how to ask him to leave when Eric jumped to his feet before she had hardly begun the gentle request; she was as far as a hint, more with raised eyebrows and a smile, eyes carefully fixed upon the buttons of his jacket, 'Sorry, sorry. It's frightfully late. How selfish of me talking on like that. Boring. Sorry.' He came towards her and bent down. In a moment of horror Lydia thought he was going to kiss her, but he was arranging the sheets. Still leaning down very near he said, losing his eyes in his meaty smile, 'I know Greg shouldn't really have tricked us, thrown us together, and I do know I shouldn't have watched you these last days (before you got ill), without you knowing. I'm sorry for that, but actually, Lydia, I'm awfully glad that ... I hope you'll be better soon.' Beads of sweat broke in his crinkly hair. 'If you want anything I'm next door. All right then? ... Goodnight then.'

Lydia let her fingers touch his hand then snatched them away, letting her eyes fall on the knot of his tie, daringly near his face. 'Eric? ... Thank you so much for ...' But it was no good, the words became convulsed in her throat and through the wall Eric heard her crying for hours into the night.

The doctor did return the next day and told her (as he pocketed the urine she had caught and bottled with difficulty in the vile, communal lavatory a floor below) that she could get up the next day and to go to the surgery on Friday when he would give her the result of the pregnancy test.

But she did not bother to go. No need to confirm the obvious.

Eric spent the next few days with his father at the "Home" returning each evening to sit with Lydia. They talked lightly, skirting all subjects that might hurt, and this achievement verged on artistry, so clever were they both to anticipate the turns of their talk and take another if some dark area loomed ahead. Perhaps the success was due to each looking out for the other's feelings. Eric's greatest concern was never to say, hint or refer to anything that might embarrass Lydia or make her remember. And Lydia's concern was to show that she was always aware of the great kindness he was paying her, and that the price for that must be a high one. She could not have been too flip, gay or optimistic, and in any case, it was easy to be none of these things because she had her decision to make, and her mind laboured upon it almost constantly until she became too tired and confused. Then she would remember that Eric would surely be leaving towards the end of the school holidays and she would descend on his conversation, relieved by his voice and his presence, which she dared not admit was dear to her.

There was one evening when Eric did say something to bring Lydia's attention to him with a jolt, because it addressed her own important subject. Eric was saying, '… it was a few days before I caught on to it, because if you notice the shop always has "Closed" on the door, but I think there must be a connecting door between "Hades", you know, where he lives, and the cellar next door, because I have never seen him going in there. But once I saw, just once, some poor fellow in there and it was Glynne behind the counter. He must make quite a packet out of it. Some of those types will pay the earth (their sort of earth, our sort of earth, because rich men have other places, don't they) to indulge their sad fantasies? I've even seen a few women lurking about there, vastly pregnant. I mean huge.' He arced his hands about his own stomach. 'Now don't tell me his Auntie left him the surgical stores too? What sort of an Auntie is that, I'd like to know? Glynne's sort, I suppose. Gosh, Lydia, you mustn't look like that or you'll have me thinking you want a rubber appliance.' His shoulders and ears jogged together for a moment with his mirth, but his hand quickly covered his mouth and he snorted his laugh. 'No, sorry. I was teasing. Sorry.'

Suddenly Lydia was moved by Eric, who had patiently endured her sullen depression; who had cooked her passable meals each evening, still gallantly insisting on using his own five-pence pieces for the gas; who had washed out her clothes after the doctor's visit and who acted as appreciative, but apologetic, audience for his own silly jokes, and who now had possibly given her a hint about where to go for what she wanted. She put her arm about his neck and kissed his cheek.

Eric had been crouching in front of the fire trying ineffectually and messily to toast a sausage on a long fork (to save coins he said). He stood up, his face a deep red, touching the spot on his cheek where her lips had pressed with one hand and holding the forked sausage aloft with the other, a beached, domesticated Neptune.

Lydia jumped back, her hand to her mouth, she realized at once that she had overstepped the bounds of this new relationship. She had done a dangerous, thoughtless thing that allowed all sorts of questions; she had deprived them both of their armour in a second of selfish gratitude, for Eric had no idea that the kiss was due to anything he had said, or that Lydia had any decision to make.

'I'm so sorry,' she said, looking directly at him, still a rare occurrence.

'No, no, really. Don't be sorry. I'm glad … because, Lydia, there's something I want to talk to you about …'

'I don't want to talk like that, Eric. Please let's not.'

'But it's about Dad. I told you he had a stroke, didn't I?' She remembered that he had told her but the sad fact seemed to have become lost among some of her own. 'I know he won't last long, Lydia, and the Matron says that's true as well.' And suddenly everything seemed too awful for Lydia to bear, she covered her face.

'I've done this, haven't I?' she said. 'I'm responsible for so much destruction.' It sounded familiar as she said it; someone else had said they were destructive, but the people who had played parts in her life seemed to exist no longer and she could not sort them out of fantasy. Eric came forward, put his arm about her and removed her hands from her face.

'Dear Lydia, you're not destructive, and you mustn't be sad, because Dad really is tired of going on. He has wanted this to happen and he has made me ready too. It was all becoming unbearable with me away and him in the "Home". I could never have moved him to live with me … even if … well … even if I wasn't alone, he would never have been well enough to leave the "Home".'

Lydia was unaware that she was pressing Eric's hand against her face as he spoke; once or twice she stroked her cheek against it, her lips brushing his fingertips. '… But I do have one confession to make. I never told him about us: you know, splitting up.'

'Thank you,' she said, and her mind began to wander back to her decision.

'Lydia? Do you think you might visit him?'

She looked vaguely at Eric then remembered what they had been talking about. 'Oh yes, of course I'd visit him. Could we go together?'

Eric hugged her to give his assent and everything was easy for him then: the sausage cooked well and quickly, his whole meal seemed to be quite a success and he found he was able to talk with confidence, even pride, about his job. He gave Lydia many details he had not wanted to before and he told her about the house, the garden, quietly dwelling on its attractions and those of the area.

Later still that same evening when they both seemed to be sitting peacefully in front of the gas fire Eric said, 'Greg would advise me not to say what I am about to say, he would say it was weak, but actually I do know I am not weak, maybe just a little too honest … Whatever has happened, Lydia, I still love you just as much as I ever did, possibly even more. I know I can get on without you, but I don't want to.'

Lydia was staring into the gas fire, her face set hard, her mouth pinched as an old maid. Glynne must know how; must know who; and is abortion so wrong? Would it hurt? How big would it be? Would it cry when it was torn out? Might she ever have another?

'… I do see I've said too much. Too soon, maybe.' Eric was

flushed again and looking down trying to control a quiver in his cheeks. He undid the frilly apron he had bought for Lydia when their evening meal together had become a ritual, although somehow it had always been him that had worn it. With his hand on the door-handle and his head hung upon his chest he said, 'Lydia, I would never do anything to embarrass you, or hurt you on purpose.'

That was it, then. She would go to Glynne first thing in the morning. She was decided. Lydia shook herself from the hypnotic glow of the gas fire. It was an old one with honeycomb filaments mostly cracked or completely broken and falling against the bars. She was surprised to see Eric had gone. For a while she thought he had gone to what he called the "chamber-pot of horrors", but when he did not return she was quite relieved, though vaguely surprised, and went to bed.

'I knew it,' Glynne said the next day settling back into his damp-smelling sofa, while Lydia stood beside an armchair twiddling a silk tassel on a cushion. 'I knew you were pregnant when I first saw you in the hall. There is something in a woman's eyes. Don't know what it is exactly but it's like a protective film between her and the real world. Don't do that, it'll come off.' He gestured towards the cushion she was toying with. Lydia dropped it and clasped her hands in front of her and then behind her. 'All the room-cleaning, too,' he said, 'little give-aways.'

Glynne moved his bulk over to a table covered with newspapers tied in bundles, papers and other leaflets. Perhaps there was a surgical stores' newsletter. He was looking for something. 'I've got a number here somewhere. You don't want a mucky job. There's dozens will do it cheap, but for a proper job you want four hundred pounds, and you say you've only got two. I don't know, but I'll see. Go away now and I'll see.' He sounded impatient.

As Lydia neared the top step leading from Glynne's cellar apartment he called after her softly, the air catching in his throat as it always did, 'Lydia. Wait a minute, Lydia.' He climbed two steps and whispered, 'It's horrible what you're going to do. Horrible. Why don't you have it and let me take it? You could. I'd love a baby, a little person, a little someone.'

Her look of disgust and horror gave the answer to his mildly insane face looming below. He had switched off the light before she reached the top.

In her room Lydia thought hard about Glynne in his cellar, the surgical store, the Antic Hel and of the hopelessness of her own life. She owed her child non-existence. That much she could do for it. She stood on a chair and pulled herself up through the skylight and sat with her legs dangling inside the room. It was a small space enclosed by slate roofs and chimney-pots, with no view but more of the same, and sky. It gave a feeling of security and intimacy. The moment was curiously happy, with the intensity that comes when the happiness is founded on simple sensations, and she never forgot the trembling light on the grey slates, the vociferous pigeons, the sun warm on her shoulders, and the world busy, unreal, invisible far below.

Even Ben seemed unreal up here so she dared herself to think of him in the present tense. She had often thought of their time together and could do that without tears these days, but she had never been able to face the truth that he must be somewhere, that he lived, breathed, talked, and with Nathalie there too, sharing all with him. It seemed unlikely that he was in his house in London; possibly he had never returned from Rabat but had gone straight to Paris and collected Nathalie. They would be singing and laughing somewhere in the dappled shadows of Europe. She felt that, wherever they were, the London house was dead and empty, and Coalbarn too.

For a long time she pondered on Ben, repressing her tears and fascinated by her own hardening. This rooftop space was quite perfect and could be made beautiful with some plants; her room, which she could see as a rectangle below her like a snapshot accidentally fallen, was not too bad either. Perhaps she would live there for years to come; become an old crank of the Antic Hel.

Later, when the sun cooled, she came down and decided that tonight for the first time she would don the frilly apron and cook for Eric. It was comforting to think that soon he would be here. She must see Victor soon.

There was a knock, but it was not going to be Eric because he always entered straight after knocking. That was one of the incongrous things about him. In every other way he seemed to be self-effacing, but his knocks were merely announcements that he was going to enter, not a request to do so.

When Lydia opened the door Glynne pattered into the room and looked about. When he saw the bed he said, 'Do you like the pillows? They are mine, you know, but it's all right I don't want them back,' and added quickly, 'not yet.' He stroked the top pillow. 'Percale. Percale's nice, soft.' He went on without looking round and still stroking the pillow so that at first Lydia did not follow him. 'It's all fixed up. Here's the address.' He reached for a piece of grubby paper from his back pockets without turning, still stroking. 'I like the feel of it against me. Against my skin. I talked to someone there who I did a favour for and they agreed to two hundred. You've got to be there in the morning. It sort of slips and slides against you, not too hot, not too cold. Like another skin. They don't say when you'll be back.'

Or if, she thought. So quickly? Did it have to be so quickly?

'You don't have to thank me.' He tried to give her a sympathetic smile but his face did not move easily into it, either from infrequency or the slack on his jowls, but he patted her shoulder as he passed out of the door. His fairy feet patted away down the stairs.

So it was settled. Now she was ambivalent about Eric's return: in one way she longed for his easy, kind company, but in another she dreaded facing the victim of her actions; already he had borne her desertion but there was still one more vast secret and that she could not share, because now she was going to destroy the little product of her infidelity and such a product she and Eric had looked forward to, planned for during their last weeks together. Kindness would be to shut her door to Eric, say she would never see him, that she did not want his company. But selfishness won out and she welcomed the thought of his return.

She prepared something resembling a stew on the gas ring and went to the off-licence and bought a bottle of 'Algerian Red', as Eric called it ('we won't go so far as to say "wine",' he said on the one occasion he had produced a bottle) because nothing was going to depress her. She had made her decision and would not be sad, she had been sad enough. She tidied the room and laid the table with things that mostly Eric had brought from his own room and left there.

Somewhere a church clock struck seven. He was late. At eight o'clock she knocked on his door even though she knew he was not there. She felt the fingers of depression tearing at the fragile cocoon of brightness she had woven about herself for that evening and started to drink the wine. Nothing to do. No one to talk to. Glynne was downstairs, of course, but by now it was not just any company she wanted. She tried to eat her stew and regretted even more that Eric was not there with his collection of bottled sauces and dried herbs which he added to the most humble baked bean. He had never been out this late before, why didn't he say?

She finished the wine and put her last five-pence coins into the meter. Now she was frightened of tomorrow and even began to ask questions of herself that she would never have dared to without the wine dazzling inside her head. Why had Ben done it? Why had he left her to this? 'If there is ever anything I can do' he had said, hadn't he? Well, she'd go there now and knock on the door of that empty house and say to Ben who was not there, 'Yes please, there is something you can do. Love me like you did before. Or if you can't, can you please blot out my life. I wouldn't ask if I could do it myself but I haven't the courage.'

For a long time Lydia cried in front of the merrily popping, raspberry-blowing gas fire until she heard the footstep on the stair, the footstep that had seemed so sinister a little while ago and now made her smile. Soon he would be knocking, entering, and she was going to tell him everything. She longed now to tell him and to have his understanding.

The footsteps reached the top of the stairs and tripped, as usual, on the last step where the carpet had rotted. You'd think he'd remember by now about that drag, and Lydia smiled again as she rubbed her face and smoothed her hair ready to greet him when he knocked. But there was no knock. Keys jingled briefly and a door closed.

Lydia threw open her door and banged hard at Eric's. How could he not have come this evening? He had come every other evening. It drunkenly flashed through her mind that she would throw herself into his arms, or take him by the hand to her room, start the evening again as though it was six o'clock and not way after midnight. She would laugh with him and have his company whatever the time was.

Eric did not answer quickly. Lydia banged again in spite of the sound of his shuffling step towards the door. It opened a crack; she could see part of his face and pushed the door wider, but stepped back quickly when she saw him clearly.

Eric's face was hideously contorted by grief. He must have been weeping for hours and still the tears were sparkling from his eyes, invisible somewhere between his puffed lids. His lips were drawn back in a parody of his smile. He put his head on one side and shook it slowly, letting out a moan, animal and eloquent. Hidden in that fleshy face his tear-filled eyes were appealing to her; he tried to speak but put his hands in the air, grasped at nothing and brought them down ferociously onto his knees, collapsing into a crouching position. He began to whimper, putting his hands over and over his frizzy hair. Still crouching and without raising his head he turned his knees to one side and shut the door on Lydia, who stood dumbfounded. The door shuddered as his sobbing weight fell against it from the inside.

Lydia banged on the door, 'Eric, what is it? ... Please, tell me. Tell me what's happened.' But she did not like the sound of her voice, she sounded numb-tongued and insincere. 'I'm here, Eric, if you want me ... here, next door ... you know,' and then the immediate shock of his grief faded from her glazed brain and she remembered how she had wanted his company, and what of his company she had wanted, and why she had wanted it. '... only, I've been waiting for you, you see. I got everything ready ...' No; not so very selfish, just human and a little drunk. But she could not keep her mind still, it kept sliding down tracks to illusory places. She returned to her room, weaved across it and found in the upturned orange box that was her larder some gin left in a half bottle that had been a get-well present from Glynne. So he had guessed all along; she had missed that little joke before.

She went back to the bed and drank it straight from the bottle. Minutes later she passed out, anaesthetized to her own anguish and anyone else's.

*

Lydia was still dizzy from drink when she entered Harley Street
at nine-thirty the next morning. Yes, Harley Street. Before she
read Glynne's slip of paper she had thought she was going to
enter the seamy side of medicine; that rusty blades and gin in a
back-alley of Paddington was her due, but when she saw
Harley Street written down the image changed. It was going to
be all right after all. Harley Street with those big brown and
brassed front doors and its waiting-rooms like Board Rooms,
smelling of Antiquax. Nothing underhand there.

Lydia still believed in medicine, that the only people who
entered that world were philanthropists and not out for gain.
Sometimes when she had been particularly low she had even
wished to be in hospital, not because she knew anything about
hospital, never having stayed in one, but because they
represented in some intangible way the security of being kept
home from school with some minor complaint and being
cared for by mother. If all else failed she could find an excuse
to put herself in the hands of medicine with the same infantile
trust that made some inmates of concentration camps
volunteer (before being forced) for medical research, believing
that the controller of the experiments sought to help mankind,
loved mankind; therefore would surely not harm one man.

With this same trust flickering away inside her, one of those
Harley Street doors shut softly behind Lydia and in the high,
mahogany, deeply respectable hall, she shyly and courteously
explained to the severe nurse behind the desk why she was
there, wondering to herself if the room she would go to (or
even the ward: there might be wards, little ones of course)
would be sunny. The sun had been shining outside so maybe
somewhere upstairs it was still.

She was waved aside and had to wait while the nurse smiled a
caked smile to a long-legged lady with a silk dress and soft
curling hair who had entered and said she must see the doctor
instantly and could not wait as she was double-parked.

'Jim,' the lady smiled looking up the curving staircase to
where a stained-glass window flirted with the sun upon the
carpet. A man in blue serge stood tall at the top step.

'Christine, my dear,' he said, 'I know, I heard,' he raised his
hand to stop her speaking again, 'you're double-parked, as
usual. Lovely dinner last night. Such fun and do thank Michael

too. That Latour … well, what can I say?'

'Jim, I can't wait about, do you know yet?'

'Of course I do. Come on up I say, the news I have for you is worth ten parking tickets.'

The lady rushed excitedly in her silk up the red-carpeted stairs, and when a door had closed on their voices leaving silence, the nurse turned to Lydia, the smile draining from her lips, contempt brewed in her eyes.

'She has terribly wanted one and she is not as young as she looks.' She rose crisply. 'This way.'

It was disconcerting to be led to the basement door although the brass upon it was well rubbed.

'Down there,' the nurse said and closed the door, leaving Lydia standing at the top of wide stone steps, a grander version of Glynne's, a white cloth screen cutting the view at the bottom. She descended slowly.

A big woman in an inappropriately tight skirt and tweed jacket came from behind the screen and said looking back, 'Oh, Lord, here's another one. We'll never be through by six.'

Lydia looked behind her to see what delivery the woman could be referring to and with an inner contraction realized.

She went on down to a cubicle created by several screens, ready to give her name, the details, but the woman never asked, she just took the money and put a rubber band with number 32 written on it around Lydia's wrist, then folded back the screen and pushed Lydia's uncertainly resisting body forward. Lydia felt no reassurance from that pushing hand so she looked back to see if there might be some in the stony face, but the screen was already closed.

The whole basement had been hollowed out into one huge, low, green-gloss-painted room with a frosted-glass panelled section running the length of one end behind which three orbs of brilliant light shone and shadows of figures moved with heads bent. Fluorescent tubes stripped across the ceiling, bathing all in harsh blue light. Camp-beds with one grey blanket each lined the walls and formed three more central lines. There must have been forty of them, every one occupied by a woman, a girl, or, as in the case of the bed directly at Lydia's side, a girl-child. But the nightmare was not the crowding, the cold, the shameless, windowless room, it was the quiet; the communal concession to defeat, broken only by someone's groan or the creak of a cross-legged camp-bed.

Lydia knew now that courtesy and polite reticence here fell on stony ground, but upbringing is hard to overcome and she thanked and smiled and nodded her way to a bed led by a blank-faced nurse no older than she was. The bed was empty but the blanket was crumpled and at its foot a pile of clothes was neatly folded. She changed into a creased and bloodstained green robe that was given to her and lay down because she was told to.

With her own stillness the quiet ebbed and the air around became filled with noises. Little noises. Noises anxious not to advertise their source or their purpose. The clink of something metal on something metal. More groans. The muted whine of the fluorescent tubes.

Lydia pulled the blanket well around her head, exposing her cold feet. The woman next door to her was lying on her back with her arms under her head, staring and still, except for frequently moistening her lips with her tongue. Some women were reading, engrossed in paperbacks, impervious to the hostility, the humiliation; so maybe if it did not exist for them it did not exist at all.

Suddenly someone let out a scream in one long breath that did not stop. All of the heaped figures sat up and looked about. The screamer was a bony-armed woman far older than anyone there. Tweed Jacket and Blank-Face surrounded her quickly and the sound of a slap resounded about the green gloss walls.

'Come on now. It's time to get dressed. It's all over and you've had your half hour.'

Lydia watched the bony woman with crepey flesh, carefully set hair and glasses, being pulled to her feet, then sank back into the hell inside her own head. She tried to sleep and pretended to herself that every time she opened her eyes it was not only sixty seconds that had passed but really several hours and that it was 'all over' for her too. Nearly half an hour passed in this way until Lydia was conscious of someone standing near her. She opened her eyes, startled; it was her turn then and she wasn't quite ready. She wanted to finish something she was thinking. What was it now ...? But it was not her turn. A girl, also in a green robe, was standing bent nearly double beside the bed with white face and trembling lips.

'Sorry, do you think I could have my clothes?' Her timid voice was shaking.

Lydia stood up quickly and tried to break the girl's fall onto the camp-bed, nearly tipping it over.

'Sorry ...' the girl said again before she fainted.

Good old English "Sorry", like the good old English "one" rising to every occasion.

"Sorry, one has just had an abortion and one is not feeling in peak condition." Sorry, girl. Sorry, Eric. Sorry I'm alive at all. Sorry. Sorry. Sorry.

'Here, you,' the blank-faced nurse girl said, 'Over there,' pointing to another used bed with another pile of clothes, this time not so neatly folded. Hours passed like that playing musical beds. It seemed everyone was allowed half an hour to recuperate, a few had longer when they really seemed to need it.

Somewhere in the middle of the afternoon the nurse came up to Lydia.

'Quickly please,' she said.

Lydia passed barefooted between rows of beds pulling her gown tight, ashamed of showing the bloodstains that were not even hers. Behind the glass panel she was blinded by the tall arc lights. There seemed to be a lot of figures all in green with skull caps and masks. Could some be apprentices?

'Give me your gown, please, and get up there,' the nurse said. It seemed she was staying and that was a comfort; for all her blank face and hardness at least Lydia could see her features and had seen her moving about for several hours. It was the nearest thing to familiarity, to reassurance she could find. But the nurse left, and as she climbed naked onto the narrow operating table the green figures did not look at her or look away; they simply tinkered and tided, ready for number 32. Lydia was confused because the table was too short to lie down, so she sat hunched, hugging her legs.

Someone wearing rubber gloves took hold of her left arm and injected it, at the same time her legs seemed to be pulled away, up and apart, but already she was losing control; her

vision was blurred and she was falling away, but all those eyes
were still upon her, following her down in her degradation. A
black, oval shape was bearing down towards her; she tried to
scream, but as in a dream the sound would not come. She saw
her own hand to go up in appeal to all those eyes and
miraculously another warm hand took hers and held fast. With
the rubber mask pressing hard against her face she twisted her
head to see who had held it and saw, before unconsciousness,
between a cap and a green cloth mask, two eyes in an agony of
pity.

In a recess of her mind something well brought-up and
grateful wanted to make her say to those eyes, 'Sorry. Sorry to
make you suffer.'

When she staggered back to the camp-bed it was her own
bloodstains she was ashamed of.

*   *   *

The rain was subsiding and through it now came a cool, shy,
late-afternoon sun. Condensation streaked the windows and
Ben leant forward with an impatient gesture clearing it from
the windscreen with his sleeve, revealing the wet-eyed world.

'... I would like to be able to tell, Lyd, that I sensed there
would be disaster in that place; that there was something in the
colour of the stones, the people's faces, but there was nothing
like that; I even quite liked the place, and Natta did too. I
don't know why we did because there were endless numbers of
soldiers wandering about from the barracks there, and they are
never a pretty sight, are they? And there was nothing particular
about the little town. Someone directed us to a small hotel,
beautiful in its simple way and the owner greeted us with great
charm.

'I can recall that night with awful clarity, the pleasure of
being clean again after the dusty roads; the cooling of the air as
we ate in the white-walled garden of the hotel; Natta's face in
the light of the fat, glass-covered candle on our table. Her way
with me that night was different from ever before and more
disarming. She was not subdued as she had been until the past
few hours, but she managed a defiant tenderness; so when she
reached across the table and took my hand to her face,

caressing it with her cheek, I was not disturbed in the way I had been in Venice; it just made me realize, again, how much I loved her. As if my whole being didn't already belong to her; but now I saw more depths, endless reflections reiterating my love. I knew then that nothing would take me away from her and I'd face all the jealousy I was bound to suffer; the jibes from other people; my own vile aging in the face of her approaching zenith; I suppose that was a decision I thought I'd reached before but this time it came as a conclusion, like the snapping shut of a book: Natta and I would be together always and that was the end of that. Nothing in the way she loved me during the hours of that night altered the feeling in me or gave me any clue that the conclusion she had reached was quite the reverse of mine.

'The next morning while we were still in our room I tried to talk about our plans; not the usual planning of routes, exciting places; this time I talked about London or Paris. I even talked about plans for Christian (although he was still something I found hard to accept), where he was to be schooled, that I preferred England for that. I only talked about him then because I thought that was what she wanted; I knew she had begun to miss him. Natta listened to me with a funny expression which finally halted me, then she shrugged; it was a kind, exasperated shrug, and she said, looking away from me, "C'mon Dad, let's not talk about all that." We had been trailing about Europe for months and I don't think once during that time she'd called me "Dad"; always, obviously, "Ben". I was worried but I didn't say anything. She was restless and suggested that we go to Caserta Vecchia, the old part of the town a little way away and higher than the newer area.

'We drove up there, the road was winding and tortuous in places but it was beautiful at the top. You know those little Italian hilltop towns where the farms and gardens spill over the edge in tiers? We wandered about the narrow cobbled streets for some time and Natta seemed quiet, sort of peaceful. She teased me if I was lagging behind her, said I was getting too old for heights, that sort of thing; I kept on about plans for the future and she stopped protesting. I assumed she was accepting them and I got quite carried away with all my ideas for our future together; she said she thought we ought to be going back to the hotel and I was in a mood to do as she wanted.

'When we got back into the car Natta became a little hilarious again, you know how she could be: shouting at other motorists, waving. She was a child; a blissful child. I was laughing at her antics but had to concentrate hard on that nasty bit of road. We were turning one of the bends; I'd already changed down to take it but was going to take off a little more speed by touching the footbrake. Nothing happened: the brake had no response; it just rattled loose under my foot. I pressed it right down to the floor, let it up and pressed again; after eternal seconds of pumping, the brake caught. When I was under control once more I looked to see if Natta had realized the danger, but she was still kidding around, this time with a lorry load of vegetables coming up behind us, but she saw me look and laughed. "Can't scare me, Dad," she said. I laughed too and tried to think what garages I'd seen in Caserta, I went dead slow after that and even the lorry of veg. overtook us with a lot of shouts and gestures, much to Natta's fury. The brake seemed to work all right after that, except for one or two lapses, but nothing as dangerous as before because we were on the flat and I was going very slowly. I didn't tell her because, although she liked me frightening her when she knew it was basically safe, she did have a horror of a real accident. She would probably have insisted on walking all the way back if I told her.

'When we reached the hotel she dashed in and I walked about for a bit checking some of the local garages. They all looked a bit dubious so I decided to talk to the man at the hotel who seemed fairly honest.

'I went to our room to tell Natta we wouldn't be leaving that afternoon, but she was already packing her case. "There's no need for that yet," I said, but she didn't stop or look at me. I crossed over to her but heard a cough over by the window, because it was on the same wall the open door had blocked my view of it when I first entered. Laurent was there. It was like seeing a Renaissance portrait of a young man with a beautiful face, wearing a long black coat and standing beside a window which revealed an azure sky and little hills with winding roads on them, you know the sort of thing.

'I didn't say anything, I couldn't, I knew what was going to happen. I sat down on the edge of the bed, hid my face in my hands. There was nothing to see in that room which wasn't going to hurt me. I felt Natta's hand on my shoulder, then her head resting on my back; she'd curled up on the bed behind me. (Did you ever notice, Lyd, how Natta would put her body into a position that matched what she was going to say; and if she thought what she was to say would hurt you, she'd say it anyway, but sort of comfort you with her body at the same time. God I loved that child. She was just perfect, wasn't she, Lyd? I mean, you knew her, it's not just me that says it.) I was shaking badly. Couldn't help it. I felt her warm hands move to hold me round my waist, "C'mon, Dad," she said (she always said that, didn't she, Lyd?), "It couldn't go on with us, you knew that. And Laurent never really left me, you know. He just wanted us to wear out whatever it was between us. I think we've done that, don't you?" Her voice was so sweet all the time, as if she was talking to a child who had to be told the worst. "He was with us in Monte Carlo, Dad," she kept saying "Dad", "and Leningrad and Moscow. But in Moscow he said if I didn't go then with him he'd leave me. Somehow I couldn't leave you then and I let him go. It was after that I knew I couldn't live without him. At that funny place, you know: the one where we had lunch in the square, he came up to me. He'd been following all the time. He really does love Christian and me." As though I didn't, as though anyone could've loved her more than me. She didn't say anything else after that and I felt the warmth of her hands go away as she turned to finish her packing.

'I still didn't look up and I don't know what I was really thinking, except that I couldn't let it happen. I heard them move to the door. Laurent had said nothing all that time and any second now they'd be gone; I heard them closing the door, it was loose on its hinge and dragged a bit. I jumped up and saw his back view in the passage with a protective arm about Natta. I shouted her name, but they didn't stop, so I shouted his too, I knew that would stop them, pretend that I accepted them as a pair. They turned back and stood together in the doorway, my beloved child with her perfect male counterpart. "Listen," I said trying to control myself, "If it's got to be like this, if you have to go, let me give the two of you a present. The car. Take my car. All the papers you need are in it."

'Laurent began to decline, but Natta grabbed his arm, "Say 'yes'," she said, "Laurent, please, please say 'yes'." He looked at her, then at me. I drew the keys from my pocket and threw them to him. He caught them and put them into his pocket: then he came across the room with infinite dignity and held out his hand to me. We shook hands. He said, "I thank you, Sir." Natta rushed to me and one last time put her arms about my neck. "Darling, Dad," she said, and kissed me. Then they went.

'I sat down again in the same position in that little room with the sun pouring in. All I had left to do was wait; sooner or later someone would be coming.

'I knew what I was doing, Lyd. I knew exactly what I was doing.

'I must have gone into a sort of trance then, for when I became aware of someone shaking me by the shoulder and smacking my cheek as though I was an old lady who'd fainted in the street, it was night outside the window where Laurent had been standing. Someone snapped the light on. The small room seemed crowded with people; the owner of the hotel who had been so charming to us was standing somewhere near the door, he was wringing his hands and saying over and over, "Dio mio; dio mio." It was a big-faced policeman who was shaking me and there were another two standing about. The Italians always do things in a crowd, don't they? There's nothing discreet about them. The policeman began to tell me he had terrible news; that I should prepare myself. What can I tell you, Lyd? How did I guess it that she was dead? Perhaps it would have been obvious to anyone. Their unhurried dramatics left little room for hope. And, after all, what had I hoped for giving them the car? I don't know: him dead? Her crying for me from some hospital bed? Nothing so clear and yet the way they ended seemed entirely by my own design. "Dead?" I asked, coldly I expect; the policeman's mouth mimed the word "Si", then he gathered himself to add, "Tutte due, tutte due". That Laurent should have been killed along with her seemed a triviality.'

Lydia, clenched with her arms wrapped about her tried to utter again her inarticulate prayer, but no sound would come.

13

Lydia walked out of Harley Street to Oxford Circus and waited with the rush-hour crowds for a bus to Victoria. She was not in pain, that came later, she just felt light and amused that people should be innocently going about their normal business; there were tourists and taxis and dummies being changed in shop windows. Nothing had changed. Only her.

When she entered the Antic, Glynne came forward from the shadows at the end of the hall. He had been waiting for her. 'Lydia, you look like death,' he said in his womanish, constricted voice as he took her arm, helped her up the stairs and onto her bed. 'There you are then. I could get you something to eat, though I suppose you don't fancy much.' She did not. 'Only, Eric's not here, you see. He's gone.' He watched her slyly out of the corner of his eye while pretending to be engrossed in pulling a thread out of the armchair. 'By the way, I've changed the sheets, the percale. Just for now, you understand.' Lydia eyed the greyed flannelette. No, we mustn't mess up the percale, must we?

'Did you tell Eric where I was?' Lydia asked suddenly, anxiously.

'No, no,' Glynne was agitated, 'not tell, but he asked and you see I thought he knew, you both being so close, meals every night and all. I said something, can't remember what now, and he guessed at once. Ever so sorry. You should have said …'

For days Lydia hardly moved from her bed and more rarely from her room (the percale never came back). Although the pain had gone, apathy kept her prostrate. But at last there did come an afternoon when she felt different, something had mended in her broken spirit. For the first time she faced her violated body. It was quite the same, quite as ordinary. The shame did not show. She washed herself and her hair, then dressed tidily. She had wanted to go onto the sunlit roof but did not have the strength to pull herself up, so opened the skylight and sat demurely beneath with the sun upon her.

It was when she was sitting in that sunlight that the door opened and Eric came in. He was going to say something about sorry and not wanting to disturb but when he saw Lydia's joyous face he simply smiled and pushed his hands down into his pockets. He raised his eyebrows and slowly opened his mouth, but before he could say anything Lydia leant forward on the chair, her thin, tired, ill face desperately searching for his understanding. 'Eric, there is something I must tell you …' He raised his hand. 'No, please, please listen,' she said, 'I didn't come on the underground, I came back by taxi.'

Eric came forward and gently brought her to her feet. 'It doesn't matter, my love, nothing matters. Come to the park with me, it's very nice there, daffodils and things.'

Rare kindness, rare man.

And in that sunny park with the dogs and the children and the limpid shadows she said 'Yes' when he asked her to marry him.

All that was nearly four years ago; since then Lydia had fitted well into the school community, she and Eric were peaceful and life was orderly, or leaving her alone. No children though, there had been complications after the abortion. She had not thought about the past. If she tried to she drew an amnesiac's blank and then some part of her would hurt, just a wrist or a shoulder, a nice external pain to draw her attention away. Until he came, that is, to the corner of her street, to watch.

*   *   *

'… And now, Lyd, I hear her voice, I see her. She torments me more than ever and there's nothing I can do. Help me, please, help me away from insanity. Please forgive. I knew that if I could find you it would be all right again: I could explain to you why I did it, why she drove me to it. They were always taking her away from me, you see. Why wouldn't they leave us alone, just to be happy together? There's something else you must know: I have Christian, our son. He's not really a stranger to you, Lyd; how well you understood his mother, help him now. He needs you. Say you're coming back. Say it to me. For Chrissake say it ... ?'

Ben and Lydia sat in silence staring before them at the world twinkling and blinking in the aftermath of its rain, and as they did a figure turned the corner, coming from the street where Lydia lived, stepping forward and on past the tree to stop, square, a few yards from the car. It was Eric. The sun spinning through his fine hair gave him a seraphic quality. He was smiling with a gentle eloquence; there would need to be no explanations; he had never asked for explanations. In his hand were the lilies and the roses she had left on the path.